INTO THE NOTHING

BROKEN OUTLAW SERIES, BOOK ONE

Dani
Thanks so much
for your support!

BT URRUELA

Photographer: CJC Photography
Cover Model: Gideon Connelly
Cover Designer: Cover Me Darling
Editor: SG Thomas
Formatting: Champagne Formats

DEDICATION

To Major David Taylor and all those heroes who lost their lives defending our freedom.

I am forever indebted to you. And to the families of the fallen who must go on without them. God Bless you all.

PROLOGUE

Xander

Present

"Confessions"—City & Colour

Inmate #0102258... That's who I am now. Xander Evans doesn't exist anymore. The man I was three years ago is now just a collection of memories quickly deteriorating. With each day spent in this hell, these four concrete walls relentlessly close in on me, inch by fucking inch.

I watched the TV shows. I was a *Lockup* addict. Hell, I had seen the very episode featuring the Missouri Correctional Facility, the same shithole I now call home. And in a sad twist of fate, I saw it long before entering this nothing. The violence. The rage. The misery. I judged it all from the front of a TV screen. Now, I'm just another animal locked up in this cage—for a crime I didn't even commit. And my entire fucking world has crumbled because of it.

Okay. I get it. That's what they all say, right? Fuck, I wouldn't believe me either. I know how I come across to people. In this mostly shitty life I've lived thus far, I know what I've done. And I know I've brought most of this shit on myself. But I can say this with certainty…I've been a lot of things in my life—a liar, a thief, a cheat—but a murderer? I'm no fucking murderer.

I loved the Watsons. And Paige… don't even get me started on her. Her face is etched in my memory. The pain still consumes me as if it happened just yesterday.

The DA told me the case against me was the tightest he'd ever seen. He said I'd get an immediate guilty verdict and due to the heinous nature of the crime, I'd likely be put to death. Admitting to a crime I didn't commit was my only salvation. But I don't give a shit about my life. I'd do anything to keep Paige from seeing what I saw that night…from seeing what haunts my dreams.

And let me tell you, I've had too many hours to process the fact that I was set up for a brutal murder and subsequently coerced into a confession.

My midday lull is disrupted by the notorious click-clack of Warden Jimmy Naranjo's alligator boots. I hear him loudly whistling whatever country song he just heard. The slow of his step lets me know I'm his likely target, which is no surprise as he's spent months now pestering me for information—information I refuse to give.

The Warden's a great guy, and I respect that he comes from a similar background, but I won't get involved in prison life politics. I just want to serve my time as peacefully as possible. It's hard enough playing this game on your own in here, with no one to watch your back. But to be a rat too? *No, thanks.*

As expected, Warden Naranjo stops just before my cell

door and leans against its frame. He tips his Stetson cowboy hat back, exposing the thick lines in his forehead and the salt and pepper gray of his Chicano hair. A matching mustache straddles his lip, and it twitches as he raps two knuckles against the door.

I analyze his attire, amused. Not at how he's dressed—hell, I'd be lying if I said the man wasn't fashionable. But his ever-changing pastel dress shirts, starched vests and designer jeans stick out like a goddamn sore thumb in this place.

"Mornin', Evans," he grunts and tips his head my way.

"Warden." I lift myself to a seated position on the top bunk.

He takes a few steps into the cell and leans against the stainless steel sink.

"We got word this mornin' that your new cellmate will be in sometime this afternoon."

I let out a light laugh. "And?"

He cracks a smile. "Well, he's not like the last one. I promise you that." He raises his weathered hands and shrugs. "He shouldn't give you any problems. And he hasn't fucked with any kids."

He scans outside the cell a bit before coming in closer. "I need you to come down to my office a little later. We have to talk about the incident with your last cellmate."

I try my best not to roll my eyes. My face must say it all though, because he quickly continues—with some authority this time. "We know you played no part. That's obvious. We have an idea of who did do it, and we think you've got an idea too."

I actually do roll my eyes this time and exhale loudly. The warden doesn't like it much. He straightens, then grabs his vest with both hands, something he always does when he gets annoyed. It's about the time his knuckles turn white I realize he'd probably rather be wringing my neck right about now.

"You can't tell me the guy didn't have it coming. What he did… I would've killed him myself if I cared enough to." I lie back on the pillow with both hands behind my head.

"Yeah, but murder is murder, Evans. I often look the other way when you try to get one over on us." He puts a thick finger up as if trying to keep me from interrupting—I wasn't planning on it. "And don't treat me like a dumbass and tell me you haven't… because we both know you have."

No argument from me there.

"I hope you'll occasionally pay me the same respect." He pauses for a moment, leaning back on his heels.

"Occasionally, Evans. That's all I'm asking for. We'll see you in a few hours." He heads toward the door, but before heading out, he looks over his shoulder at me. "CO Towson will be down to grab you in a bit. You help me, I help you. Roger?" I nod, and with that he's gone.

Our talks aren't usually so brief, but I assume he'll have plenty more to say at our get-together later. Warden Naranjo loves to pry, I love to fight, and we both love to win. In a way, we're serving life together.

We have a lifetime to do this dance.

TRUMAN VALLEY SHERIFF'S OFFICE
OFFENSE/INCIDENT REPORT
CASE REPORT #08931
REPORT NARRATIVE
DATE: 05/09/2013
OFFICER: Deputy Jacoby Virgil

INVESTIGATION: On 05/09/2013 at approx. 0030 hrs, I received a call from dispatch to respond to 1 Watson Wineries Drive in Truman Valley in reference to a homicide.

I arrived on the scene and met with the caller, Xander Evans (DOB 02/13/1985), who first encountered the victim, Teresa Watson (DOB 06/19/1968), before calling 911. Mr. Evans was distraught, but calm enough to communicate. He informed me he heard glass shattering and a loud yell from the main house while he was in a detached living quarters, located a few hundred feet behind the main residence. Both are situated on a winery of several dozen acres on the outside of town, which is owned by the Watson family. Mr. Evans stated he had been staying in the living quarters and working as an assistant to Watson Wineries for a little under two months. He is not of any relation to the victim. Evans also informed me that the husband of the deceased, Jack Watson (DOB currently unknown), and daughter, Paige Watson (DOB currently unknown), were on a hunting trip near Twain Lake. Teenage son, Caleb Watson, was at a friend's house for the weekend.

Mr. Evans stated that, upon hearing the commotion, he dressed and headed to the main residence. He entered an unlocked back door and almost immediately came upon the body of Mrs. Watson, facedown on the kitchen floor. He checked for a pulse, concluding that Mrs. Watson still had one but it was faint. He removed the suspected murder weapon—a Bowie hunting knife found in the sink—before calling police and conducting a search of the home.

The victim had multiple stab wounds to the back, head and neck. An autopsy is currently being conducted.

Mr. Evans consented to a search of the guesthouse without issue, which turned up several items belonging to the Watsons, including credit cards and checkbooks. Several pieces of jewelry were found that we have reason to believe were owned by the Watsons. All items were located inside Mr. Evans' luggage. Marijuana and paraphernalia were also discovered.

Mr. Evans has been taken in for further questioning. A more detailed search of the residence and land is necessary. Immediate family has been notified and are en route to the Sheriff's office.

Case open pending homicide investigation.

End of Report

CHAPTER ONE

Xander

March 2013

"Maybe This Time"—Sherwood

THIS BAR IS NOT UNLIKE THE MANY I'VE STOPPED AT ALONG the way in my nine-year journey. I've stayed in hundreds of backroad towns and gotten wasted at just as many hole-in-the-wall bars.

Don't get me wrong, there's an unmatched charm to this place. Sure, it's got your typical deer heads, rusted garage signs and the jukebox playing Alabama in the background. But it also has the faint, comforting smell of cedar and a collection of people you'd expect to find in hippie Oregon, not the middle-of-nowhere Missouri. With two empty bar stools on either side of me, a chilled pale ale before me, and twelve hours of driving behind me, I'm in my happy place right now.

Six beers down and I'm still better than the hick across the bar from me. Slouched in all his inebriated glory, his massive arms cradle a Bud and two shots. Before I can analyze him further, a stunningly beautiful woman, early twenties with a confident stride, makes her way toward a nearby takeout counter. A middle-aged man with the same dirty blond hair, probably her father, hands her a twenty and heads for the restrooms on the other side of the bar.

I watch her as she leans against the counter, a cotton tee and small jean shorts doing little to hide her magnificent curves. It's incredibly difficult to break my stare, but it's been a long time since I've seen someone so damn beautiful. A pair of piercing blue eyes catch mine before I'm smart enough to avert my gaze.

She's not offended though. Her smile is playful and innocent, yet with a hint of mischief. It's the kind of smile Hollywood starlets would envy, and I can't help but smile back. No one like her has walked in here all night, and no one like her will walk in after. I'd put money on that.

Before I know it, my drunk friend to the left has stumbled off his stool and toward the girl I've been ogling. He reaches her, his hands groping for anything and everything. When he captures a handful of tits and ass, her eyes widen and her mouth curls in disgust.

None of the dozen or so other people in the bar seem to notice or care much. Just another drunk asshole in another rinky-dink fucking town. Before I can even think, I'm off my stool and on him like a starving lion on a freshly killed carcass. I'm driven solely by instinct.

And a drunken desire to impress this woman.

CHAPTER
TWO

Paige

"She Walks In Her Own Way"—The Kooks

IT'S NOT UNLIKE THE DOGS IN THIS TOWN TO GET GRABBY whenever the opportunity presents itself. So I'm not the least bit surprised when I see it's Benji Mathis who's pawing at me in his usual drunken stupor. The guy is a tumor in Truman Valley, and the exact reason we have the reputation that we do. This town is not the town I once knew—not by a long shot. And it's because of guys like him.

Just as I'm about to put a Converse in Benji's balls, I see the sexy guy from the bar has leapt from his stool, a look of anger etched on his face. I freeze. I can do nothing as all three hundred plus pounds of Benji Mathis crumples to the floor. The stallion of a man who rushed from his barstool faster than I could process a thought has Benji pleading for release, his arm bent in a way I'd more likely see in a UFC fight than at Whittaker's on a Thursday night. That's something I never thought I'd see in my lifetime. Besides my ex, Cody, no one is more feared in Truman Valley than Benji. And yet here he is at the mercy of a man who, not five seconds ago, I was eye-fucking the shit out of.

God, I wonder if he noticed.

I'm trying not to act desperate, but it's been six months since I ended things with Cody, and let's just say he was no pro in the sex department. I've had pints of Ben and Jerry's during my period last longer.

I spot Dad just outside the bathroom in the same incapacitated state I'm still in, locked in observation of this stranger taking matters into his own hands. The man grinds up harder on Benji's arm, inducing a pathetic whimper.

"I don't know who you are, or who raised you, but where I come from, we're taught a little thing called respect," the sexy stranger says, his biceps bulging with the strain of keeping Benji down. His eyes are locked onto Benji as everyone else in Whittaker's now watches, some with their cell phones aimed at the action. For the first time ever, Whittaker's is dead silent.

"Let… Me… Gahhh… Go…" Benji manages to say between gasps.

"I'll cover your bar tab, but you're going to get the hell out of here. Understood?" Benji wails in pain when the stranger once again cinches his arm, which looks to be near its breaking point.

"Yes. Yes. God, yes! Just please…" The pain snuffs out his words. With that, the stranger releases his grip and Benji stands and stumbles awkwardly toward the door. He turns and grunts. "This ain't the end, motherfucker." As he makes his way out, the man just shrugs and nods at me.

Dad approaches and extends his hand. "Well shit, son, I think you just saved me some dirty work." The stranger immediately shakes it, while the onlookers pocket their cellphones, go back to their beers and continue their loud conversations.

"This is my daughter right here… my baby. And I don't like that kind of shit one bit." He motions to me and then throws an arm around my neck, ruffling my hair with his other hand. He's been doing it since I was a kid, and it's probably the most comforting feeling I know. Also one of the most annoying when there's a guy like this in the room.

"It's no problem at all, sir. I don't like that kind of stuff either." The stranger quickly turns and heads in the direction of his stool, but my father follows.

"Hey, you know what? We're getting this pizza here and got plenty of beer at the house. How about you come back and have dinner with us? As a 'thank you.' It's the least we can do." The stranger turns and smiles, and it's then that his mossy hazel eyes absolutely captivate me.

Correction, they make me go completely stupid. They're the kind of eyes that make you forget everything.

"Oh wow, I appreciate the offer, sir, but I just got in from a brutal road trip. I'm about ready to get some sleep." He looks at me and smiles, and instinctually, I look away. I curse myself for my sudden and complete lack of confidence.

"Tomorrow then," my father says. "The missus will cook us up something nice."

The stranger pauses for a moment. "Tomorrow? Yeah, I think I can swing that." He extends a hand. "My name is Xander. Xander Evans." My dad's hand meets his again.

"I'm Jack. This is my daughter, Paige." I wave. "We live just outside of town at Watson Wineries. You must've seen it coming in off the interstate?"

"Well, I didn't know what it was, but I certainly saw it. Quite the place you have there."

My father laughs it off and follows the stranger—or Xander, I guess it is—to the bar. I follow close behind having grabbed our pizza from the takeout counter.

"Alright, well, come on by at seven tomorrow and we'll set you up right."

"I'll be there." Xander smiles and returns to his stool.

We make our way toward the door, and it's then that I realize I haven't said a word to this man. Not one. As my father and I depart Whittaker's, I can't help but dread tomorrow and hope to hell that Xander doesn't show up.

But at the same time, I hope he does.

———————

The wait is excruciating. I'm seated in a recliner in the living room as my garlic bread finishes in the oven. Mom puts the final touches on her famous spaghetti in the kitchen and Dad is out in the vineyard working late as usual. My younger brother, Caleb, is likely in his room playing video games where he can so often be found. The clock reads 6:58 p.m., and I have to fight the urge to bite my freshly manicured nails—a battle I find myself losing.

It's not that I'm nervous to talk to the guy. Not trying to sound conceited, but I was the prom queen, for Christ's sake. Boys do *not* intimidate me. Hell, who am I trying to convince?

This is no Missouri boy. I could tell that the first time I laid eyes on him. The people here—most of them, at least—walk around with a chip on their shoulder, like they've got something to prove. But Xander...he seems different. So sure of himself. So confident.

Maybe I'm just bothered by the fact that I didn't say anything to him. *Not one word.* The guy made Benji freakin' Mathis yelp like a damn dog. I mean, come on. The least I could've done was say thank you to him.

The doorbell rings, and Mom comes from the kitchen wiping her spaghetti sauce-stained hands on her apron. I know I should get up and answer the door for her, but my legs are locked in place. "Caleb! Come get the door, please," she calls up the stairs.

I hear his bedroom door swing open, crashing into the wall behind it as the doorbell rings again. He stomps to the top of the stairs.

"What the hell? I'm busy, Mom! Why can't you get it?" She rolls her head back in annoyance, spotting me huddled in the corner. Her patient eyes are outdone only by the warm, radiating smile that never seems to leave her face. Not even when my soon-to-be sixteen-year-old brother is acting like a total asshole.

And they thought I was bad. He makes 'teenage me' look like a damn saint.

"I can get it, Mom." I start to get up, but she motions for me to sit back down. With a smile she heads to the door and opens it. Xander stands with a bottle of red wine in his hands and a nervous look on his face. I can't help but giggle at the thought of him purchasing a bottle of wine to bring to a winery.

A black V-neck grips his body and the sight of it takes the laugh right out of me. His amber hair sits perfectly on his head with no sign of product, as if he woke up that way.

"You must be Xander. Please, come in." Mom sidesteps and he slips past her as I approach them from the front room. I catch her checking out his biceps and then the muscles in his back before she looks at me, wide-eyed, and mouths *'wow.'*

I roll my eyes as she takes the bottle from him.

"My name is Teresa. I'm Paige's mom and Jack's wife. It's so great to have you!" She shuts the door and hands the wine to me as we make our way to the kitchen. Xander catches my eyes and nods. I do the same and smile, trying my best not to look like a little girl. I feel like I'm completely failing in my attempts.

"It's great to be here, ma'am. Thank you for having me." The back door sliding open pulls our attention, and Dad walks in, his overalls stained green and brown from a long day's work.

He greets Xander with a smile. "Good to see you could make it! Sorry, I'm running a bit late, but I gotta grab a quick shower. I'll meet y'all down in a few."

Dad slips his work boots off and makes a beeline to Mom as I pull the garlic bread from the oven. His lips meet her forehead and stay there for a few moments. Her eyes close and she takes him in, day of sweat and all. I can't help but smile. To see them is to know what true love is.

"Babe, you alright in here?"

"I'm fine, honey. Dinner will be done soon. Go clean your stinky butt." She playfully pushes him away.

"You know you love this stinky ass!" He juts out his rear and shakes it a little, giving us all a good laugh. Then he grabs a Bud from the fridge and kisses my mother on the cheek. "I'll go take that shower, dear." He observes the room, eyeing each of us. "Where's Caleb, by the way?"

Mom rolls her eyes and shrugs her shoulders. She's been doing a lot of that since my brother hit puberty.

"In his room, where else?" She smiles, but carries something else in her eyes—something not smile-worthy at all. I hate that my brother makes her feel that way.

My dad huffs out a sigh, rubs Mom's shoulders and proceeds upstairs.

I pull out a chair for Xander and he accepts with a nod. As he sits down at the kitchen table, I realize I've still yet to say a word to him. I can tell by the way he stares at me, he's likely trying to figure out if I'm mute or not. My mouth opens, but nothing comes out. He just smiles and it's then I catch a whiff of his cologne. It's intoxicating, causing the words to become even more tangled up in my throat.

"Ugh," I croak, my mother giggling in the background. I sneer at her then turn back to Xander.

"I'm Paige."

"I gathered that." He shoots me a smirk. I manage my way into the seat across from him and rest my elbows against the table.

"So, you aren't from around here?" It comes out of my mouth sounding far more critical than I intended, and my mother shoots me a look from the stovetop—the kind of look that's usually followed by a very motherly 'Paige Lorraine!' For the good of my already bruised ego, she refrains.

"I mean... we have like two thousand people in this town. We all know each other. That guy you, um, made look like an idiot last night was in eleventh grade English with me. Of course, he was only in the class because he'd already failed three grades at that point." He laughs. Sadly, I'm serious.

"You're right, I just got in town last night. A few hours before the… the altercation." His sly and mysterious smile captivates me. It's both hard to look at him and hard *not* to look at him. "I'm originally from Florida, but I've been all over the place awhile now. Came up from Georgia yesterday. Columbus."

Mom lets out a loud *ughhh* and whips around to face us.

"Xander, how rude of me! Can I offer you something to drink? Water, soda, beer?"

"Beer, yeah. Beer would be great." He gets the words out with a quickness. Hell, maybe he's a little nervous too. I slip back into my chair a bit, my shoulders settling.

"I'll take a beer too, Mom!" I call to her.

As she pops the tops and sets them before us, Dad comes down the stairs, to the dining area, and pulls out a chair of his own. He observes the room, smiles, and takes a seat. My brother, scrawny and desperately attached to a horrible emo fad, comes in behind him. He plops himself in a chair and grumbles under his breath.

Dad just chuckles and shakes his head. Spotting the beers in front of Xander and me, he licks his lips. "Honey, can y—" Before he can finish, Mom slips a beer in front of him. His Mizzou Tigers koozie, faded from the years, is in its rightful place. He chugs it and lets out a loud, satisfied sigh. He shakes his head.

"Where are my manners? Xander, cheers!" He lifts his beer and Xander meets it with his own. "Thank you for coming to our home, and for last night. Welcome to Truman Valley…a once great town quickly being overrun by the type you've already encountered." He shakes his head solemnly and takes another long swig. "There's a lot of good in this town, but a whole lot of bad, too."

Xander nods, maintaining eye contact with my father throughout, something I always notice and Dad always appreciates.

"So, where are you from?" Dad asks as Mom sets down pots and pans full of Italian sausage, spaghetti sauce and noodles on placemats on the table. I join her, grabbing plates and utensils for everyone.

"I was just telling the ladies that I'm originally from Florida. But I've been traveling around for quite some time now."

"Well damn, where at in Florida? My family is from Plant City. We had a big strawberry farm out there. I was pretty young... don't remember much of it."

"I'm actually from Ocala... right by there. I got out pretty much as soon as I could though." He laughs, but it's one of those laughs meant to disguise something else entirely—something deeper. "I've been to Plant City before though. It's a lot like Ocala." He laughs again, genuinely this time. "A whole lotta nothing."

"So you say you left early...you a military man?"

Xander quickly raises a hand. "No, no, nothing like that. I've thought about it. I have friends that are military, and I respect them a lot for it. I think though, in the end, I'm just a little too selfish." He stops abruptly, as if he wishes he could take his words back. But my father nods approvingly, and Mom finally takes her own seat at the table.

"I saw how you operated last night. Witnessed it with my

own eyes. There was nothing selfish about that."

Xander scratches at his beer label, nervously laughing off Dad's comment, and then we all begin shoveling food onto our plates. Everyone other than my brother, that is, who is pulling his own brand of hunger strike. Mom's learned to not let it bother her so much.

Dad has halved his usual rapid eating pace tonight for our guest, and between swallows, he peppers Xander with questions. It's not that he's nosy, just naturally curious.

Ok, maybe a little nosy.

"So what brings you to our neck of the woods?" he asks through a mouthful of spaghetti. Mom glares at him, though it goes unnoticed.

Xander takes small bites, carefully dabbing his mouth with a napkin after each one. It's one of those cute, polite things a guy will stop doing once he's comfortable enough with you.

"I was coming up from Columbus, Georgia. Spent the better part of three years down there...and it just came time for me to move on. By the time I hit your town, I was in desperate need of a beer and a bed. The beer of which, I had plenty..." Xander laughs and lifts his empty beer. "Could I bother you for another, by the way? Or I could get it myself."

Mom jumps to her feet, grabbing his empty bottle.

"My pleasure." She smiles and makes her way to the fridge, emerging with three bottles, as she already knows two more requests will be coming shortly. She hardly drinks, but the same can't be said for my father and me.

"You said you've been on the road awhile? Where else have you been?" Dad asks.

"Well, before Georgia, I bartended in Miami. Place was

too busy for me. I spent a little time in Jacksonville and Orlando before that, more construction and some bouncing. Savannah and Charlotte for a little bit too."

"Can I be released to my room?" my brother interjects.

"Just go, Caleb," Dad says, a bite to his tone. Caleb gets up as quickly as he can and makes his way up the stairs. The slam of the door cuts the awkward silence in half.

"Well then, I didn't think the spaghetti was that bad," Mom jokes, grabbing my brother's plate and taking it to the trash.

"Ma'am, honestly, it could quite possibly be the best spaghetti I've ever had," Xander says as he piles more onto his plate.

My mother smiles a broad, honest smile as she places my brother's dish in the sink. I'm smiling too because, my god, this man is something else. Based on looks alone—but in a semi-sexy kind of way—I'd think about turning around to avoid him in a dark alley. But to hear him speak… his chivalry and respectfulness is something else. Something I haven't seen much of in the eligible men around these parts. At least not in the last ten years, which is when I started paying attention.

"She is one *hell* of a cook." Dad slaps a hand against Mom's ass as she returns to the table, and I put a hand over my eyes in feigned disgust.

"Get a room!" I yell as Mom sets the beers on the table.

"Oh, don't give me that shit, young lady. How do you think you got here?" Dad turns his attention to Xander. "Your family must miss you being gone all the time?" he asks.

"Daaaad!" I give him my best what-the-fuck look.

Xander just smiles. "No, really, it's no problem at all. I've met a lot of friends along the way, and I've done my share of talking." He clears his throat, swigs, then continues.

"As for family..." He trails off, his eyes darting nervously to the floor.

"You don't have to say any more," Mom says softly, her tender voice pulling his eyes to hers.

"Yeah, seriously... *Dad.*" I stare at him, but he doesn't see me. He's still looking at Xander, presumably waiting for him to respond. He's so damn stubborn sometimes.

"Well, it's a bit too heavy for tonight, but I don't have much in the way of family. Spent a lot of time in foster care, so my friends are my family." He takes another swig of his beer. Whatever his past is, he's accepted it. Or he's perfected the *look* of acceptance.

"Well, I can understand that. Not to that extent, I'm sure, but my old man was a real bastard. Mother wasn't much better." Dad lifts his eyes to the ceiling. "Lord knows I'm not speaking ill of the dead, only the truth." Mom gives my father a knowing look, placing a hand on his and rubbing it softly with her thumb.

She gets up and collects our dirty dishes, dumping them into the sink with a clatter. She makes her way back to the table quickly. Though she'd never admit it, she's as interested in the answer as Dad and I. But just as she sits down, Xander abruptly stands and walks to the sink. He begins cleaning the dishes and Mom stands without hesitation.

"Please, I'll get that later. You're a guest," she says.

"And as a guest, I feel like I should do my part. You cooked, so I can clean a few plates off." Mom reluctantly sits back down. With his back to us, Xander continues talking while he washes the dishes. "Eventually, I'll end up in Washington. I have some, uh, friends up that way. But I'm in no hurry. This is kind of my 'discover me' period, I guess. Traveling the country and seeing what all it has to offer." He finishes with the plates and sets them on the rack to dry. Then he dries his hands and returns to his seat.

Dad nods with a look of approval. "That's not a bad idea at all. I've told Teresa for years I wanna sell the winery and retire to the open road. Just a Winnebago and my girl. That would be perfect." He looks Mom in the eyes as if Xander and I aren't even here.

Dad works long hours and he does it for us and for those years he'll spend with my mother by his side, four spinning wheels below.

"One day, honey," Mom says, smiling and gripping his hand tightly. She looks back to Xander. "I think it's a wonderful thing you're doing. Most people lack the courage to go somewhere new... somewhere no one knows them. It takes a great deal of strength. Jack knows all about that."

Dad remains quiet, unaffected.

Xander takes this in for a moment before speaking again. "Well, really, it probably would have been more courageous to stay in Ocala...with people I knew all too well. Have you ever been there?" He laughs.

"No, I haven't," Mom says.

"I stopped there on my way to Miami once. Started hearing *Deliverance* banjos the second I stepped out of the car!" Dad laughs heartily and scoots his chair out, then rises to his feet.

"Xander, we've got a pretty nice fire pit out back and more than enough beer. How's a few more sound? You got anywhere to be?"

"I think that sounds like a damn good idea, sir. The schedule looks wide open tomorrow," he says with a wink.

"Alright, well, no more of this 'sir' business. Okay? And God knows I respect and love the hell out of her, but in this house"—he points to Mom—"no 'ma'am' either. It's Jack and Teresa, alright?" Dad cracks a smile, a tipsy twinkle in his eye.

"Yeah Jack, sounds just fine." Xander says, standing and following Dad to the back door. I collect the empty bottles and grab four more before joining them.

Mom cut me off, along with herself, a good hour ago. That's one of the pleasures of having Mom as a boss.

Dad and Xander do most of the talking, and their laughter breaks the still night air in waves. Out of nowhere, Dad bats wildly at his legs as embers curl his leg hairs into blackened stubs. His beer tumbles to the ground as he jumps quickly to his feet.

We all laugh hysterically with each bumbling move. It takes Xander a moment before he eventually catches me staring from across the bonfire. It's the kind of stare best executed after a few. He looks back at me, smiling through the dancing flames as Mom and Dad's hysterical laughter rings loudly behind us.

"Well, I'll be… I think I've reached my damn limit!" Dad says between laughs, drawing my eyes from Xander, though I'm reluctant to look away.

"Yeah, I might need to get back to the motel before I'm no longer able to drive," Xander says, rising to his feet and fumbling with his keys.

"No, you can't drive! You've had as much as they have!"

Mom scolds. She stands to meet Xander. "I'll take you there."

"What about my truck?" I ask, relieved that my tipsy ass won't have to drive.

"Caleb's got a learner's permit. He can drive my car behind us with Paige."

Dad stands again and throws an arm over Xander's shoulder. "I need some help with the vineyard—at least for a few months. I have a lot of work that needs to be done and not enough of me to do it." Dad points to the guesthouse above our garage. "We've got a nice little place up there, and seeing as you have no particular timeline, I say you stay awhile and help out. I'd be paying you of course."

"Sir, uh, no disrespect, but are you—?"

"Jack."

"I'm sorry. Jack, are you sure you know what you're asking right now? We've had a lot to drink." Xander looks to Mom. She just smiles.

"Positive. Be over here at nine," Dad says, making his way to the sliding glass door.

"We are one hundred percent positive, Xander," Mom adds before she follows Dad to the door. He's still struggling to open it and I can't help but laugh.

"Well, there is one thing. I have a dog. I don't know if that's a problem."

"You have a dog?! What kind?" My voice comes out way too high-pitched.

"Yeah, a German Shepherd named Rowdy. Been with me for a few years."

"We lost our pup a few months ago to cancer. Haven't had the heart to get another one yet. I hope to see you and Rowdy in the morning," Dad says, finally walking into the house.

"Xander, I'm gonna get Caleb up, and have him meet you guys out front, okay?"

"Sounds good. Thanks, Teresa." Xander smiles and Mom heads in after Dad.

And now we're alone. The fire's dying down between us, but the cricket's chirp is alive as ever. The bright country stars light his face in a way that makes him look like a dream—a sultry, beautiful dream.

"So, were they serious?" Xander asks.

"How are you not drunker?" I unintentionally ignore his question, but I wait for my answer anyways.

"More drunk, you mean? How am I not 'more drunk'?" He smiles and winks. I don't say anything, and he continues. "I've done my fair share of drinking over the last few years. I am twenty-seven, after all."

God, that smile.

"Oh, well you only have three years on me."

"Were they serious?" he repeats, ignoring my comment.

"Why? Would you consider it?"

"I *am* considering it—if it were legitimate. How are *you* not more drunk?"

"My mother cut me off, remember?" I roll my eyes. "She loves to treat me like I'm still fifteen. Anyways, it was a legitimate offer. My dad may be drunk, but he knows what he's saying."

Xander sits quietly. He looks to be deep in thought.

"Well, I think you should." I smile, the kind of smile that is meant to say so much more. "I guess we better go meet my mom, but just so you know, I hope to see you and Rowdy in the morning too. You forget the dog, and you might as well just take your ass right back down that gravel road."

CHAPTER
THREE

Xander

"Therapy"—All Time Low

Sunlight floods the dingy Sunshine Valley Motel room, filling my foggy eyes and making my temples pound. Six hours of toss-and-turn-riddled sleep and the repercussions of last night are making themselves perfectly clear. A drinker I may be, but resistant to hangovers I am not. With age, it seems, the worse they get.

I'd love nothing more than to stay in bed, but I fully intend on taking the Watsons up on their offer. I could use the money and, hell, there's something about this family that's comforting. Something like what I had at Fort Benning. Something a guy like me soaks up every bit of.

Family is foreign to me. Always has been. When I get even a glimpse of it, it's hard to let go.

I manage to shift my legs over the edge of the bed and drag

my body from the mattress, but that's about all I've got. My large torso hangs weightlessly over my knees. My stomach lurches, calling for me to lie back down. I swipe a bottle of Aleve from the nightstand and down four of them with a swig of last night's water. Rowdy is wide awake now and pawing at my feet, his vibrant eyes unyielding. He wants breakfast, and he's relentless until he gets it.

"Not yet buddy...*please*." I nudge away a crowd of beer cans and grab a pre-packed bowl from the nightstand, the vibrant green and purplish weed tempting me from its mouth. I'm immediately thankful I had the wherewithal to pack it last night, as doing so this morning would've been a bitch.

I light it, take a drag, long and slow, and release the billows of smoke in little O's. Rowdy hops at my feet for his morning chow. I take another drag and feel a tingling sensation trail down my back and arms.

"Alright, buddy, I got ya."

———

My 1970 Ford F-100 is loaded with most of my belongings, which equates to two military-style A-bags, my guitar and a backpack. Not much, but it's enough. Rowdy relieves himself one final time before our five-minute trek to Watson Wineries. The hangover has subsided a bit, and I silently thank the weed gods for that.

With a tip of my Browning cap to the Sunshine Valley Motel, I load Rowdy onto the bench seat and hop in alongside him. And with that, my adventure in Truman Valley truly begins.

It's not hard to spot Watson Wineries. As Jack stated last night, it's the first thing you see. You can't help but notice miles of grapevines in neat rows that act as a gateway to the town of Truman Valley.

Large wrought iron gates give way to a never-ending gravel driveway. The two-story, white-as-snow farmhouse with navy blue shutters—hand-built by Jack's father, as I was told last night—centers the endless rows of grapevines around it.

I park, open the door, and step out of my F-100 with bags in hand when Rowdy comes rushing out behind me. He nearly knocks me over in the process.

"Well hello, Mr. Evans, you're late," Paige says, squatting down to welcome Rowdy as he runs into her arms. "Aw, what a beautiful little baby you are."

Another girl walks right past Paige and Rowdy and she stops just before me . She extends her hand and smiles weakly. "I'm Brandi."

"I'm Xander. Nice to meet you, Brandi." I shake her hand gently and release it, my eyes barely leaving Paige. "Late? I thought your dad said to show up at nine? That was tough enough as it is."

"I know. I'm just messing with you."

The soft smile she gives makes my heart buzz. Perfectly pearl-white teeth are set behind lips ideal for kissing. Decked out in short shorts and a tank top, she's wearing her hair curly today, her golden waves pushing the limits of a hair tie. I find myself even more attracted to her like this.

"He's been up since like six, though. I don't know how he

does it. I woke up in a whole lot of pain this morning."

"Yeah. Tell me about it. Well, if you guys want, you can take Rowdy here inside while I'm working. Is it okay if I throw my stuff in the guesthouse?"

"Yeah, yeah, you're fine. Door's unlocked. Dad's in the field and said just to meet him out by the barn," Paige says as she leads Rowdy to the house. Brandi reluctantly follows.

"Enjoy your first day of work, Xander," Paige says over her shoulder. "Don't you worry about Rowdy here. He's in good hands." The three of them head through the front door, closing it behind them and leaving me with the quiet countryside to figure out what exactly just happened. Two minutes in and I've already managed to get my dog stolen. It's not surprising he's the star of the show, that's usually how it works out, but I figured I'd get a little more attention at least.

I head back to the truck and unload it. I lug my baggage up to the guesthouse and drop them off inside. I'm taken back by the size of the place, which looks like a mansion compared to the motel room I stayed in. There's a kitchen and bathroom all the way in the back, a bed and vanity just before it, and living room with two loveseats and a TV when you first walk in the door. I could definitely get comfortable here.

When I'm done exploring the new place a little bit I head to a large maroon barn with paint chipping at the corners, set back a bit in the middle of the vineyard. Jack is huddled under the hood of a tractor, a grease rag tucked into the side of his overalls. His arms are buried in the engine.

"Jack, it's Xander," I call out. I hear a thud from Jack's head meeting the hard steel hood. He lets out a groan and then a quiet laugh.

"Shit, I'm so sorry," I tell him. "I thought you heard me coming."

"No problem at all. You'd think I would have, as quiet as it is. I think I'm still in a daze from last night." He shakes his head and smiles. "Or maybe I'm just getting old."

"Yeah, to be honest, I woke up and thought maybe your offer was a dream."

"Nossir. But I'd be lying if I said I wasn't drunk as all hell by the time my head hit the pillow last night. I definitely need some help out here," he says, then hesitates for a second before continuing, "and I like you."

Flattered, but not knowing what to say, I mumble, "I like you all too, sir."

"Good. Well then, we should get along just fine. It won't be terribly hard work, but they'll be long days. I'll pay you handsomely for your assistance, and I hope you'll at least stay with us until mid-summer. And remember, just call me Jack."

"That sounds great, Jack. I'm happy to help in any way I can. What kind of help do you need? I've done a lot in my life, but not much in the way of winery work."

"Not a problem. I'll always be around to direct you, and it won't take long to get the hang of it. Some of what I'll need from you goes beyond the winery. Did my wife discuss her business last night? I can't for the life of me remember."

I scan my brain but come up short. "I know she mentioned owning a business at the bonfire last night and that Paige works with her. I don't think she gave specifics though. That, or my drunken memory fails me."

"Okay, well she and Paige run Watson Metalworks down on Main Street. You see it down there yesterday?" Jack leans back against the tractor, wiping an arm across his sweat-beaded forehead.

"I remember seeing the sign for it…big metal sign welded together, right? Looks badass, like it belongs outside a heavy metal venue or something."

"That's the one… My wife is a sculptor. Only I guess it's sculpting with a twist. She hits junkyards, recycling facilities, pretty much wherever she can find scrap metal. We're talking anything from screws to forks to bike rims. Whatever she finds that strikes her fancy, and she welds them together into sculptures using those parts. Started it years and years ago as a hobby, but things have really taken off over the last few years. Got so busy that Paige even started working for her when she finished college."

He stands a bit taller now, pride pouring from his words. It's the kind of pride a man *should* have for his wife and daughter. It's endearing, but the only thing I can think of is how in the hell he can be so talkative this early in the morning… and after so much booze the night before.

"Watson Metalworks is one of the most popular stores in at least the nearest five counties and the internet side of the business has just started to explode this year." He grabs another rag, this one clean, from the other side of his overalls and wipes his forehead again. This man sweats like he's just finished a marathon. "Listen to me going on and on. Long story long, she often needs my help, which takes me away from the million-and-one things I need to do around here. They get so caught up on a new piece, shipping out orders or dealing with customers, they can't seem to pull themselves away very often. A few years back, I could complain and make Paige do it, but I'd be lying if I said the store isn't making as much money as this damn winery by now."

I can barely make out what he's saying. My head feels like a helium balloon seconds away from takeoff.

He cocks his head to the side. "You alright, Xander?"

"Yeah, I'm hanging in there."

"You look like shit."

"I feel like shit." I smile—or attempt one, at least—and he laughs.

"Well, if I learned one thing in the Army, it's that you've gotta work through hangovers." He lifts himself from the tractor, laughing as he passes by. "Let's go get you acquainted with the winery."

CHAPTER FOUR

Paige

"Prairie Girl" –Rah Rah

I SIT BACK DOWN IN THE FRONT ROOM, GRABBING MY NOW lukewarm coffee and taking a nauseating chug of it. Only the Bailey's helps keep it down.

Rowdy lies at my feet, rolling onto his back and pawing at me for attention. The sight of it is almost too much to bear. It's been hard since our pit bull, Scout, died, so it's nice to have a dog around again.

"Holy fuckin' balls, bitch. You didn't say he was *that* hot!" Brandi plops down beside me and swipes a forearm dramatically across her forehead.

"I did tell you!" I reach a hand down and oblige Rowdy's begging. He laps a tongue against my arm in appreciation.

"You said he was hot, but he's like… *smoking* hot. Dibs on that shit!" She laughs.

"*Dibs*?" The sound of my voice takes me back a bit. I didn't mean for it to come off so… territorial.

She curls a lip and shoves me. "You bitch. You like him!" She swats my arm. "I mean, I don't blame you, but I'd think with your parents right upstairs, he'd be off-limits."

She's right, of course.

"I don't like him! I don't even know him. He could be a complete creep." I don't even believe my own words.

"Okay, Paige, I've known you for how long now? Going on fifteen years. I've known your parents about the same. Your dad isn't going to let some creeper near his family, so he must have seen something in him. He's good at that shit."

She's right. My dad has always been protective of our family, especially with my mom and me, and at times, it's almost too much.

"He was over here for like five hours last night drinking and talking with Dad. You think I like him? My dad's in love. And the way he didn't hesitate to put Benji in his place, I just think Dad's got a good feeling about him."

"Shit, I've got a good feeling about him too… and it's in my panties." She laughs and motions toward her crotch. "If I had been working and saw him do that to Benji's fat ass, I would've let him fuck me right on top of the bar…and I would've let everyone watch."

"Brandi!"

"I'm serious. Fuck it!"

"You're ridiculous."

"Paige, don't tell me you didn't notice that anaconda stuffed into his jeans?"

"*What*?! What the fuck are you talking about? Anaconda?

I wasn't looking at his damn jeans." I laugh, finding it hard not to love this girl who has become like a sister to me. She's the craziest bitch I know, but she's got my back no matter what. She's had it since day one. She's never really had much in the way of family, so she became an unofficial member of ours a long time ago.

"Why *wouldn't* you look at his jeans? That's where his dick is! Well, you definitely missed out on quite a show! I'd bet he's packing at least a niner. Maybe even a ten." She says it so matter-of-fact that I can't tell if she's serious or just pulling my leg, but the chiming of the grandfather clock makes it irrelevant. I'm already late for work.

"Listen, I've gotta go, you little nympho. Can you put Rowdy in the guesthouse whenever you leave? You work at Whittaker's tonight, right?" I stand and Rowdy hops up instantly to join me.

"Yeah, I'll probably just hang out here and head out around five. You gonna stop by tonight?"

"I might. It depends when Mom lets me leave. The way it's looking, I won't get in to work until about ten."

"Alright, well text me if you end up going. And, dear Lord, please bring that fine-ass specimen with you. I'm gonna go take a long nap in your bed and dream about Mr. Anaconda slithering into my cave." She stands and heads toward the hallway.

"You have got to stop reading those romance novels."

"Oh no, it's not the romance novels. The erotica ones are what really get my pussy percolating." She cackles and makes her way down the hall to my room.

"You need serious help, you know that, right? How are we even still friends?"

She turns her head, feigning a look of disgust, and then she flashes her wide, beautiful smile. "You love me, whore, and you know it."

She blows me a kiss and disappears down the hall.

———————

I slip through the front doors of our shop, my hands full of lattes and donuts. Mom just rolls her eyes and laughs. A welder's mask sits over her long brown hair, which is tucked beneath a blue bandana. Our latest project is in front of her, half-finished but actually starting to look like a dragon.

"Tough morning, my dear?" Mom pulls off the welder's mask, setting it aside and sliding her reading glasses on top of her head.

I set the lattes and donuts on the massive wooden work table amongst different metal pieces and parts picked from junkyards and garage sales. There are also several projects in varying stages of completion. Mom never works on just one project at a time. Her mind is always going.

She's taught me a little of the skill over the years, and though I truly enjoy it, I'm primarily the business side of Watson Metalworks. I got my degree in finance at Mizzou, and I've been running the books here ever since. I give Mom shit all the time, but she really is the greatest part of my life.

She came from the wrong side of the tracks, worked her way through art school and met Dad along the way. Their love is something I dream about. It's something I long for. Not just yet... but one day.

"It wasn't too bad. Brandi came over late last night, so she kept me up talking awhile. You know how she gets."

"Did your new friend ever show up.?"

"Why is he *my* friend? Dad's the one who took him in like a lost puppy... And yeah, he showed up right before I left."

"Oh yeah? Those two were quite drunk last night. I didn't think either would remember." She slips her glasses over her wise eyes and sits back down on her stool. Then she pulls pencil-drawn plans from a drawer and starts going over them. As if talking to the papers, she asks, "What was he wearing?"

"Mom?!"

"What? I'm just imagining a wife beater and a sexy pair of jeans. Maybe some work boots and a bandana." She closes her eyes and throws her head back, letting out an exaggerated sigh, followed by a wicked laugh.

"Both you and Brandi need sex addiction therapy." I head to my desk just a few steps away, take a seat and power up my computer.

"I'm forty-five, dear. That means I'm in my sexual prime."

My thought: Mom and Dad naked, the sound of skin slapping skin.

My reaction: coffee creeping its way back up my throat.

"Please, mother of mine, keep all talk of your sexual activity with my father to yourself. I may not eat the rest of the day now!" I ball up a piece of paper and throw it at her head. It hits her squarely in the forehead—twelve years of softball weren't wasted—and falls to the ground.

"The sexual activity we should be discussing"—she leans in and whispers as if telling a secret—"or lack thereof, I should say... is yours!" She chuckles.

"Mom, I think we have talked enough about my sexual

activity to last me a lifetime. As an employee of Watson Metal-works, I could no doubt sue you for sexual harassment. Don't you make me go there."

"Well, good thing I'm your mother then, huh? And re-member, I can still fire you." She winks. "Now spill the beans!"

"Fine, he was wearing a wife beater, damn it. And holy shit, I almost fainted."

"Did Brandi get a look at him?"

"You know she did."

"I can only imagine how that went."

"If I wasn't there, I'm positive she would've undressed on the spot."

"Oh boy, I love that girl, but I hope he steers clear!" She stops fiddling with the plans and looks at me. "Who was he eyeing more?"

"Huh?"

"You were both in PJs, I assume?"

I nod. "Well, a tank and short shorts."

"And I assume you both spoke to him when you saw him, right?"

Another nod.

"So where were his eyes? On you... or on her?"

I think about this for a moment, not immediately recalling who exactly he was looking at. But as I scan my brain for the events that transpired earlier, I'm pleased with what I find.

"Me." I can feel her smile.

"You liiiiike him." She makes kissing faces and gets far more of a kick out of it than I do.

"You and Brandi, I swear. What the hell am I going to do with you two?"

"You know you love us." Mom smiles and déjà vu hits me from my conversation with Brandi earlier. They are so alike. *Too* alike sometimes. But God, how I love them.

CHAPTER
FIVE

Paige

"Hope"–Tim Legend

MOM MANAGED TO FINISH THE DAY'S SCULPTURES IN record time, and she currently has a pot roast in the slow cooker. It fills the house with a delightful aroma, making my stomach growl with anticipation. Dad helps set the table. He's in from work far earlier than usual and he helps Mom set the table.

The chill early March air bites at my skin as I cross the gravel driveway to the guesthouse to get Xander for dinner. Just as I reach the door, I hear an acoustic guitar being played flawlessly, followed by the muffled sound of Xander singing. I can't make out the words through the door, but the beauty in his voice is obvious. It's sounds somewhere between Aaron Lewis and Kurt Cobain, with a touch of gravel but also sweet and alluring. He hits every note perfectly, holding it just long enough.

There's pain in his words, but something else too. It's hard to tell. Maybe hope?

Before I even realize it, I've spent five minutes with my ear against the door. When he finishes his song, I snap back to reality. I rap two knuckles against the door and hear an 'oh shit,' followed by the loud clatter..

"Just a second!" he calls, his voice cracking. A moment passes and then I hear, "Alright, it's open." I walk in and he's sitting on the bed, his guitar case stuffed underneath it but still peeking out.

"So, I was told to get you for dinner, but that's just about the last thing on my mind right now."

His eyes dart across the room.

"What do you mean?" he asks, knowing full well he's caught. His bashful state makes him that much more appealing in my eyes.

"I heard you. You are so talented."

He cracks a nervous smile. "What? I just had the radio playing."

My eyes roll, and my hands hit my hips. "You little shit, play something for me!" He looks shocked and feigns offense. "No way. I've never played in front of anyone."

"You just did. I was outside the door for a good five minutes. Now play for me."

"Nope. Never." He crosses his arms. It's just about the cutest thing I've ever seen.

I'm pouting now. The kind I've practiced many times throughout my life. First, to get what I wanted from Dad, and later, from boys I've dated. I like to think I've mastered it.

"Listen lady, I'm sure that look works on these little Missouri boys, but growing up in Florida a man learns better than to trust a woman with a good puppy-dog face." He gets up and nudges me just a little with his hip as he slips past me and out the door. "Now, what's for dinner?" he asks without turning back.

"I'll have you know this look has been proven to work everywhere! I'm international, baby!" He's through the back door of the house before I even finish my sentence.

Mom scoops up the plates as Caleb slinks back up to his room. Although he only pecked at his food, the rest of us did the exact opposite, filling ourselves to Thanksgiving Day levels. Mom scurries past me and slides a hand across my shoulders, giving me the wide-eyed 'I'm going to say something and you're going to go with it' look.

"So Paige, with the wine festival next weekend, I was thinking maybe it'd be a good time for Xander get out and about and get to know some other people in town."

"Mom, he's still getting settled in. I'm sure he'd like to take some time getting used to us before being bombarded by the whole town." Mom takes a seat again, smiling.

"What makes you think he'll be bombarded? We aren't a town of flesh-eating zombies, dear. If he's going to be staying through the summer, he's going to want to meet some other people besides us."

"Mom, why are you talking about him like he's not here?"

"You started it!" She pokes her tongue out at me and then turns her attention back to Xander.

"So, Xander, what do you think?" Without letting him respond, she begins her sales pitch. "I don't know if you know this or not, but this part of Missouri has a lot of really good wineries. They're all across the state. Not that I'm biased or anything, but my husband's pinot noir is the best. It's been voted number one in the state, six years running. And that's out of about twenty-five!"

Dad smiles appreciatively at her. He reaches a hand over and caresses the back of her neck.

"I think the festival sounds pretty good. I like a good pinot noir," Xander says.

Our faces say it all.

"What? I swear I do. I've grown to appreciate wine in my old age."

Dad laughs as he gets up. He pats a heavy hand against Xander's shoulder.

"You've got a *long* way to go, kid."

Xander's eyes follow Dad as he grabs more beer from the fridge. There's a mischievous smile on his face. "Shit, what are you pushing, seventy? Seventy-five? I guess I do have some catching up to do."

Dad crows, having trouble placing the four beers in front of us. "You better watch it, fucker! Remember who's signing your paychecks."

"Jack Michael, language!" Mom says sharply, though a smile is tugging at the corners of her lips.

Dad motions his beer toward Xander. "He started it."

My Chewbacca text alert brings a wide smile and approving nod from Xander.

Brandi: Hey bitch, I kno ur off. Visit meeeee!

"Oh shit, I've actually gotta pass on another beer, Dad. I told Brandi I'd go up to Whittaker's after I got off. She'll be a baby if I don't go for at least a few."

"Perfect. Why don't you take Xander with you, then?" Mom asks. "But if you two have more than a few, you call me!"

She gives me the motherly finger wag, but she knows me better than that. I would never drink and drive. We lost a special member of our family to a drunk driver a few years back It really messed the family up. Since then, it's not even a question.

"That's if Xander wants to go," Mom adds.

"Yeah, I'm up for it." His eyes meet mine. "You driving or am I?"

"I got it," I say, sliding from the table. I smile to myself at the thought of how impressed he's about to be.

Xander stands, as does Mom, and he stretches, patting his stomach.

"Ma'am, that was probably the best meal I've had in my entire life. And I'm not even kidding. I feel like I should be paying you for letting me eat here."

Mom laughs and opens her arms wide. "As long as you're living here, you're a Watson. Now bring it in. I'm a hugger, and with that 'best meal' line, you've now become my favorite person in the house."

She hugs Xander, disappearing into his arms. When she releases him, she makes her way to me, grabbing me and pulling me in.

Her lips meet my forehead. "You be safe. Call me if you need anything, okay? Love you, baby."

"Okay, we will. I promise. Love you too, Mama."

CHAPTER SIX

Paige

"*Downtown*"—Majical Cloudz

I PULL MY '69 CHEVELLE SS FROM THE GARAGE AND THE growl of the 454 big block catches his immediate attention as he exits the guesthouse. His eyes are wide and fixated on my powder blue beauty. He climbs in the passenger side with the same expression on his face as I pull down the gravel drive.

"Are you fucking kidding me right now?"

"What?" I ask, acting clueless.

"Uh, this car. It's amazing. How long have you had it?"

"You're totally going to judge me."

"I won't judge."

"Well, it was kind of a sixteenth birthday present from my dad." Immediately, he huffs and rolls his eyes, and I give him a stern look in response. "Hey jerk, you said you wouldn't judge."

"I'm not!"

"Oh yeah? What's this, then?" I do my best impression of the attitude he just gave me, but he just cracks up.

"Okay, okay… so, sixteenth birthday. But why a Chevelle?"

"I've always wanted one. I begged and begged, and Dad always said if I kept a 3.5 or above my first two years of high school, then he'd get it for me."

"And I take it you did?"

"4.0, thank you very much." I wink and instantly feel as if I've been too cocky. He doesn't seem to mind though.

"Well shit, I'd buy you a Chevelle, too. I squeaked by with a 1.5 at best. School was about the last thing on my mind. I always assumed I'd play guitar for some famous band or something. Who needs school if you're a rock star, right?" He chuckles to himself before looking back over at me. "So after you got the car, did your grades go to shit?"

"No sir. I kept them up, for the most part. I don't want to talk about my grades though. Let's go back to this music thing. Why *aren't* you fronting a famous rock band? You're amazing. Honestly!"

"I've got a pretty gnarly case of stage fright. It's about the only thing that does really get to me. Singing, sharing a part of yourself with others… that's never been my life. Never what it's been about."

"So what *has* it been about then?"

"That's a whole other story for a whole other time."

"Well, we've got all summer." I pull into Whittaker's lot and park. Scanning the lot for my ex's truck, I'm relieved to see it's not here.

We head inside the half-empty bar and Brandi squeals when she sees us. Making her way around the counter, she gives me a huge hug, nearly knocking me over in the process.

"Thank you! I'm sooooo fucking bored!" She lets go and eyes Xander from head to toe. "Well, hello again, stranger. Long time, no see. You get a hug, too."

She stands on her tiptoes and wraps her arms around him with a squeeze before letting him go.

"Good to see you too, Brandi," he says.

"How was your first day with the old man? He's a fuckin riot, right?" She makes her way back around the bar and sets two cocktail napkins down. We each take a seat and she starts making my usual vodka, water and lime. "Xander, what are you drinking tonight?"

"Grab me one of the Schlafly pale ales, please. And yeah, it wasn't bad at all. He's a real good dude."

She sets my drink down, pops the top off the beer and places it in front of Xander.

"Ethan is coming up later. Did he text you?" Brandi asks and I check my phone. There are two unread texts from him.

"I guess he did. What time?"

"He said 'around eight.' Then he said 'maybe nine.' I don't know. You know how all over the place he is." She rolls her eyes and wipes the counter aimlessly with a dirty dish rag.

"Yeah, no kidding."

As she tends to a regular across the bar I turn my attention to Xander. "Ethan is a good friend of ours. Weird guy, but he's sweet. The three of us went to school together, and he's had my back with some stuff in the past."

I bite my lip, fighting back the memory of Ethan grabbing Cody off me, only to get the living shit beat out of him. It was the first time Cody came after me, and it was the first time I left him.

Not long after was the first time I took him back.

"That's cool. A friend of yours is a friend of mine," Xander says, sipping his beer and then flashing me that smile I'm already too smitten with.

"So that 'whole other story at a whole other time' business… seems like as good a time as any." I nudge him with my elbow.

"No, that's not really bar talk. It's not really 'Hey, I just met you' talk either." He laughs and takes a swig of his beer. I know I should leave it be, but his vulnerability when I bring it up makes me selfishly want to know. It makes me *need* to know. In the end, I guess I'm as curious as my father.

"How about twenty questions?" I ask.

"I hate twenty questions."

"How about five questions, then?"

He cracks a smile and lifts an eyebrow. "How about three?"

"Deal!"

"So, have I mentioned how much I fucking hate Tuesdays?" Brandi's voice cuts right between us. Xander looks relieved.

Me? Not so much. "Damn it, Brandi!"

"What?"

"Oh nothing. Can you grab me Fireball though? Pretty please. Two of them." I look at Xander. "You're taking one."

"Three. I am too, bitch! Fuck Tuesdays!" Brandi calls out from across the bar as she begins filling the shot glasses from the Fireball chiller.

"Question one. You said you've been traveling awhile now, right? Do you ever get tired of it? Ever feel like settling?"

"Damn. Starting out with the heavy hitters, huh?" He eyes

the shot glasses as if hoping it will somehow make them fill faster.

"Need me to go easier on you? Maybe a finger or two first before I go in with the whole fist?"

He looks at me in disbelief. "Did you really just say that?"

"Just answer the question, two fingers or three?"

"What am I going to do with you?" He laughs and shakes his head. "Shit, I didn't even know you could talk when I first met you. I'm relieved to know you're more than able." He holds up a balled fist. "And no, I'm good with the fist. I've had practice." He says with a wink.

My face contorts in disgust at the thought and he drops his hand, poking a tongue out at me.

"Anyway, to answer your question, I kind of settled in Georgia. As settled as I've ever been I guess. It never really did feel like home though. Come to think of it, I can't say anywhere ever really has. Sometimes it's easier that way."

"Were you always in foster care?" I immediately regret asking. It isn't my place, but my damn curiosity has gotten the best of me. "Never mind. I'm sorry I asked. I shouldn't have."

"It's okay, really. It's not really a big deal to talk about." He clears his throat. "I spent the first few years of my life—seven or eight, I guess—with my biological parents. The rest were spent in foster care," he says, swallowing hard. "I don't have much in the way of family and Ocala stopped being home quite a while ago."

Brandi brings shots over, interrupting our conversation. She sets ours down and lifts hers up. "To Xander getting acquainted with the beautifully miserable town of Truman Valley."

"I'll drink to that," I say, raising my own, and we proceed to down them. She tosses the plastic shot glasses in the trash and makes her way around the bar to make her rounds.

"So did any of the foster homes actually feel like home?" *No filter I'm telling you.*

"Is that your second question? Shit, actually that would be your third. Aren't I supposed to get one?"

"No, they're both just parts of the first question," I say with a coy smile.

"You're killing me. Making up your own rules now?" He laughs and shakes his head. "Okay, okay, so to answer your question, no, none of them did. And that counts as the second question at least. As for *my* question, I want to know what the hardest thing in your life has been." The way he says it comes off so condescending.

"What? You think because I didn't spend time in foster care that I haven't struggled? Seriously?"

Xander's face turns red, his mouth gapes open. "Wait, wait, wait… down girl! Are you always so quick to assume? You were asking about one of the toughest parts of my life. I figured I'd even it out a little." He puts a hand on my shoulder. "Okay? I meant no offense. I swear. You don't have to answer that question, okay? It was stupid."

"No, it's alright." I hesitate for a moment because I don't often talk about my past, particularly with strangers, but something makes me want to tell him. His presence is comforting.

"My ex was abusive," I blurt out, bringing a look of shock to Xander's face. I can feel his eyes burning a hole through me, so I continue talking to fill the awkward void.

"We were high school sweethearts, and for a long time

things were normal. In college, he was the star quarterback. He was highly rated and supposed to go into the NFL. But he pissed hot for steroids and ended up getting his scholarship taken away. He started drinking more and doing drugs, and that's when everything changed."

My mind takes me back to the exact night, one I'm not likely to forget. Drunk and hopped up on something, Cody pushed me around at my parents' lake house. Only Ethan and Brandi were with us and, unfortunately, Ethan paid dearly.

I didn't know what to do. I loved Cody. I really did. He checked every box I had before everything changed. I thought I was doing the right thing. I thought I could change him.

"I'm so sorry, Paige. I feel like shit for how I came across earlier," Xander says, his hand meeting my shoulder again.

"It's okay. I've kind of learned to accept it and move on. It was just a lot. Once the abuse started, it never really stopped, and I just had no clue how to get out."

"How *did* you get out?"

"It took a long time. I opened up to Mom after a little persistence from Brandi. I wanted to tell someone for so long, but I was so scared. Near the end, I thought he might really hurt me. Like something worse than the bumps and bruises. Dad was the last one I wanted to tell, but Mom eventually convinced me otherwise. He went over to Cody's house and beat the ever-loving shit out of him. Told him if he ever saw him around me again, he'd kill him. I've been lucky enough to only run into him a few times since. It's such a small town... kind of a hard thing to avoid."

"I can imagine. If I ever see that prick..." Xander's voice trails off and he cracks his knuckles. His eyes are intense and lost in the row of top shelf liquor.

"Don't worry, I think he got the hint. I didn't see it, but I heard my dad didn't go easy on him. Shit travels fast in small towns."

"Yeah, it was the same where I'm from."

"Cody and your buddy from the other night run together," I say, motioning my head to the spot where Benji Mathis was at the mercy of Xander just a couple nights ago. "They're really doing their best to turn this town to shit. They deal meth and some other stuff with this guy, Russ. Real pieces of work…all of them. "

Brandi approaches with two more shots and sets them in front of Xander and me.

"Tell me you're not talking about that horrible ex of yours. Have some shots. Lighten things up a bit."

"I'm okay with how the conversation's going," Xander says, a smart-ass smirk on his face. He raises his shot glass in the air and nods to Brandi before taking it.

"Okay, your turn. Don't you go thinking I've forgotten about this game of ours." I smile and poke him in his side.

"Okay, okay, let me think…I've got major Fireball brain right now." He rubs his temples and closes his eyes. "Oh, I have one… has your brother always been such a dick?" He laughs, as do I, and then he puts up a hand. "Completely kidding. He seems… uh… nice."

"Hey, you don't have to sugarcoat it for me. I know full well how much of a dick my brother is. But he's been through a lot in his life. He was in foster care himself awhile. Went through a few families and didn't have the best experiences. My parents couldn't conceive after me, but they desperately wanted another kid so they adopted Caleb when he was seven." My gaze drops to the floor. "Probably sharing a bit too much there. I drink and the word vomit commences."

"No, you're totally fine. I like it. I feel like shit for being judgmental though. I would've never guessed he was adopted. He looks just like you guys."

"Don't feel bad. How are you supposed to know? Anyway, I have my next question for you, mister."

Xander clears his throat dramatically. "I think you mean *last* question, lady. And that's disregarding your three-part first question," he says with a laugh.

"Ugh, fine! Last question."

"Shoot."

"*Friends* or *The Office*."

"That's a terrible question. How the hell am I supposed to choose?" He stands and tips the stool against the bar.

"You're going to have to," I tell him.

"No, what I have to do is piss. You'll have to wait for your answer." He winks and makes his way to the bathroom.

CHAPTER SEVEN

Xander

"Mind Reader"—Dustin Lynch

UPON EXITING THE BATHROOM, I NOTICE ANOTHER GUY—presumably Ethan—has taken up a stool right next to Paige.

Before taking my seat, I extend a hand to him. "I guess you're Ethan. How're you doing? I'm Xander."

He takes my hand, limp wristed, and then quickly lets go. "Yeah, I know who you are. Brandi can't stop frickin' talking about you." He rolls his eyes and shakes his head. "You'd think you piss gold or something."

"Damn Ethan, you on your period, buddy?" Paige says with a playful laugh. He's not as impressed as I am by her joke.

"No, no, just giving Xander a bit of shit. A little rookie hazing, no?" He looks at me with an odd smile and I nod, though I have no idea what he's talking about. "How have the Watsons been treating you, my man?" Ethan asks, pushing his oversized glasses back up the bridge of his nose. He has mechanic's hands, oiled and rough, and they fidget constantly. That being said, this guy doesn't look like any mechanic I've ever met.

"I have no complaints," I say. "Mrs. Watson is quite the cook. She's been fattening me up."

"Yes, yes she is quite the cook. I've spent a lot of time at that house. I've known the Watsons since I was just a kid. I think Teresa would likely adopt me if she could!" He looks to Paige excitedly, almost manically. "Right?"

"Well, she sure does miss you helping out in the kitchen. She doesn't get much help from her own kids," Paige says, forcing an awkward laugh and then she calls for Brandi to bring more drinks for the two of us.

Ethan scoffs and snaps his fingers at Brandi, indicating he wants another drink as well, though his is still three-quarters full. She ignores him. Rolling his eyes, he huffs and turns to face me. "I suppose you'll be at the wine festival this weekend?"

"Yeah, everyone keeps talking about it. I guess I'd better,"

"Yes, you'd better." He smiles again, his crooked teeth peeking from behind chapped lips. This guy is into Paige, and he makes no attempt at hiding it. It's almost amusing the way he interacts with her. At first I thought maybe he was gay, but the way he looks at her…I don't know. It's creepy.

"By the way, Paige," I say, trying my best to shut this dude up. He's already starting to annoy me. "I've decided it's a question that cannot be answered."

She shakes her head as I take a new beer from Brandi and lift it in appreciation. Ethan looks to me, confused.

"I said you have to answer it." She smirks. "Rules are rules."

"Answer what?" Ethan asks.

"Better show, *The Office* or *Friends*," Paige says, her eyes still on me. "So, Xander?"

"That's easy, they both suck," Ethan interjects.

"That's not an option, Ethan. Xander, go."

"If you're holding a gun to my head, then… I guess… *The Office*." Paige throws two thumbs down and boos.

"This is a shit conversation." Ethan's haughty voice is grating on my nerves.

"So let's talk about you then, Ethan. What do you do?" I ask before chugging my beer. I tried to mask my annoyance, but it's not something I'm very good at. Especially after I've been drinking. The rate at which it's going down now is scary. We are about to enter Xander drunk territory, as my buddies who serve would say, which never turns out very well for me.

"I'm a mechanic at my dad's shop. Not my dream job, but it pays," Ethan says.

"So what is your dream job?"

"Hell if I know. Not a goddamn mechanic, that's for sure."

"Hey, I know the feeling. I've done everything from electrical installation to construction and roofing. Now, I'm picking grapes. God knows where I'll be or what I'll be doing a year from now, but none of it's ever what I imagined I'd be doing." I look at the empty shot glasses. "Hey Ethan, you want a shot? Paige, I don't know about you. You gotta drive."

"Wait, wait, wait. I want one!" Paige whines. "I'm sure as shit not driving after all the shots I've had. Are you crazy? We can just have Brandi take us home after the bar closes. She spends the night pretty much every night anyways."

"Okay, cool, and Ethan?" I ask.

"Yeah, I guess, but what are you having? I don't do the strong stuff."

"Nah, we're just doing Fireball."

"That *is* the strong stuff." I try my best not to laugh, but it tears from my mouth regardless. Paige starts laughing too, and Ethan's face turns bright red.

"Fuck you guys," he says, flicking his hand our way effeminately.

My laughing stops abruptly. Any other man saying those words to me would've been beaten senseless. I stow the feeling away, not wanting to ruin the evening. Instead, I motion for Brandi to grab three more. She starts to fill four. *So much for our DD.*

She brings the shots, balancing them against each other as only a seasoned bartender can, and sets them in front of us. Ethan grimaces when he lifts his. I want to laugh again, but I refrain. It takes everything I have not to ridicule him.

"Cheers!" I say and we take the shots. Three of them stay down. One comes right back up in a trail leading to the bathroom, our laughter a soundtrack behind Ethan as he scurries away. Paige and I laugh for a good five minutes as Brandi bitches about how she "won't be cleaning that shit up".

Ethan comes back with a stick up his ass and barely speaks. I'm too drunk to give a shit, though I can promise you I wouldn't care stone cold sober either. This dude is a fucking creep. And right now, he's lucky he's Paige's friend.

Ethan leaves soon after his Smirnoff Ice is finished with a hug for Paige and a cold shoulder for me. We spend an hour or so more at the bar watching ESPN, talking sports and dropping a few more shots. After Brandi gets off work, Paige and I settle in the back of her Honda Civic.

By the time the engine starts, she and I are already leaning together in a drunken heap, eyes closed and borderline passed out. I can hear Brandi huffing in the front seat, complaining about having to drive or something like that. I don't really care though. Right now, the smell of Paige's hair has my drunken senses in overdrive. Her soft hair falls onto my chest, her head resting against my shoulder. I prop my head against hers, and with each bump, my chin brushes against her forehead. Each time, she giggles and swats at her face before nuzzling back in.

The ride could've lasted forever and it would've been alright with me. Unfortunately, it doesn't. I feel the car come to a stop and open my eyes. Paige does too. Before we can shake the sleepiness off, Brandi has one leg already out the door.

"I'll see you in your room, Paige. Hurry your ass up. I'm tired." Her look of annoyance passes from Paige to me, but then it softens a bit. "I'll see you in the morning, Xander."

She slams the car door and makes her way into the house. Paige's eyes follow her all the way to the door, then she slowly turns to me, a look of confusion on her face. Out of nowhere, she bursts into laughter, holding two hands to her mouth. I start laughing too—the drunken kind of laugh brought on by just about anything…and everything. Paige puts a hand to my chest, trying to catch her breath. She squeezes and it sends sensations to places they shouldn't go. She squeezes my chest again.

"Jesus, how often do you work out? Like every day?"

"I try to. I actually was going to ask you where I can go around here."

"The Truman Valley Community Complex is your only option. Seriously though, these pecs."

"Yours aren't so bad either." I give her the cheesiest wink in the entire world. I can feel it. *How fucking corny am I?*

She removes her hand, but she still has a smile stretched from ear to ear. "Xander Evans, I want to know you."

"You already know more than most... and it's only been two days," I say. It's the truth, after all.

"I wanna know more."

"Why?" *Fuck, I really don't even care why. I want to know more about this girl too.*

"I don't know." She slips her bottom lip into her mouth, nervously darting her eyes around the driveway.

"You have to have a valid reason before I share anything." I smile my biggest smile, trying my best to keep her right where she is, but as she yawns, I know our night is coming to an end.

Paige opens her door and gets out, and I reluctantly follow. She comes around to my side, just a foot in front of me, and pokes a finger into the same pec she was squeezing just moments ago.

"I don't need a reason. You, sir, will tell me because I'm adorable and because I asked nicely." She blows me a kiss, and turning on her heel, she makes her way to the house. I can't help but watch her as she walks away, her beautiful ass firm and teasing me from beneath short jean shorts. I wish she'd turn around, no matter the trouble it would inevitably cause.

She doesn't.

I stagger to the guesthouse, and as I reach the top of the

steps, I stop in my tracks. A rustling in the vineyard draws my focus. Shaded by the darkness, it looks as if there's a figure among the rows of grapevines, the moon reflecting off what could be eyes…maybe glasses?

Hell, I'm drunk off my ass. I rub a stiff palm across each eye and look again.

Nothing… *Damn Fireball.*

CHAPTER EIGHT

Xander

"Higher"—The Ready Set

I MANAGE TO AVOID PAIGE FOR THE BETTER PART OF THE week. I get the feeling she's avoiding me too. We both know nothing good can come of this. I would never disrespect this man in his own home, and I wouldn't ruin the good thing I have here—or the good money I'm making, for that matter.

But damn. When I'm around her, she's got every last bit of my attention.

I guess it helps that Jack keeps me in the vineyard most of the day. It's not terribly difficult work, but they are some long hours under the sun. I enjoy his company though. He can bullshit with the best of them, and if there's one thing you learn to appreciate in a man after hanging out with military guys, it's a good bullshitter.

He pours a bottle of water over his head, holding out another for me.

"No, I'm fine, Jack."

"I think I'm just getting old," he says, grunting loudly and tossing the water bottle into a wheelbarrow.

"Pretty sure you've been old for quite some time." I keep my face as straight as I can, but it's moments from cracking. He takes the sweat soaked rag from around his neck and flings it directly at my head. I dodge it easily and pick it up, preparing my own throw.

"Dude, you even throw like an old man!" I toss it at him lightly, and it falls to his feet.

"Don't let the diminishing arm speed fool you, kid. I still got old man strength, which means I can still kick your ass." He sticks a forefinger into my chest and brushes past me, laughing his ass off.

"I'm not so sure that whole old man strength thing is real, Jack. The science just doesn't add up." He laughs heartily again, making his way toward the house. Before he enters, he turns back around. "C'mon in for a second. I need you to run an errand for me."

I follow him inside, where he grabs his wallet from the counter and pulls out two twenties.

"The ladies have made their demands. Can you stop over at Whittaker's"—he grabs a small piece of paper from the counter and hands it to me—"and pick up some lunch? I guess they're tied up."

"No problem at all." I take the cash from him and start out the door.

"Grab something for yourself too. I don't need any change."

I look back, a slanted smile on my face.

"Who said you were getting any change back?" I wink at him and he laughs, brushing me off with his hand.

"Get the fuck outta here, you turd."

"Turd? You're really showing your age there, old man. Nobody says turd anymore."

———————

Watson Metalworks takes up an entire block in downtown Truman Valley. The huge welded metal sign sets itself drastically apart from the rest of Main Street in a way that draws the eye almost immediately. Large windows cover the entire face of the building, and inside I can see it's broken up into two sections: a display room with different metal sculptures lining shelves on the walls and in display cases scattered throughout the room. In the other, larger room, I can see Teresa busy at work on a sculpture. It looks like a dragon, or maybe a bird, I can't quite tell.

I open the front door and enter the display area. A delicate tone sounds as the door swings shut behind me. Almost immediately, Paige's head pops around the corner. Her eyes go wide when she sees the greasy bag in my hand.

"Yesssssss!" she says. "Meatball sub!"

She walks around the corner, the Watson Metalworks polo delicately clinging to her beautiful curves. I laugh as she skips toward me and snatches the bag from my hands.

"Took you long enough, stranger. Hmmph!" She turns, swinging her hair enough to whip me in the face with it, and she prances to the studio

I follow close behind, almost as if I'm on a leash. *Shame on you, Xander.*

"Xander!" Teresa calls as she sees me. "I was about to send out a search party."

"Sorry, ma'am, Brandi's working." Both Teresa and Paige look at each other, knowing full well what I mean.

"Oh well, then I'm shocked you made it at all!" She grabs the bag from Paige and digs out her Caesar salad in a hurry. "And didn't I talk to you about calling me 'ma'am' already?"

"No, ma'am, I don't believe you did." I crack a smile.

"Well, it's Teresa from now on, you got it? We're gonna break you of that eventually." She squints her eyes, attempting to look tough.

"Yes, ma'am." This time it's completely out of habit, but they burst out laughing anyway.

"You're a mischievous one!" Teresa starts to dig into her salad, and I notice Paige is already halfway through her meatball sub. She hasn't even bothered sitting down.

"Did you get anything for yourself?" Teresa asks.

"Yeah, but I was starving so I ate my burger while Brandi talked my ear off."

I take a seat while inspecting the different projects in front of me. "So what are you guys working on?"

"Well, the real question is, what are we *not* working on?" Teresa says. Her eyes scan the dozen or so metal sculptures scattered on the table, eventually landing on the one right in front of her. "At some point this is going to be Falkor from the—"

"No way!" I cut her off without thinking. "*The NeverEnding Story*. I love that movie."

"Me too!" Paige is wide-eyed, presumably excited I've seen the movie too. "I tell her every day that I'm stealing this thing before it ever gets to a customer. That, or she's making one for me after this."

"I don't think I ever want to attempt this again. Absolutely the hardest project I've ever done, and I regret ever agreeing to do it."

"Well, I'm blown away by the ingenuity it would take to do something like this."

Teresa turns red, looking to Paige and then back to me. "Can I keep you?" she says, and Paige giggles.

"That can be arranged," I say with a smile. "So how did you even get started with this?"

"Well, my daddy was a welder. About the only good memory I have with him was learning the trade." Teresa spoke so freely, without altering her tone or expression. I respect a person's ability to be so open. It makes me want to be open too.

"He never did this kind of welding, just your usual stuff. Once I got out of art school, I sculpted—mostly with clay—and then I kind of got the idea to combine the skills. It took a long time to get it all figured out, but once I did, it sort of became an obsession."

"No kidding," Paige says, rolling her eyes.

"Hey, you didn't mind when this obsession paid for your college degree," Teresa says, nudging her daughter playfully with her hand.

"Oh, I know, Mama. I'm just yanking your chain."

"You better be," Teresa says, smiling and then turns her attention to me. "So, Xander, you excited for the festival tonight?" Teresa asks.

"Yeah, I am. It sounds like it'll be a good time. It's been fun watching Jack the more we've gotten things together for the festival. No nerves at all. With how big this competition is, you'd think he'd at least be a little nervous. I guess that's what winning five years in a row will get you, huh?"

"Six," Teresa corrects me with a smile. "Honestly, he's always been that way. Even when the winery first started. He's one of the most level-headed people I've ever met. As I'm sure you've come to find out, he puts everything he has into the vineyard. Win or lose, he's proud of it."

"Well, I'm looking forward to having a bottle or two tonight." I smile and rise from my stool.

"Or three or four or five," Paige says with a sly smile. Teresa gives her the typical stern motherly look and Paige just shrugs.

"What, Mom? It's the wine festival!"

"You just better be careful, young lady. I won't be bailing you out."

"Oh my God, Mom. Seriously? I think we'll be okay. Right, Xander?"

"Don't you worry Teresa. I'll make sure she stays out of trouble." I stand and slip the stool back under the work station. "Anyways, I should probably get back before boss-man starts cutting my pay."

"Oh, you're definitely docked at least a hundred dollars already. Keep it up and you'll soon be working for free," Teresa says, laughing and pretending to crack a whip. She stands and walks over to me, wrapping me up in a hug. *She's a hugger, all right.*

"Uh huh. Figures you'd talk crap and then hightail it out of here."

"Bye, Paige," I say, a smile spread wide across my face.

"Bye, Xander."

The sky is full of beautiful amber and fiery orange as the sun dips into the horizon. The evening breeze sways the tree branches rhythmically. It's so damn beautiful in this part of the country at this time of year—better than any place I've been so far.

The rocker creaks and groans against the guesthouse porch as my foot bobs back and forth. I fall into somewhat of a trance, the beauty of the country settling me.

I have an ice cold beer in my hand, one of several I've had while waiting. I try my best to keep my white button-up stain free, which, for me, is a feat in and of itself…beers or not. It's one of the many things Jack and I have in common.

I'm not often a man who spends a lot of time in front of the mirror, but tonight I had reason. Though it pains me to admit it, I spent twenty-something minutes getting my hair just right—and shamefully scowling back at myself, of course.

But what can I say? I've never craved someone like I do Paige, and while I know all the reasons she and I can't hook up, it just makes the prospect of it that much more appealing.

It makes her untouchable. And I like untouchable. That's not something a man can even help.

Jack and Teresa have already made their way to the festival. We set everything up earlier, but Jack has to get his pinot noir in to the judges. Paige and Brandi are on something like the second hour of getting ready, but with a few beers and the evening as beautiful as it is, I don't mind the wait.

We can't leave until Ethan gets here anyway. Brandi made sure he would be available to DD tonight. Probably a good idea as I can hear the girls whooping it up in the main house with

90's hip-hop blaring, likely on their second or third glass of wine.

It usually takes five minutes to get into town, but it took us a good twenty this go-around and ten more to find a good parking spot. Plenty of time for the women to fill the SUV with a flurry of rap lines, make-up touch-ups and tipsy selfies… and for us men to sit in the front in awkward silence. If traffic were any indication, the entire town truly does come out for this thing.

Roads are blocked off and people walk the brightly lit downtown area in all directions. Rows of tables with tents and various community entities are in every direction. There's Whittaker's serving sliders and craft beer, Brooke's Books with new and used paperbacks, and Sunshine Cleaners with business cards and smiling faces. Archie's Sporting Goods has set up a basketball net, and there's a line of excited kids alongside the table. VFW Post 63 is located beside them, taking donations, and you can't miss the Club Rapid girls with over-sweetened shots and skimpy clothes.

Then you have all the wineries. They make up the bulk of the tables, and each one offers free samples. The sight instantly gets me excited. My buzz is already well on its way and free alcohol shines like a beacon of continued happiness. In the middle of everything, set up in the town square is a huge dance floor with a stage set behind it and a band pumping out 80's rock.

"Dad and Mom are way in the back… in front of the shop. It's way too far of a walk not to stop for a few samples first," Paige says, winking at me and pulling Brandi to the first booth. The banner reads: Aerie's Wineries - Grafton, Illinois. "Four

Adlerschreiens, please." She turns back to me. "This is one of my favorites!"

By the time we make it to the Watsons' tents, we've had about a hundred samples. A warmth coats my face and crawls slowly up and down my arms. The corners of my mouth ache from smiling. I'm not even quite sure what I've been smiling about.

Just below the massive Watson Metalworks sign, there are two tables with tents over them. One table sports a banner for the winery and has the three different wines we produce in a hundred tiny plastic cups. On the other table, there are two sculptures. One is of a dragon poised to attack, and the other is a medieval warrior made from various everyday items. His helmet is a small stainless steel bowl, his jaw part of a bike chain with screws for teeth. In his hand, he's wielding a mace made out of an egg beater and screws.

"Hey, guys! You finally made it!" Teresa says, her voice registering at a high drunken octave. She walks around the table and gives both girls their hugs. Ethan and I are next. "Grab some wine! Xander, have you been able to try any yet?" Without letting me answer, she snatches up a few plastic cups and distributes them to each of us.

"I've had a few, but I've saved the best for last!" I take the cup from her and down it.

"That's what I like to hear," Teresa says slipping two more cups into my hands.

"Paige, have you taken him to Aeries?" She looks at me. "Aeries is our favorite. After ours, of course"

"Yes, Mom, that was our first stop?" Paige scans the crowd, nervously. It seems as if she's looking for something—or someone.

"I haven't seen him yet," Teresa says.

Paige turns quickly to look at her. "I just didn't want any surprises."

"Fuck him! He's not going to ruin our night!" Brandi says, a drunken slur beginning to make itself known. She grabs another cup anyways. Ethan tries to grab one as well, but Brandi shoots him a glare. "You better watch it, you gotta drive me home!"

Ethan rolls his eyes, but does as he's told and lets go of the cup.

"Mom, we're going to go walk around a little bit. Where's Dad?" Paige asks.

"He's talking with the judges in the judges' tent. If you head there now, you should be able to catch him."

Brandi passes around two more cups a piece to all those allowed to drink and we finish them off before departing.

The judges' tent isn't far and sits just behind the stage. The blaring amps send vibrations throughout my body. The pulse of the drums makes me wish I had my guitar. I've never experienced playing on stage, or with a band. I was always too nervous to play in front of people. But it's something I've dreamed about since I was a little kid. Losing myself to the music. Letting the sound, the beat, the words, and the pain take over. And then—to let it all go.

Just as we reach the tent, Jack comes barreling out, his face bright red and a huge six-beers-down grin plastered on his face. He takes Paige into his arms, lifting her slightly off the ground and shaking her gently.

"My princess!"

"Daddy!" Paige giggles. "Let me down!"

He finally does and puts his hand out for me. I take it, and he pulls me in for a bro hug. Surprised, I accept it, and out of the corner of my eye, I can see Ethan shooting me a sour look, his brow furrowed.

I give Jack a couple extra pats on the back for good measure and then pull away.

"Xander, my boy, good work this week. Now, come get a beer with me. This fucker Stan, whom I usually deny being friends with, makes a damn good APA. Oh, Ethan, you come too, man."

Jack leads the two of us away, and I hear Brandi chuckling behind us. I turn and wave, primarily to Paige, but they both wave back.

"Bye bye, afterthought!" Brandi's words have some bite to them, and Ethan glares back at her. Jack hardly notices, while I'm stifling a laugh of my own.

After three beers with Jack and Stan, along with the generous amount of wine samples, I'm stumbling a bit as I make my way through the crowd. Ethan struggles to keep up. I walk with a purpose and I know only one speed.

"Hey, man," he says, still trying to catch up.

I don't slow my step, or even turn back to him. From over my shoulder, I ask, "What's up?"

"Hey, man," he repeats, "can we slow down a little? We don't even know where they are." Ethan finally makes it to my side, and I see sweat has taken up most of his forehead and his glasses are fogged. A greasy sheen coats his forehead. I slow up a little as he removes his glasses and wipes them down with his shirt.

"I don't have either of their numbers," I say. "Did you text them?"

"Yeah. They haven't texted back. You don't have Paige's number?"

"No."

"Why not?

"I don't know. There hasn't been a need, I guess. Why?"

"Oh, just curious. You guys seem to be hitting it off. I figured you would've already exchanged numbers by this point... if not more."

The condescending way he says that stops me in my tracks. After a few steps, he stops too.

"You got a problem with me, man? I work with the Watsons... Paige is a friend. Whatever it is you have in your head, get rid of it." I keep my tone neutral—or as neutral as I can—but I'd like to take his glasses off his fucking face and throw them. Would I be allowed to hit him then?

"I just want to know what your intentions are with Paige. She's a dear friend of mine. It's my business to ensure her... um...safety. I feel that way for all the Watsons."

I want to tell the fucker I'm pretty sure Paige only keeps him around out of pity—and Brandi because he's her lap dog. But I hold back. I'm not going to stir up any shit with a friend of the family.

"Listen, you don't know me, man, and I don't know what relationship you have with the Watsons. While I can respect it, you also need to know I'm not going to put up with this shit. I'm not trying to judge you, because I don't know you. Do me a favor and show me the same respect."

I turn and walk away without letting him get a word in.

When I spot the Watsons' tents and Teresa drinking from a large wine glass behind the table, I breathe a sigh of relief.

"Hey, man," Ethan calls out from behind me, his voice grating my nerves. "No need to get harsh with it. I'm just looking out."

I don't bother looking back—or even answering, for that matter. Instead, I greet Teresa with a smile. "Hey, Teresa…have you seen Paige and Brandi?" I ask, just as Ethan catches up.

"Hey, guys! They were just here to grab a bottle, and I believe they were headed toward the dance floor." She looks at her wrist as if a watch is there. "It's about that time anyways, if I know my daughter!" She smiles widely and offers up a glass of wine—in a real glass this time—which I happily accept.

"Are you having a good time?" she asks, eyeing me as I take a big drink. She readies the bottle for another pour. Their pinot noir truly is a thing of beauty.

"I'm having a great time!" I nearly shout, but not on purpose. "Jack took us over to Stan's, and we had about a keg of craft beer. It was like I was in heaven. The guy had some great war stories too. I could've sat there all day."

"Oh god, Stan is something else. Only believe half of what you hear. He's harmless though. Well, go find the girls, and here"—she fills my glass almost to the top—"take some for the road." She lifts the bottle up for Ethan, but he waves her off. I lift the glass to Teresa in thanks and make my way to find Paige and Brandi with Ethan close behind.

CHAPTER NINE

Paige

"Goodnight Moon"—Go Radio

I'M SO DRUNK I DON'T FEEL LIKE I HAVE CONTROL OVER MY arms anymore, as if they're completely separate from my body. The wine bottle I snagged from Mom is just moments from shattering into a hundred pieces all over the dance floor as Brandi and I make our way across it. Brandi periodically snatches my arm for balance which threatens to bring the both of us down.

The band is playing a killer version of "Sweet Home Alabama," and she and I are doing our best to make complete asses out of ourselves. When I see Xander heading toward us, my brain tells me to stop dancing like an idiot, but my body doesn't respond. I continue gyrating and thrusting as if I popped right out of an 80's music video. Instead of laughing at me, Xander hops onto the dance floor and starts doing the most ridiculous "lawn mower" move I've ever seen. He quickly shifts to a lasso-ing cowboy that draws laughter from some of the others on the dance floor, but he hardly notices. He keeps going until he's just a foot away. I stop dancing and look back at Brandi to see if she's seeing his sweet moves, but she's in her own little world right now. I then see Ethan glaring intently at Xander as he dances, a judgmental look on his face. Brandi takes a seat at the table just to our right, pulls her heels off and tilts her head back with a sigh of relief.

I look back to Xander, who has stopped dancing, and I grab his hand to pull him toward the table. "I think it's time to crack this bottle open. What do you say?" I ask.

"Sounds like a damn good plan," Xander says, taking a seat and tugging his shirt back and forth for circulation. Sweat has taken up much of his v-neck and he looks completely uncom-fortable.

"Where did you guys disappear to anyways?" I ask taking my own seat next to him.

"We were at Stan's the whole time. That dude can talk."

I laugh. "Tell me about it. You oughta see him and Dad out by the fire pit with a case of beer. It's a riot!"

"I can only imagine," Xander says. Ethan joins us at the table. He crosses his arms and wears a pathetic frown. I try my best to ignore him as Xander continues. "It's like a never ending pissing contest. Which is fucking great as a bystander."

"Yeah, it's free entertainment. Can't beat that, baby." Though my 'baby' was completely innocent, I see Ethan cringe and he grumbles under his breath.

"Who drove a stick up your ass, Ethan?" I ask.

"Well, Paige, it's not always fun being the DD." He snarls a little, showing the slight yellow stain of his teeth.

"Give me a break! You don't even like drinking that much," Brandi says to him as she struggles to pull the cork from the bottle.

Xander finally takes it from her and finishes the job, pouring a glass for each of us—including Ethan. He holds it out to him as Ethan inspects the glass.

"DD can have a little, too," Xander says. "Take it, bro." Ethan reluctantly accepts the glass and eases up, nodding his head toward Xander in appreciation.

We're enjoying our wine and resting our feet when the band starts playing the first few notes of "Sweet Child O' Mine". I just can't help myself. I grab Xander's hand and drag him toward the dance floor. He only fights it for a moment.

Once on the dance floor, he takes my other hand and whisks me around effortlessly. To my surprise, he can actually dance. Moving and swaying to the music, he guides me so well I don't even have to think. I'm relieved to know the "white boy" dancing was just an act, though this man could make just about anything look good.

As the band hits the chorus, I start to lose myself in the moment with Xander. My hands are held gently in his. His eyes get lost in my own, and a smile tugs at the corner of his mouth. Then, as he spins me, I catch Brandi coming toward me quickly from the corner of my eye. Concern is etched on her face. From behind her, I see my ex barreling forward, his eyes glazed over and mouth open. We've stopped dancing and both Xander and I watch and wait. Xander steps in front of me as Cody approaches. Behind Cody are his lackeys, Russ and Benji.

Benji has one of his sausage fingers outstretched and

pointed right at Xander.

"That's the motherfucker from Whittaker's, Cody. That motherfucker *right there!*"

The three of them stop in front of us. Cody, who is at least two inches taller than Xander and about two times wider thanks to a weekly shot of testosterone, sizes Xander up. The other two are even bigger, but Xander stands firm. Ethan and Brandi are standing, but staying back.

"You know that's my woman, right, boy?" As usual, Cody is chewing on a toothpick that sits in the corner of his mouth. While he's talking, it bobs as his lips move.

"From what I hear, she hasn't been your woman for quite some time." Xander stands taller now, though I didn't think it was possible. "And from what I see, you're drunk as fuck, high on something, and interrupting a damn good time."

The band continues to play, but now pays more attention to the action than playing the proper chord progressions. There's still activity around the booths, but everyone on the dance floor is now watching to see what Cody will do next. I'm concerned as I have seen far too many times what alcohol does to his temper. I don't need an encore.

"Xander, let's just go." It comes out almost a whisper, though I intended it to be much louder.

"No, we are going to settle this right here, right now. There is no issue here." Xander points to himself, then to Cody and back again. "Your boy was out of line at Whittaker's, and I acted only as I would hope any other man would in the situation. You do know he got manhandled because he was pawing at *your woman*, don't you?"

Cody looks back at Benji inquisitively, who scoffs and

shakes his head.

Xander points his finger at Cody again.

"You. I don't even know you. I have no issue with you… other than the fact Jack Watson made it damn clear that you were to stay away from Paige. Yet here you are."

Cody grinds his teeth and digs his fingernails into his palms so hard his whole hand turns white. "*Fuck* Jack Watson." Cody looks back at Benji and then to Rusty with a smirk before turning back to Xander. "And *fuck* you." He jabs a finger into Xander's chest, but Xander doesn't waver.

"It's Cody, right?" Xander doesn't let him answer. "Listen, Cody. I don't normally let any man put his hands on me, and I don't believe in giving out warnings in life. They're kind of like participation ribbons in youth sports, you know what I mean?" Again, he gives him no time to respond. "But because I'm having a good time, and because I don't want to ruin the good time of all these people, I'll give you a pass on this one. Usually that kind of thing elicits some serious facial rearrangement." Some of the crowd boos Xander for this, but he pays them no attention.

Just as Cody is about to speak, he continues, "I'm going to tell you what I told your buddy over there." He points to Benji. "I'm a man who's all about respect. I'll give it, and I expect it in return. If you can't give it, I suggest you get the fuck out of my face. And I suggest you mind the warnings of Mr. Watson, no matter what you may think of him."

Just beside the stage, I see Dad standing and listening in. He approaches us just as Cody takes a step closer—so close I'm sure Xander can smell the whiskey on his breath.

"Cody, you need to get your ass out of here real quick.

Don't ruin this night for all these good people," Dad says, a plastic smile on his face.

Cody looks at Dad and then back to Xander. He stares for what seems like an eternity.

"This ain't over, motherfucker," Cody finally says before turning around and leading his minions away.

"Why do I feel like I've heard that before?" Xander says with a smile. Cody either doesn't hear it or just doesn't care to respond, because he continues to grumble as he pushes his way through the crowd. Dad pats Xander on the back and heads back toward the tents.

I take Xander's hand and pull him in close. "Let's go home," I whisper, and somehow it comes out far sexier than I mean it to.

"What, like all of us?" He stutters and his sudden nervousness is endearing. I come in closer.

"No, like you and me." He looks at me.

"How are we going to get there? What about your Dad? The contest?" The look on Xander's face is priceless. Like a kid about to let down his parents.

"He wins *every* year. It's pretty much a guarantee at this point. Plus, I always leave early. They don't care if we go." I take a few steps forward holding onto his shirt and making him follow. "C'mon, we can walk. It's only like two miles." I pause momentarily, plotting my next bargaining tool. "Unless you're too chicken shit to walk a lady home at night."

Brandi sits bored at the table and Ethan fidgets in his seat, his eyes on our every movement.

"Hey now," he says. "Let's not get crazy. If you promise your dad won't care, then I would love to walk you home. My world is starting to spin anyways."

"Good!" I take his arm and lead him to the table where Ethan and Brandi sit. Barely slowing to a brisk walk, I say, "Good night, Brandi. 'Night, Ethan. We're heading home."

"Are you fucking kidding me?" Ethan shouts, his voice in a tone I haven't ever heard from him before. We don't acknowledge him.

"Good night, lovebirds!" Brandi calls out from behind us.

I don't turn back. Neither does Xander. I just put up a hand and wave, my other hand gripping his bicep. His pulse plays games with my fingertips.

───────※───────

It doesn't take any convincing from Xander to get me into the guesthouse, nor does it seem I have an option anyway. The wicked little smile he passes me as he leaves the guesthouse door wide open makes sure of that. Rowdy comes barreling out as expected and nearly knocks me over in his excitement. Xander calls for him to go back inside and Rowdy reluctantly obliges, his ears darting back and eyes drifting back to me.

I follow behind Rowdy as Xander orders him up onto his bed. He then grabs two beers and I take a seat. Popping their tops, he hands me one, and sits across from me on another love seat. I gulp the beer, nervous about my emerging feelings and what I might drunkenly do tonight. I know damn well what I want to do.

And I'm scared as hell about it.

"Xander Evans," I say in the sweetest tone I can muster. I don't want to think about the what ifs. Not right now at least.

Right now, I want to live in this moment.

"Yes, Paige Watson?"

"Will you sing for me, please?"

"What makes you so special?" He smiles, but he has a new look of nervousness.

"Well, that's a dumb question. I'm pretty awesome."

He doesn't say anything, but smiles timidly.

"You know I won't judge you, right? What if I close my eyes?"

As if contemplating whether to play or not, he looks down at his guitar case beneath the bed and then back at me, but remains silent.

"I would never in a million years judge anything that you say. I think you're an amazing guy, and you've come so far after all you've been through." I stop for a moment, wanting to say the right words, and hoping, at least in some way, I am. "I would just honestly appreciate you sharing that part of you with me. Just for tonight."

His eyes are locked on the guitar case and then they flit around the room as his leg bobs nervously. Finally, he stands and walks to his bed. It takes everything I have not to squeal with excitement.

He squats, pauses for a moment, his hand against the guitar case handle, and then he pulls it out.

He slowly unlatches the clasps and lifts the lid, his movements noticeably shaken either from alcohol, or nerves, or both. He manages to pull the guitar out and removes a pick from its strings. He takes a seat with it, his eyes never leaving the ground. His breathing is heavy, his eyes fixated on one specific point in front of him. Nothing else. He clutches the pick tightly, knuckles white as the pick is pressed firmly against the strings but not moving.

"Your eyes," he says, his still focused on the floor. I cover my eyes with my hands and hear him settle back on the couch, and after a moment—and a few awkward notes—he starts to play. His playing is beautiful, and heartbreaking, and moving all rolled into one. He transitions from chord to chord effortlessly, strumming with the ease and fluidity of a pro, and it's only a matter of seconds before my hands fall to my sides.

Xander's eyes are closed and he's hunched over the guitar. Then he begins to sing.

Have I become an illusion?
So desperate and disillusioned.
And am I to blame for it all, after all
I chose to be born to you

Am I desperately distracted
From life, like it's a cancer.
A self-inflicted question I've been asking
Cause you've never had the answers

To all the memories, and all the tragedy.
And all the hopeless insecurities.

To all the failure and all the heartbreak
And all the second rate remedies

I'm gone, I'm leaving, there's no looking back now.
Believe me, I'm lying, there's no use in trying.

He stops abruptly after the first chorus, and I realize that my eyes have closed on their own this time. I was as lost in the music as he was. The beauty in his voice, the depth to his words… it overwhelms me. *He* overwhelms me. I open my eyes and see I've scooted all the way to the end of the loveseat. My legs are nearly brushing against his. I lean forward, elbows on my knees and chin in my palms, when he finally opens his eyes.

"Why did you stop?"

"I…I don't even know what the hell it is I write about," he says. His voice quivers. "I just write the music as words come together in my mind. It's ridiculous."

He's beginning to turn red, and all of a sudden I want to take him in my arms and tell him how amazing he is. How lucky parents would be to call him their child. How lucky a woman would be to call him her man.

But I don't say anything, and for a few moments, neither does he.

"It's stupid," he finally mumbles.

"It's not stupid. I think it's amazing that you're able to express yourself so clearly through music. It makes me feel so many things. It makes me feel, if only for a song, what you feel…or what you felt…" I pause, because what I want to ask won't be well received, but maybe—just maybe—he'll open up to me.

"Xander, what happened with your parents? Is that what the scar is from?" I point to the five-inch-long, one-and-a-half-inch thick scar on his right forearm, something I've been meaning to ask about, but I've been putting off. I think I've been scared of the response. I can tell by the way the color leaves his face that my fear is well founded.

"Scratch that, Xander." I pull in closer. I want to take his mind away from wherever it's just gone and I do so the only way my drunken brain knows how. "What I really want to know is how badly do you want to kiss me?"

He cocks his head, his eyes wide with bewilderment. He stammers but doesn't form any actual words. I lean in closer to him…closer and closer and closer until I can feel his breath against my neck. My lips meet his ear, my voice low and seductive. "If you ever hope to kiss me, Mr. Evans, you'd better quit that dirty little habit of yours."

With that, I pull away from him and stand, nodding my head toward the tin of chewing tobacco on his nightstand, and then I make my way to the door. As I open it, I turn back in time to see him realize what I was motioning to. He looks back at me in a near panic. His eyes are even wider now. I've noticed him trying to hide his nasty habit from me for the past week. I was waiting for just the right time to break it to him that his dirty little secret was no secret at all. And that face right there… that makes the wait completely worth it.

I'm one foot out the door when I hear him finally form a response.

"What makes you think I even wanna kiss you anyways?"

With a playful look over my shoulder, I leave the guest-house without bothering to respond.

I enter the back door of the main house and close it behind me. For a moment, I lean against it and shut my eyes. The night plays over in my head.

Am I crazy to think this man could be different… that he's not like all the rest of them? Everything about him seems so genuine.

Just as my giddiness reaches pathetic levels, I hear a loud crash tear through the dark house, my brother yelling, followed by another crash. I head upstairs and begin to make out a little of what he's saying.

"Fuck you, fuck you, fuck you… *Fuck you*!" I hear the loud thud of what sounds like a remote control hitting the hardwood flooring, then the indistinguishable sound of hand meeting cheek.

Caleb's bedroom door is cracked just slightly and I peer inside. My brother's face is cranberry red, turning more so with each vicious slap. A PlayStation remote is shattered in pieces on the floor—as is the PlayStation itself. He kicks the main bulk of mangled PlayStation before punching himself in the face this time, not with all of his strength, but enough to do damage. Left, right, left, right, until blood trickles from his nose, over his lips and down his chin.

With one more punch to the face, I make the decision to stop him. I open the door slowly so it doesn't surprise him, and his eyes rip from the floor to my own. His teeth grind against each other audibly, a combination of pure anger and surprise on his face.

"What the fuck are you doing in here?!" Spittle tears from his mouth, nearly hitting me in the process. He looks like a rabid dog ready to bite and maim anything or anyone that gets in its way.

"Cody was there. We came back early." His anger immediately turns to shame, and he looks around meekly, the hate in his voice now subtle. "Are Mom and Dad here too?"

"No. Just Xander and I. What are you doing up here, Caleb?" His anger returns. He looks at me as if he'd like to kill me.

"That's none of your fucking business. Get the fuck out of my room!" He goes to close the door, but I block it with my foot. His eyes pierce straight through mine. I flinch, half expecting him to swing at me next.

"I'm your sister. Of course it's my business. Now, what the fuck are you doing up here?"

He thrusts a shoulder into the door again, but he's not the strongest teenager so the door hardly budges against my foot.

"If you tell Mom and Dad, I can't promise you I won't hurt you." I can hardly believe my ears. And I can hardly believe the conviction in his words.

"Excuse me?!" I push the door into him, and it throws him back a bit on his heels. "I'm bigger than you are, Caleb. Don't think for a second I won't hit you back. And I'm gonna make it hurt. Don't you *ever* threaten me again." I thrust my finger just inches from his face. "Do you fucking understand me?"

"Get the fuck out of my room!" He says it louder now, his voice trembling.

"Just understand this, little brother. If you ever, *ever* threaten me again, I'll not only tell Mom and Dad, but I'll break every piece of fucking entertainment you have up here. You need some help. Seriously."

I remove my foot and he slams the door in my face.

CHAPTER TEN

Xander

"Looking Too Closely"—Fink

LOUD, FRANTIC KNOCKING ON THE GUESTHOUSE DOOR tears me from my alcohol-induced sleep. My eyelids are heavy and each knock reverberates in my head as if my ear were up against a recently struck gong. Rowdy lets out a bark, and then another, and the sharpness of it makes my brain throb even more.

"Xander," I hear Paige say, her words barely audible. "You need to come out here."

I open my eyes and lift myself up, snapping at Rowdy angrily to cut his shit. I catch my reflection in the vanity across from me and see that red has taken over the whites of my eyes. My hair is disheveled, and I can't help but chuckle as I realize I passed out still wearing my jeans and white button-up—a true sign last night was a bender.

Paige's voice comes through the door again, "Xander, get up!"

"Just a second!" I call, my own voice fueling the headache's intensity. I'm slow to get up. Shifting my hands to my hips, I arch my back and try to stretch out the stiffness. I finally make my way to the door and open it.

The mid-morning sun streams in like a spotlight, forcing my eyes shut and an arm up to block it. Once my eyes finally focus through the beaming sun, I see Paige with a look of concern on her face. Jack is pacing by the back door of the main house with his iPhone to his ear.

"Paige, what's wrong?"

"You just gotta come see this." She starts down the steps and I follow behind her. Rowdy races past us to the yard to relieve himself.

It doesn't take me long to see what "this" is. Just as I reach the last step, I spot my truck, right where I left it but now sitting on four flats. I approach the truck and upon further inspection, I notice obvious stab marks in the wheel wells of all four tires.

"Dad's on the phone with the sheriff now. It's got to be Cody," Paige says, coming up behind me.

I turn to her. "There's no doubt in my mind. Can you call Ethan? See if he can get a tow truck over here?"

"Already done. He'll be here soon. I'm going to call Cody now. This is bullshit," Paige says, her voice full of anger. She lifts the phone to dial, but I put a hand over it.

"If your dad is calling the sheriff, we should just let them handle things first before calling anybody." She pulls the phone away and starts dialing anyway. Stubborn one, this girl.

"Fuck that, he's going to get a piece of my mind. This is just so childish and stupid. It's been six damn months!" She lifts the phone to her ear, and I can hear a faint ring on the other side of the line, followed by someone answering.

"Don't 'who is this' me. You know who the fuck this is! We found your little present this morning, and we're calling the sheriff. Do you think you can get away with this?"

I hear a muffled response come through the receiver. Paige shakes her head ignoring my hand as I reach for the phone.

"Don't play stupid. You know exactly what I'm talking about," she says, a hand to her hip and foot bobbing wildly. I find it hard not to smile at just how cute it is the way she's getting so worked up, as if her Chevelle had been the victim.

In an instant, the anger in her face fades and tears begin to build up in her eyes. She puts a hand to her mouth and pulls the phone from her ear, shaking her head. With her free hand, she taps the speakerphone button and a flurry of insults in Cody's thick country twang pours from the receiver.

"...don't you fuckin' worry about me, bitch. You understand? I do what I want when I want to, and no cunt is gonna have any say in that." If it wasn't already, that word brings my blood to a boil. A few tears roll down Paige's flushed cheeks. "I'll be god fuckin' damned if I let you ever control me again. You're worthless, bitch. Fuckin' worthless."

Before I know what I'm doing, I snatch the phone from her hand and press 'end.' I hand it back to her without a word and then march straight over to Jack by the back door. He still has the phone to his ear.

"Hey, Jack. Can I talk to you a second?" He asks the caller to wait and drops the phone to his side.

"What's going on, Xander?"

"I need you to end the call. There's not much that's going to come out of it anyways. I'm not going to press charges."

"Are you sure?" he asks, looking confused.

I nod. "Yeah, positive."

He lifts the phone again and I make my way back to Paige.

"Paige, I need you to take me to this dude's house," I say.

"Xander, no." She wipes a hand across her cheeks and then against her tank top. "It's not the first time he's talked to me like that. It's no big deal."

"If it weren't a big deal, you wouldn't have had the reaction you did. I don't care if it's the first time or the fiftieth, he will *not* talk to you like that. No man should talk to a woman like that."

She shakes her head and a look of acceptance creeps across her face. "Xander, please, let's just forget it. You don't want to get involved with the likes of him. He really doesn't have a whole lot to lose."

"And you think I do?" I snap, though I didn't mean it to come out that harsh. "Sorry, I just could care less, to be honest. I won't let him get away with this. If no one ever stands up to him, he'll never learn. I'll find the house myself if I have to. Hell, I'll walk there. So please, either help me out here, or—" I stop, finding no good way to end the sentence.

"Okay, okay, no need to get grumpy. I'll take you there. You just have to promise me you won't do something stupid. Please, Xander. Promise?"

"I promise not to do anything stupid as long as he refrains from doing something stupid."

She rolls her eyes but then heads toward the door just as Jack hangs up the phone and walks toward me. He looks back at Paige, confused, as she heads inside.

"Where's she headed?" he asks, gesturing behind him.

"She's going to get her car keys."

He looks as if he already knows. "Going for a drive, are we?" he asks, though it comes off more like a statement. "You sure that's a good idea?"

"It's not for me, Jack. I could give two shits about the flat tires. If he thinks I haven't had worse…if he thinks something like that is going to get me going, well, he's fucking wrong. People like him don't phase me. What I won't sit back and let happen is how he talked to Paige like she's fucking garbage. I've never heard a man talk to a woman like that."

I think about this lie for a moment. My dad used to talk to my mom like that all the time. But they didn't really count.

"Be careful," Jack says, "You want me to go with you?"

"No, Jack. Thank you, though. I can handle this."

CHAPTER ELEVEN

Paige

"Open Arms"—RKCB

I PULL THE CHEVELLE UP TO THE BEATEN-DOWN TRAILER, one of many that tarnish the beautiful Missouri land that lies beyond the trailer park. Seeing this particular trailer again after so long sends a swift shudder down my spine. Xander must notice my unease because he places a hand on my knee and gently squeezes it, which relaxes me instantly.

"This it?" he asks. All I can do is nod.

"I want you to stay here. If anything crazy happens, I want you to call the cops. Don't get out of the car." His words are stern, and though my first reaction is to give him shit for the bossiness, I refrain. Right about now, the authority he's exuding is getting me kind of hot. It's how a man should be.

Xander climbs out of the car and shuts the door behind him. As if on queue, the rickety trailer door flies open, creak-ing at its joints. Cody stands in the doorway behind the screen door, his shirt off and basketball shorts hung low on his hips. He has a beer in one hand and a shotgun in the other. He glares at Xander first and then at me in the driver's seat.

"What the fuck do you want?" Xander doesn't flinch or back down in the slightest, even at the sight of the gun. He scans Cody, taking him in. "You hear me, boy?"

"Oh, I hear you, but you're saying all the wrong words. What I want to hear is how sorry you are for the way you spoke to Paige earlier. What I want to hear is how you'll never do it again. And I'll tell you straight up, I wanna hear it real fucking quick."

Cody shoves the screen door open and takes a step forward, blocking it from closing with his right hip. "And what the fuck are you gonna do if I don't?" Cody snarls, spitting a wad of tobacco juice and spit on his porch floor.

"Oh, I can promise you," Xander says with a smile, "this is no threat. At least for now. I have no intention of fighting you right now. I respect Paige too much for that. Respect, which you are noticeably lacking. What I can promise you is this… if it continues, I'll beat your fucking skull in. I won't even give you a chance to speak."

Cody smirks, spitting again, and Xander continues, unimpressed by Cody's tough guy act. This is an act that has scared the shit out of me time and time again.

"I'll beat that silly smirk off your face," Xander says. "I'll make you swallow your own fucking teeth. If you think I'm kidding, please test me. You won't speak right for the rest of your life," he continues, so matter-of-fact you'd think he was giving a stranger driving directions.

Cody doesn't take this well. He steps forward, letting the screen door slam behind him, and he handles the shotgun as if he's about ready to use it.

Xander doesn't seem to notice.

"You can act as tough as you want, country boy," Xander says, his voice remaining calm but firm. "You can handle that shotgun. You can spit your dip. But at the end of the day, you've got no idea who the fuck I am. And I can promise you, you don't want to know. The way I grew up, words mean nothing. How you handle your fists is the only language anyone understands. You following me?"

He waits for Cody to say something, but nothing comes out. If this were a cartoon, two billows of thick smoke would be pluming out of Cody's nostrils. His hand clutches the beer so tightly that the can crumples between white knuckles. He drops it to the floor and kicks it at Xander, hitting him square in the chest.

Xander pays no mind. He still has yet to move. "You've owned this town for how long, Cody? You got that way through fear, am I right? Pouting and staring and crushing beer cans. Maybe flashing a shotgun here and there. And you scared a few people. Maybe you beat a few up real good. Word traveled fast and now here you are." Xander finally does move taking a step forward. Cody stands just a little straighter; his chest just a little wider. "But at the end of the day, what is that, really? You may scare them, but you don't fucking scare me. And you never will. You ought to get used to that."

Cody grunts, taking two more steps forward. He sets the shotgun up against the porch railing and heads down the stairs, stopping right in front of Xander.

"And what the fuck are you gonna do about it?" Cody asks. It's at this point that I open the car door and take one step out. Xander looks back at me and puts a finger up.

"Please, Paige, just stay in the car." As I'm about to settle back into the Chevelle, I see Cody charge toward Xander with a raised fist.

I want to scream. I try my best to yell his name, but the words won't come out. Xander turns around just in time to catch Cody's fist in the jaw with a loud thud. Xander staggers back from the force, but otherwise looks unaffected. He steadies himself just as Cody comes at him again, ready to continue his attack.

I scramble from the car, not even sure what exactly I will do, but before I have a chance to do anything, Xander thrusts two fingers—and only two fingers—just below Cody's sternum.

His eyes flash white and he crumples to the ground quicker than I can even process what I just saw. As Cody lies motionless, Xander turns, gives me a wink and walks back to the car. I try to turn and join him, but I can't move my legs. My focus is locked onto Cody's crumpled body, comically positioned as if he were just hit by a semi.

"Babe, come on. He'll be awake in a few." Xander climbs in and shuts the door. *Babe?* Yeah, that'll get my feet moving.

I join Xander in the car and start it up. Pulling out of the trailer park in a hurry, I'm still trying my best to wrap my brain around what just happened.

"What the hell was that?" I ask.

"Just a little trick I learned a while back."

"Little trick? That was more than just a little trick. What, are you like CIA or something?"

"No, nothing like that."

"Soooo….."

"I have Army buddies, remember? Some of them did some hardcore stuff overseas. They taught me a few things

"Again, what exactly did I just witness?"

"I hit him in the solar plexus. It's a big bundle of nerves in the mid-torso. Knocks 'em right out… as you just witnessed."

"But you only hit him with two fingers."

"Less surface area, so the force is stronger at my fingertips than it would be had I punched him there."

"Remind me never to make you angry," I joke, but at the same time I wonder so much more about this man. It seems as if I've only scratched the surface.

He looks at me, his face no longer playful but very serious. "You have absolutely nothing to worry about—ever. I don't hit women. I never have, and I never will. You know that… or at least you should."

"Oh, I know. But still, you keep those fingers away from me." He chuckles, then puts a hand over his mouth. It looks like he's ready to burst out in laughter. It takes me a minute to understand, but when I do, my face turns bright red. I swat his arm. "Context, damn it. Context!"

CHAPTER TWELVE

Xander

"Kiss Me"—Ed Sheeran

THE ALARM CLOCK SCREAMS AT ME TO GET UP FAR EARLIER than I'd like it to. Last night after work, Jack asked me to meet with him at six a.m. I'm hoping it's not regarding the incident with Cody a few days ago. When Jack did ask me about it, I kind of just shrugged him off and made up a lie. He didn't look like he believed me.

Regardless, there was never any police involvement after the fact. Not that I see that as a realistic course of action for a guy like Cody. Surprisingly, there's been no repercussion at all yet. I'd be kidding myself if I thought it wasn't coming. It's only a matter of time.

Eyes closed, I swat a hand over the snooze button, and out of nowhere I feel Rowdy's cold, wet nose meet the side of my cheek. He nuzzles into me as if bartering for my eyes to open and the food bowl to be filled, then he slathers the side of my face with saliva. I open my eyes and can't help but laugh at his big brown eyes staring back at me. He lifts a paw and bats at my arm.

"*Alright!*"

After feeding Rowdy and letting him out to do his business, I make my way to the main house.

"Morning, buddy," Jack says from the kitchen table as I come through the back door. A cup of coffee is cradled between his hands.

"Morning, Jack. The ladies gone already?" I pour my own cup of coffee and sip it, taking a seat across from him.

"Teresa is. Paige is getting cleaned up at the moment."

"So, what's on the agenda today?" I ask.

"I'll actually need you to run up to St. Louis with Paige here in a little bit. Say around seven?" My ears perk up, my attention all his. That's nearly a three-hour drive— just the two of us. This is not the conversation I thought I'd be having with him right now.

"No problem at all. What are we doing up there?"

"She's gotta hit a big junkyard the ladies always go through for parts, and I'm going to have you hit the wine supply depot in Grafton while you're at it. Paige knows where it's at, and they know you're coming. They'll have everything ready for you once you get there. I'd have her do it all herself, but that's a lot of lifting. Plus, there's not an ice cube's chance in hell anyone is driving my truck!" He lets out a hearty laugh and rises to his feet, then sets the cup in the sink.

"Oh, okay." I stand, adding more coffee to my mug. "I've never been to St. Louis. It'll be nice to see it."

"It's a real nice city, especially this time of year. Make sure you guys take some time to drive by the Arch. It's definitely something to see. A drive-by is just fine though. You don't wanna be getting into those tiny-ass elevators. It's just asking for an anxiety attack."

"Wait a second," I say. "There's an elevator in that thing?"

"Yeah, and if you have claustrophobia, you're likely not to come back down conscious." He shivers and then shakes the thought away. "Anyhow, I'm gonna go get changed. I'll see you when y'all get back."

"See you then."

He heads upstairs and I take my coffee with me back to the guesthouse, my mind running a mile a minute. I'm both excited and nervous at the same time. Of course, I couldn't be more thrilled to spend some time with Paige, just the two of us, but the more I let this girl in, the harder it is to keep myself from wanting her. I can't want her. I can't…but Lord knows I do.

I'll stick to my guns, though. I *will* keep myself from ever being with her. There's just too much to lose. What's the point, anyway? My time here is fleeting. In three months or so, I'll be back on the road, headed to Washington to see my little sister for the first time in twenty years—a sister who likely remembers nothing about me.

With the St. Louis Arch two hours in our rearview mirror, Paige and I are just an hour or so away from Truman Valley. The truck's bed is filled to the brim, and my worried eyes have been cautiously checking it the entire ride. Most of our time together so far has been spent with the windows down and music blaring. Paige has somehow taken over my radio and forced country music onto my helpless eardrums. I don't much mind though, because watching her belt out every tune is both hot as all hell and just a tad funny. She wasn't lying… the girl really is tone deaf.

A road sign catches her attention and she abruptly turns the music down.

"Hey, so I almost forgot. I was hoping we could stop somewhere before we go back."

"Sure. Where at?"

"Well, it's my favorite place in the world. Somewhere my family and I always go. It's just a few miles down the road off Exit 45. Is that okay?"

"Of course." This girl could ask me to watch paint dry, and I'd be *all* for it.

A few minutes later, I see exit 45 and take it. There's nothing except a plethora of trees and one old, abandoned gas station. Just as my doubts begin to rise, I notice a beautifully constructed wooden fence with a large sign atop it that reads: TWAIN LAKE. Paige points to a small dirt road just past the sign and I take it, careful not to spill anything out of the truck bed as I do.

We cruise down the road a mile or two, the woods around us thick with a richness in the leaves you only really see in the heart of spring. I notice an opening just in front of us and catch a peek of the lake and all its shimmering glory. The lake glints majestically from the midday sun and it beckons me toward it like a mirage.

Just before the lake, there's a fork in the road. A few houses line the shore on all sides. Paige directs me to take a left, and

I do so. The sprawling lake stretches into the horizon. As we pull down the road, she points to the first lake house we come across, and I see a dock jutting out from behind it.

"Here. Pull in here," she says with a smile.

"Are we going to be trespassing? Because this looks like gun country." She laughs and shakes her head as I park.

"We're in Missouri. This whole *state* is gun country. But no, there's no one here, and we definitely aren't trespassing."

"And how do you know?"

"You mean beyond the lack of any cars in the driveway? Because it's ours." She climbs out, shutting the door behind her, and I follow right after her.

"Wait, what?" She's several paces ahead of me, heading straight for the dock. "Hey lady, wait up!"

She turns her head without slowing and says, "Hey, mister. Keep up!"

I jog a little until I'm just beside her.

"So, this is your place?"

"Yeah. Well, my parents'. My dad and I come up here a few times a year to hunt hogs. And usually the whole family will take a trip here for spring break every year. Come sit on the dock with me."

"Wait, so you hunt?" I ask, genuinely surprised. "I feel like there's so much I don't know about you."

She pops off her shoes once she hits the dock and sits down, dipping her feet into the water. I take off my own shoes and settle down beside her.

"What, do I not look like a girl who knows how to shoot?" She glares at me. "I'll have you know I've been shooting since about the time I started walking."

"Well damn, color me impressed." She smiles and scans the lake, her eyes squinting through the beaming sun.

"There's quite a bit I don't know about you too, you know." She looks at me with mischief written all over her face. I'm afraid of what's to come. "That changes right now." The joy she's getting out of this is far from subtle.

"Oh, does it now? Am I going to regret coming here?"

"Probably," she says with a devilish smile.

"Another game of twenty questions?"

"It was three questions, mister, not twenty. This is more like one question and one request."

"Oh God." I roll my eyes. "Yep, I'm definitely going to regret this."

"Don't be such a downer. There's a lot I want to know about you, and I hope there's a lot you want to know about me too. We don't have a whole lot of time here, so you just let me do what I want. Mkay?"

"I feel like I should've taken shots before this." I think about the fifth in the glove compartment. I wonder how I could grab a few shots without being figured out. I come to terms with the improbability of it, but the urge is so strong I can nearly taste the bourbon.

"Oh shush, quit being a drama queen!"

"Hey now, woman. I'll do my best to play nice, but if you ever call me a drama queen again, I'm done with you!" I smirk and playfully swipe a leg against hers. "So what's first, request or question?"

"I think request would be the best way to start, but you have to hear me out before you say no, okay?"

"Uh-oh. I don't like the sound of this."

"Come on now, I have a feeling you can handle it. Now, no interrupting until I'm finished. I'm serious!"

"Okay, okay. Just get it over with already."

"So, Whittaker's has an open mic night every month. It's coming up next weekend, and I want you to do it." My head is already shaking before she even finishes her sentence.

"No freaking way, woman. Not a chance in hell. You do remember I told you I've never sung in front of anyone, right?"

"Yes, you did. And then you sang in front of me, and hun, you are amazing. It's not fair to keep that kind of talent to yourself. You heard my vocal skills in the truck—or lack thereof, I should say. I only *wish* I had a voice like yours. You need to share it with other people."

"No freaking way," I repeat, my head still shaking as if I were a four-year-old refusing broccoli.

"Listen to me, Xander. I know I said this was a request, but you can just consider it a requirement. I will make your ass go up there. Beyond your vocal and guitar skills being ridiculously impressive, your lyrics, your writing… it's beautiful. You could connect with so many people in this world through your music if you wanted. I'm not bullshitting you. I really think you have incredible talent, and it would be so disappointing if other people never got a chance to hear it."

"I've never done anything like that before. And I don't think Truman Valley is the place I want to start."

"You won't ever start. You don't want to, and I know it can't be because you think you're bad. We both know full well you aren't. I think you're just afraid." For a moment I'm offended, but before I can proceed, I realize she's right.

Spot on.

"You can't let fear control who you are. I've seen you in action. You don't let fear control any other aspect of your life. Why this?"

"I think it plays a bigger role in my life than you realize." My gaze drops to the water, and my legs kick nervously back and forth, splashing the cool water back toward us.

"Well, that's something I hope you share with me one day, but right now, this is about your music. I don't think anything in this world should keep you from sharing this amazing gift God's given you."

"I honestly don't even know how to respond. I don't even know if there is a god. If there is, he sure hasn't been there for me. Listen, I get where you're coming from, but this has been a lifelong fear. Would I love to get up there and play? Fuck yeah. But I'm scared shitless about it. I feel like I'll just go up there and freeze."

"Maybe you will… though I highly doubt it. But how will you know if you never try?"

"That's not helping any," I say, flashing a nervous smile.

"Don't be the guy that lives with regrets. Maybe it doesn't bother you now… but one day when you're old and gray, you'll regret having never tried it…just to see what it's like, ya know? You're amazing, Xander. Share it!"

"Easier said than done."

"Maybe so, but nothing ventured, nothing gained, right? You're so damn strong, Xander. Don't let something like fear control who you are."

"And why would I do this all for a woman I've only known for a week and a half?"

She looks at me, lips curled in disgust. "Well, thanks for

that. Maybe I've only known you for a week and a half, but I've come to respect you as a person, and I like to think you feel the same about me."

"Of course! I didn't mean it like that, Paige. I respect the fuck out of you, you know that. I wouldn't have confronted that douchebag the other day if I didn't. I'm just saying this has been a fear that's messed with me my entire life. It's going to take a whole hell of a lot to get me up there. And, honestly, I don't think anything or anyone really could."

She shakes her head in disappointment. "Well, that's really sad to hear. I think you're making a mistake. And don't for a second think I won't be pestering you all week about it."

"Pester away, woman. I can't be phased."

"Really? So being piss scared about what strangers think of you is you being unphased? Hmm…"

Damn it. She's got me there.

"Let me think about it, okay? It's not as easy as just saying yes."

"Actually, it is."

"Ugh! Didn't you say there was a question too? I think I'm ready for that now."

"Don't be so sure." She laughs.

"Oh god."

"Listen, I'll move on to the question, but this isn't over."

"Alright. Alright. The question now, *please*."

"You're not going to like this one either. Actually, you'll probably hate it, but you have to know it's only because I care for you. A week and a half or not, I truly do, and I want to know more about you. More than surface-level shit. I wanna get to know the *real* you."

"I've been nothing but real with you."

"Oh, I know. I just mean we haven't talked much about you and your life. I know you mentioned it a little at that first dinner, but based on your song, I know there's so much more to it." She hesitates, biting her bottom lip nervously.

"Xander, what happened with your parents?"

My heart sinks. Of all the potential questions running through my mind, that's not the one I thought she would ask. In this moment, I'm without words.

"I know it's personal. I know I probably shouldn't ask, but I want to know. I want you to feel comfortable sharing that kind of stuff with me." The look on her face as she says it lets me know I'll be telling this girl whatever she wants to hear.

"Why do you want to know?"

"Why? Damn it, Xander! Do I have to come right out and say it? I like you…a lot. I think you're an incredible man, and while I love bullshitting with you, I want to know more. I want to know the path you took to get here. I want to know what you're running from."

"God, Paige, I like you too. You must know that. I think the absolute world of you, but that's just not something I freely share. It's hard for me to talk about. And you know I'm leaving in a few months anyways. I mean…" My voice trails off, because I honestly have no clue what to say.

"What exactly does that mean, Xander? What, two more months and you'll just hightail it out of here and never talk to us again? I get that you're leaving, but why exactly does that mean you can't share anything with me?" Her tone becomes more agitated and I want more than anything for us to just enjoy our time out here; to not let the future get in the way of right now, but I can't find the right words to say.

"I mean, if it's only a stopover," she continues. "If my family and I mean nothing to you, then fuck it. What's the point?"

"Paige, stop!" I put an arm around her and pull her in close enough that her perfume fucks with my senses. "I didn't mean it like that. I love your family. It's been really amazing getting to know them. And you? I've never felt so connected to someone so quickly in my life." Her breathing picks up. Her eyes close. "You calm me. You make me feel carefree. It's something that doesn't usually happen for me. I just mean, no matter how I feel about you, there's not a whole lot I can do about it. I work for your father, and in a few months I have to leave. I would never play with your feelings like that."

She opens her eyes, sinking a little more into my arm, and she bats her eyelashes innocently. "And why do you have to leave?"

I want to give her the truth. I want to spill it all, but the truth is shit and communication isn't my best attribute. She looks me in the eyes, locking hers on mine, and rests a hand against my cheek.

"Kiss me," she says, catching me completely off guard.

"Paige, I—"

"Kiss me," she repeats. "No more bartering. No more excuses. Just kiss me."

There's not a doubt in my mind that I want to kiss her, and in this moment—this perfectly beautiful, unexpected moment—any concerns as to why we shouldn't be together disappears. I see her in a way I haven't seen someone for as long as I can remember. All I feel is the heat of her body against mine, the race of my beating heart, and a yearning to stay just like this forever. I take one last longing look into her eyes and then place my lips against hers. They move effortlessly with my own.

When we part, her eyes are still closed. My hand stays right where it is, and I rub my thumb against her cheek. She slowly opens her beautiful eyes.

"I've wanted that since the day I met you," I say sincerely.

"That makes two of us." She smiles, nuzzling her head into my palm. The way the sun glints off her face is perfection.

Without warning, and completely unbeknownst to me, I get the undeniable urge to spill it all; to tell her everything. I haven't talked about it in a long time; longer than I can even remember. Now feels like the right time Now *is* the right time.

"My parents died when I was seven. Murder-suicide," I blurt out. My voice seems foreign to me. The words don't seem real. But they are.

My eyes are no longer on hers. My hand drops back to my side as I wait for the oncoming judgment. I don't care what anyone says. You spill a thing like that and people look at you differently. What I get instead is her arm around my waist. She sets her other hand softly against my knee.

"Oh, Xander. I'm so very sorry. I should've never asked."

"No, hun, it's okay. I want to share this with you. I really do. I just didn't know if I'd actually be able to say the words. I never have before. To anyone."

"Well, thank you for sharing with me, Xander. I can only imagine how hard that could've been. Just know I will never judge you because of your past. I will never look at you any differently than I do right now. You are amazing. Absolutely amazing."

I look at her, admiring the sincerity in her eyes, and I pull her against me again, setting my chin on top of her head. For this next part, I can't look at her. It would just be too hard.

"They were heroin addicts, and my father had a bad trip. He shot my mother in front of my sister and me, and then put the gun under his chin."

Paige pulls back, her eyes wide and mouth gaping, but she says nothing.

"My sister was only two. We went into foster care immediately after, since there were no other family members to take us. My sister was adopted. I never was. Paige…" I look at her again, tears welling in my eyes. "I could never express to you what losing her did to me. What being in foster care did to me. I've grown past it—the foster care part, at least—but it's something that always lives with me. You ask what I'm running from? It's that. Florida means nothing to me but tragedy."

"God, babe, I'm so sorry. So, so sorry. What about your sister? Where is she?"

"I haven't seen her since then, and it fucking kills me. I managed to get the adoption information a few years back, but I've been too chicken shit to go see her. She won't even remember me, and would she really even care to meet me anyways?"

"Of course she would! You are blood. You can't think like that."

"I know. I know. Well, you asked why I have to leave in a couple months. That's why. I looked her up, and she's been in the Army for the past five years. She's currently stationed at Fort Lewis in Washington. I've been on a long journey building up the courage to see her. I never thought I actually would. I've let different things in each town keep me just a little bit longer. To occupy my headspace and help me to forget about the sister I lost. But I can't." As hard as I've fought to keep them at bay, the tears are flowing now. I try to hide my face from her, but she pulls my chin back.

"Xander, don't you ever be afraid to let me see the real you. Not ever." She wipes both sides of my face and then takes my lips against hers. They're soft and supple, and instantly I feel okay. I feel relieved.

I feel alive.

We kiss and talk on the dock for an hour, losing track of time, losing ourselves in the moment. This girl owns my attention.

She's someone I could love... and it scares the shit out of me.

The ride back to Truman Valley has a healthy dose of country music with Paige belting along out of tune, her hand resting on my knee. The longer it sits there the more my mind races with all the unanswerable questions this situation brings. It's not what I should do, it's not what I want to do, but I'm afraid that falling for Paige is inevitable at this point.

After unloading the new junkyard acquisitions for Paige and Teresa, I make my way back to the house.

Rowdy relieves himself and goes back to his favorite teddy, of which I have to replace every three days or so. Jack waves me down from the barn. It's only two p.m., but he's already sweated up a storm, his overalls coated in grease as usual.

"How was it? You see the Arch?"

"Yeah, I find it even harder to believe that thing has elevators in it. No way in hell I'm ever getting in there." He laughs, pulling a large, stainless steel cylinder from the barn, a nozzle protruding from the top. ORGANIC PESTICIDES, INC is printed on the label.

"Yeah, it's a trip. How'd everything go business-wise?"

"No problems at all. Paige took a few hours to collect everything she needed, but the wine guys were easy. I was waiting awhile for Paige to get done browsing." I smirk, rubbing away the beads of sweat beginning to trickle down my forehead.

"Well, I hope that means you're up for some outdoor labor. We've got some plants to protect. Something's been killing them off lately, and though I think it's no accident, I have to take precautions." He points toward the cylinder as he heaves another one from the barn. "And then I need you to grab Caleb from school at five-thirty. The ladies are going to be busy organizing the new inventory. Go get changed and I'll grab you a mask."

"Alrighty. Sounds good. I'll be out in two." I turn and head to the guesthouse.

⸻

The Truman Valley High School parking lot is bustling with kids and cars are log-jammed in the small parking lot at the front of the school. I pull into a lower lot with a little less chaos, and text Caleb to meet me.

Five minutes pass and there's still no response. To my left, a group of teens emerge from the woods, which catches my attention. There are four of them. One of them is trying to get away. Three of them are swinging wildly and trying to pull the other back into the woods. I peer in their direction to get a better look. They've yet to see me.

It's fucking Caleb.

His frail arms cover his face. His black, oversized band tee is ripped. His mouth is bleeding. *Fucking faggot*, I can hear them say. *Fuck you, emo pussy!*

I open the door, slamming it behind me, and it draws their attention. They immediately stop hitting him, but their hands remain tightly gripped to the tattered remains of his shirt.

"What the *fuck* do you think you're doing?" My voice, far from calm, tears from my mouth in a growl. The kids, no older than fifteen and small themselves compared to me, immediately release their grips. Their beady eyes stare in confusion before they turn and take off running. They run as fast as their little pretzel stick legs will allow until they're out of sight.

Caleb doesn't react for a moment. He stands, eyes fixed to the ground. Fresh beads of blood trickle down his lips.

I take a few steps forward and his head pops up, his eyes locking on mine. There's no more humiliation. Only rage.

"*Why did you fucking do that?*" He swipes an arm across his bloody lips and spits a blood clot from his mouth. I almost can't believe my ears. I just saved this kid from a complete ass kicking and he's mad at me.

"What the fuck are you talking about, Caleb? Get in the truck." I turn and head back toward where I parked when I hear him take a few quick steps closer. If looks could kill…

"They would've stopped soon. They always do. Why did you fucking do that?"

"Dude, fuck that. I'm not going to just watch that shit happen to you. Get in the truck, Caleb. Come on." A few teachers and students have noticed us. The teachers quickly avert their gaze as if they never even saw the beaten boy crying on the pavement.

"They'll never leave me alone now," he sobs. I look around awkwardly, unsure of how exactly to respond. I'm not cut out for these kinds of situations.

"Caleb, *get* in the truck," I say sternly and he finally complies. I follow, throwing him a towel from the bench seat, and he presses it to his face as he climbs in.

"Why do you let them hit you like that? One, two, three, it doesn't matter...you gotta hit back. They get bored with the ones that stick up for themselves. It's no fun anymore when you're getting hit right back."

He looks at me and scowls, the bloody rag clutched tightly in his hands. "And how the *fuck* would you know anything about that?"

"You fucking kidding me, kid? You think I was always in shape? You think I grew up two hundred pounds? You think I grew up easy? Fuck no. When I was fourteen, I was your size. When I was fourteen, I was in a fucking orphanage."

He's no longer humiliated or angry, only skeptical. "You're fucking with me, right?"

"Nah, I'm not the type to fuck around. I'm serious. Just like you, I grew up in a boys' home."

"Are you fucking with me?" he repeats.

"I'm not. You don't want to go toe to toe with me on what a rough life means. You had it hard, no doubt about that, but you got it really fucking good now. Your parents love you. They take care of you. They're there for you. It's more than a lot of kids have. It's more than you or I had starting out. It's something I never got." I hold up two fingers. "Two things you gotta take away from this conversation. One, start working out... start hitting a heavy bag, start fighting back. Play a fucking sport or something, for Christ's sake. And two, don't ever think you got it so bad again, because really, you don't. You had it damn hard, and by the grace of God you found people that truly love you. Appreciate that. Got it?"

He looks stunned, his mouth wide, as if my words were in a foreign language. Either that, or they were the worst thing he's ever been told.

"Got it?" I repeat. He nods his head very, very slowly.

The rest of the drive back to the Watson house is pleasantly quiet.

CHAPTER
THIRTEEN

Paige

"Monster Lead Me Home"—Sara Hartman

It's been four days since Xander and I spent time on the dock. Four days since our first kiss. Four days since I felt my heart grab hold of him.

We haven't seen each other much, other than at family dinner where conversations are mostly generic and light, and flirty eyes pass between us at all available moments. Caleb has seemed to lighten up lately, which doesn't necessarily mean he's been pleasant, but he eats now at least.

I've wanted to spend more time with Xander alone, but he's been working late with Dad every evening and passing out soon after dinner. I can only assume he is scared shitless about my little open mic request, but it hasn't stopped me from putting Post-it note reminders on the guesthouse door. And in the guesthouse. And on his truck door.

That man *is* playing. I don't care what I have to do.

As I position another Post-it note against the guest-house door—my last day to do so before Whittaker's open mic night—I hear the rustle of Xander's work boots against the gravel driveway behind me. I turn and his beautiful smile greets me, looking more effervescent than usual from the contrast of his deepening tan. The dirty wife beater clings tightly to his abs, the sweat making it almost see-through. It takes everything I have not to stare; or not to stare *that* much at least.

"Did I catch you off guard there, stealthy?" He smiles again, seeming to not notice my sudden hot flash—or at least giving me the courtesy of not pointing it out.

"You've been avoiding me, mister." I shake a finger at him, stepping down from the guesthouse porch, trailing the porch rail with my finger.

"No, ma'am. I've just been busy. I have a job to do, you know." He stands just before me, eyes glancing at the back door of the main house.

"They aren't here. You know that." *Am I being too flirtatious? What if he's avoiding me for reasons other than the open mic night? What if he regrets the kiss?*

Before my thoughts get the better of me, Xander takes me into his arms and looks into my eyes. He stares for a moment and what should be awkward feels far too comfortable.

He doesn't just look at me. It's like he sees right through me.

Xander kisses me, softly at first. Just lips. A little tongue now, and it's like electricity travels back and forth from my mouth to his. His hands slide down to my ass, settling there, then he pulls me into him. A gasp escapes my mouth, but he kisses me even harder and longer. An ache takes hold.

He breaks the kiss and pulls me inside the guesthouse, closing the door behind him. His hands brace my hips firmly, but he pushes me carefully against the door. He grabs my wrists and pulls them above my head, holding both of my hands with one of his own. His other hand cradles my face. He kisses me again making everything below my knees feel useless.

For what is probably only five minutes—but feels like much longer—he kisses me, his hands touching the skin beneath my shirt. He fights to keep them from where his hands shouldn't go. But where I want them so damn bad.

I don't want him to fight it, but I'm glad that he has the willpower to. This man's restraint is impressive.

He pulls his lips away from me slowly, and all I can do is stay right where I am, eyes closed, resting in his arms and my lips ready for his.

"I'll sing tomorrow."

My eyes open instantly. "Are you serious?"

He leans in so close I can feel his warm breath on my lips. "For you…" he breathes the words against my mouth, "and only for you. But you have to sit right in the center of the bar, so any time I get nervous, I can look at you."

Just take my fucking heart, damn it.

I grab his cheeks and pull him in for another kiss.

"You don't even have to ask. I'm there. I'll always be there," I say, kissing him again, pouring every ounce of promise into it. Then I reluctantly leave the guesthouse, since my parents will be back shortly.

His hand fidgets against my leg nervously, his guitar case held tightly between his legs. As we make our way to Whittaker's, I can see another pep talk is in order. I find him irresistibly cute when he's nervous. To see this man who's obviously strong become so vulnerable is quite endearing.

I place my hand on his and squeeze it lightly, drawing his attention. He looks at me, catches my wide smile and shoots me a nervous smirk in return.

"You're going to do great, Xander. I have no doubt."

He laughs genuinely and says, "That makes one of us!" The laugh fades and he picks at the edges of his aged case.

"Stop! You're going to kill it. I've heard you before, remember? Just play as if only for me."

He looks at me, his eyes sincere. Grabbing my hand, he pulls it slowly toward his lips as I park the car in Whittaker's lot. I'm trying my best to keep my attention on the lot and not his perfect lips meeting my skin.

Goosebumps race across my skin. Little hairs stand on end. He stirs a heart that's been idle for quite some time and it's hard to make sense of it all.

He pulls my hand from his mouth and then places it on his knee. Smiling, he says, "Right in the middle, remember?"

"I won't move a muscle." I wink and hop out of the car, my heart still pounding in my chest. Xander follows soon after.

The crowd is light for an open mic Friday night, but I've been coming here long enough to know it won't stay this way. I won't let Xander in on that though.

He makes a beeline for the bar where Brandi waits impatiently, a goofy smile spread across her face. Xander orders two Jamesons and a Coors as his nervous eyes flit around the stage at the other end of the bar where amps, cords and mics are being set up. He downs both Jamesons in the time it takes him to pass me my Coors.

I see Bryson Whittaker, the owner of this establishment, emerge from a back office and I meet him near the bar. He lets me know Xander will be fourth up, which causes my stomach to churn a little. Whittaker's will be busier by then.

I meet Xander back over by the bar as he downs another shot of Jameson. His guitar is tucked against the bar behind a stool as if he hoped no one would see it. My hand touches his back and glides up to his shoulder. I give it a good squeeze or two.

"Don't be nervous. And don't be so drunk you can't play."

He glares at me with a playful smirk fighting to break through. "Woman, you know three shots of Jameson for me is just a warmup." Just as he says this, Brandi brings another shot. He looks at me guilty.

"You're going up in like forty minutes, I remind him. "Just relax." His eyes go wide and he quickly throws back the shot that was just placed before him.

"Xander!" I say as sternly as I can.

"Alright. Alright. I'm good now." He motions to Brandi for one more as if I'm not right in front of him, then acts surprised when he turns to see my best 'what do you think you're doing' look.

"Just one more." He puts both hands together and pretends to plead with me.

"Xander, you have as many as you want. I'm not your mom. But I don't want to hear it when you're too drunk to sing and you're booed off stage."

"Nah, I'm good. Promise." He takes the shot, slamming it quickly back down to the bar top, and he exhales loudly. It's not long before he catches my scowl. His cockeyed smile and glazed over eyes make it apparent my look isn't going to be very effective.

CHAPTER
FOURTEEN

Xander

"Who Needs Air"—The Classic Crime

THAT LOOK. THAT LOOK RIGHT THERE IS EXACTLY WHY Paige hasn't left my mind for weeks. The little pout, the darting eyebrows, the judging eyes. They're certainly intended to be serious, but it just makes my damn heart explode.

The corner of her mouth quivers, a sure sign that a smile is dying to break loose.

"Just one more, I swear," I say in my best little kid voice. The liquor is kicking in, drowning out all apprehension of singing in front of others—for now, at least. The only thing I can even see in this moment is Paige. Everything else around me is just a blur.

"*One* more, mister. That's it!" She turns and heads toward one of several small tables in front of the stage. Right in the middle, like I asked. An employee taps the mic and calls out a slow 1-2-3. A confident, long-haired country singer type stands backstage looking out among the crowd as if he doesn't have a care in the world. *Lucky fuck.*

Paige glances back at me. Lifting an eyebrow, she shoves the other chair out with her foot, inviting me to join her. Reluctantly, I do.

The first three acts are good. *Really* good. And as I wait for them to call me to the stage for my go at it, I feel as if the blood just might burst from the top of my head. A lump sits heavy in my throat, so much that it makes it hard to swallow. Paige's hand sits on my knee, squeezing, as it has been for the first three sets. It does little to quell the nerves that make me feel as if I may spontaneously combust at any moment.

I hear my name called. I know it's my name, but it sounds distorted, like it's coming from a mile away. I don't move. My eyes are fixated on the center of the small oak table. Maybe if I stare long enough I'll disappear.

Paige squeezes my knee and then nudges me with her elbow.

"Xander," she says, "you're up."

I still don't move. Panic sets in. I can feel a tight constriction in my chest. My breathing feels thick and arduous.

"Xander, baby, you're up." I snap out of my daze and look over at Paige. She appears genuinely concerned. "Are you okay?"

"Yeah, yeah, sorry." I wipe a sleeve across my forehead and rise to my feet, grabbing my guitar case from the ground.

"Are you sure? You don't have to do this. We can leave." I look into her eyes. Nothing but sincerity and concern. I'm drunk enough to block out everything else now. All I have to do is focus on her.

"I got this. I'm only singing for you, right? And you'll stay right here? Right where you are until I'm done?"

"I won't move a muscle, babe." She winks then brings both hands together to welcome me to the stage. After a brief hesitation, I make my ascent. A few of the other patrons join her in clapping, making the bar not seem completely depressing, but most sit back with blank stares on their faces and an air of arrogance surrounding them. I fight to block them out. I try to see only her.

Once on the stage, the lights are bright and hot as hell, though I can't say whether it's the nerves or the lights making me sweat so profusely. Peering through the beams of light out at the crowd, I can't see anything in particular, just distorted figures. *Has it been an hour I've been up here?* It sure fucking feels like it right now.

I strum a chord awkwardly. Feedback from the amps causes the crowd, which seems to have doubled in size since we got here, to release a collective groan. There's a random 'you got this' from the crowd. Then I hear heckling from the back of the room. I squint through the stage lights to see Cody and Benji leaning against the bar, beers in one hand, the other cupped to their mouths. My heart sinks. As if this couldn't get any worse.

I strum again and it sounds just as awkward. Apparently, my nerves have overtaken my fingers. It feels as if they aren't even a part of me anymore. Benji boos loudly. Just as I'm about to retreat back down the stage, I finally spot Paige just where I left her, looking sweetly up at me.

Feeling in my fingers returns. My heart slows. The crowd around her completely disappears this time. It's only the two of us in the guesthouse. I'm singing for her—and only her. I repeat the words as if they are my mantra. I strum again, perfectly this time. The beautiful sound fills the bar, bouncing from wall to wall, silencing the crowd.

Another chord. Flawless. I'm regaining control. I complete the intro and transition right into the first verse. As I prepare to sing, it feels like the words may never escape my lips. But they do. And they do for her.

I've found my way through.
Caught the waves, the ocean blue
I lose myself sometimes too,
But I am me.
Here I am.

Benji and Cody heckle louder now. After a quick snap of her head in their direction, Paige looks to me again and smiles. It's all I need to continue.

I've found my way to you.
Somehow, still so lost, still so confused.
But if I could be that man for you.
That's what I'll be
Here I am.
It's in the way she looks at me.
Her eyes, they see things I can't see.
Her faith brings out the best in me.
So here I am.
It's in my past, this path, unkept.
And after all the tears and questions left
You were there
So here I am.

I finish the song and wait for an onslaught of boos. I can see it so clearly in my head. They'll boo me until I'm laughed off the stage. I'll hang my head, pick up the pieces of my shattered dignity and drag my ass back to the house. But there are no boos beyond the two idiots in the back. In fact, the applause is more than I could have ever imagined. My focus is only on one person in this room though, and her smile, wide as can be, is like a lighthouse through a storm. It's clarity.

It's everything.

My time is up, but the crowd wants an encore. I spot the bar owner watching from the side of the stage and he gives me the okay. Benji and Cody's boos have gotten progressively louder in an effort to drown out the applause and calls for more. My eyes dart in their direction and I glare, then smile because I know exactly what to play.

"This one's for the two dumbasses in the back. To everyone else, thanks for your kindness. I've never done anything like this before." I wink at my two 'friends' by the bar and begin strumming again. They've stopped booing and now look as if they may rush the stage at any moment. I know they won't, though. Damn, how I wish they would.

Have I been here far too long now?
There's no respect here anymore.
And if I tell you that I'm leaving,
Would it be like it was before?

We can't all be perfect too.
You've kept that crown for a while.
If you knew what I've lived through.
Would you still be in denial?

I've felt these four walls close around me.
Hands clenched tightly 'round my neck.
I've felt the weight of all your bullshit.
And taken it from off my back.

We can't all be just like you,
But we can wear your plastic smile.
I could bullshit my way through too,
But I could never touch your style...

I finish the song with a round of applause. The nerves I felt before have now given way to a near euphoria. A box is checked on the bucket list and, more importantly, I have the desire to do it again. And I owe it all to one girl.

I find Paige in the crowd. She stands and claps wildly. I make my way toward her as the next musician takes the stage. In one fluid motion, I drop my guitar case, sweep her into my arms and carelessly kiss her. I don't know for how long. I don't know who's watching. I just know that never have I had a moment so perfect in my life, a natural high that seems to surge throughout my body.

"You wanna get out of here?" I whisper into her ear. She nods, the smile still stamped on her face.

Just as we exit the bar, I'm pushed from behind, nearly falling face first to the pavement. I stumble but catch myself and turn to see Cody with balled up fists and gritted teeth.

"Motherfucker, you think you can come into my town and pull some bullshit MMA games on me, insult me and take *my* girl? Do you know who the fuck you are dealing with?" Cody's face has turned a shade of red I haven't seen since my father's when he'd beat on my mom in a heroin-induced rage. I need to get Paige out of here.

"Listen, you hit me first. I came to your trailer to talk, not fight. That shit's on you. You came in tonight and started heckling me. I'm not playing these games with you, man." The multiple shots begin to make peaceful resolve an improbability. The more I look at him, the more I want to fuck his world up.

"Two things you gotta remember. This town…"—I point to the main street behind us—"is not yours. And she"—I gesture at Paige—"is not your girl."

Cody's lackey blocks the door with his back keeping anyone from coming out. I hand my guitar case to Paige and motion toward the Chevelle.

"Are you sure?" she asks, hesitating.

"Yeah, babe." She heads toward the car, but Cody takes a few steps along with her. I do the same, acting as a blockade between them. I follow her all the way to the car until she's able to get in.

Suddenly, Cody's bloodshot eyes shift from me to the road behind us. His tense shoulders drop a bit. His balled hands unfurl. I glance back, keeping him in my peripheral, and see what caught his attention. A police cruiser drives by slowly, and the cop's eyes are locked on us. I see my exit. Though I'd like to wreck this guy—both of them for that matter—I have to be smart.

I climb into the passenger side and Paige immediately backs out of the parking spot. Cody still eyeballs the cruiser as it creeps along, and then he looks back at us, cursing under his breath. I smile and flash a middle finger as they fade in the rearview.

We're only minutes from the house when the liquor that gave me the confidence to perform takes a turn for the worse. It takes a hard fucking right turn. My head seems to melt into the seat cushion. My limbs are cooked noodles.

Paige's voice sounds like it's coming from the end of a narrow hall. "Babe? Did you hear me?"

Her voice breaks through and my vision steadies. "Wait, what?" I mean to say more, but it's all I can manage.

"I told you not to drink so much." There's a bite to her words. Unnecessary bite.

"I'm not drunk. I'm just tired."

"Tired, my ass. You just passed out mid-conversation."

Did I?

The events of the night are fading already. I'm angry. But why?

"I said, you don't always need to provoke them. I know they start a lot of this shit, but they're not really people you want to fuck with. There's a lot of them. As much as—"

"You think I can't take him?" I cut her off, hardly even realizing what I'm saying. The words fall freely from my lips. "You think I'll ever let a pussy like that make me afraid? That's what he wants. I know guys like that. They talk a big game, but they ain't shit."

"Oh seriously, drop the tough guy act." Whatever sweetness she carried into the conversation has dissipated. "It's not just about Cody. I know you can take him. I've *seen* you take him. This is about all of them. Cody, Benji, Russ. They're fucked up guys. They're friends with a lot of other fucked up guys. I've seen them do some really messed up shit to people."

"*I've* done some really messed up shit to people," I blurt out, the anger simmering deep inside. "Whatever you think about me...whatever you *think* you know...you don't know the half of it."

"I *want* to know all of it!" She parks the car and I look around, unaware we were even on the Watson's property. My head pounds relentlessly.

Paige grabs my shoulder and squeezes gently, drawing my attention.

"I want to know it all," she repeats, softer this time.

"There's way too much to share, Paige. More than I'd ever want to."

"Don't you think talking about it might help you move past it a little?"

"I *am* past it." My words are unconvincing.

"Are you? You've opened up to me. And I can't tell you how much I appreciate and respect that. But I just want you to know, you can trust me. I'm here for you. I mean that."

"It's just too much, Paige. It's all too much. I'm tired. I'm going to go in." I open the door and move to get out when she grabs my arm and pulls me back in.

"Can I come with you...just for a bit? We don't have to talk. I just want to lie with you." She smiles, weakly, and everything in me wants to say yes. But I won't. *I can't.*

Not tonight. Tonight, I just need to slip into a drunken slumber and let this conversation end before I say something I truly regret.

"I'm tired. Let's talk tomorrow." I get out and close the door behind me. Paige follows, meeting me on the other side of the Chevelle and taking my hand into hers.

"Okay, Xander. I understand. Get some sleep." She pulls me in close, rises to her tiptoes and wraps her arms around my neck. Then she presses her lips against mine. I want to hold her there and never let go. But I won't. *I can't.*

Not tonight. Not when I'm like this.

"Good night, Paige." I kiss her again, a quick peck, and release her. Stumbling to the guesthouse, I can feel her still behind me. I stop and turn back toward her.

"Good night, Xander." She turns on her heel and then she's gone.

———————

I wake up still wearing my jeans and tee, boots still tied tight to my feet, and I'm sprawled on the love seat. Empty beer cans that weren't there the night before line the coffee table, a half smoked bowl beside them. Morning light cuts through the window, my eyelids helpless against it. I swipe my shades from the end table and put them on. Rising to my feet with a heavy groan, my stiff back cracks from neck to tailbone. The walls spin and a fog sits heavy in my head. I grasp for memories from last night, but they're spotty and unclear.

I know Paige was upset with me—or withdrawn, at the very least—but I can't for the life of me remember the details of our conversation. This isn't the first time alcohol has gotten the best of me. I always reasoned that I just liked to have a good time. But nearing thirty and with the good times steadily accumulating, it's hard not to start wondering if there's more to it.

Too many mornings like this. Too many drunken mistakes.

I make it to the kitchen, grabbing a water and four aspirin before I realize something's missing.

Rowdy.

I have a tendency of letting him out when I'm drunk or stoned and forgetting to let him back in. He usually hangs around outside the front door, but he's known to take off on an adventure for stretches of time too. I'm crossing my fingers for the former, though there's no sign of him when I open the door.

I see Jack is already outside working in the barn, which means it's sometime around eight a.m. He's there even on Sundays, just like clockwork.

Rowdy isn't anywhere in sight. I slink toward the house, hoping to go unnoticed… conversation with anyone sounds like a bad idea right now. My brain still isn't functioning properly, and I'm sure I look like a homeless junkie. Fortunately, I make my way inside undetected, and after checking the kitchen, I find myself in front of Paige's door. All is quiet and still.

I put an ear to the cracked door and listen. Nothing but the light whir of her ceiling fan. I edge the door open further and slip my head in. The shades are still drawn, casting a shadow over everything, but I can see Paige fast asleep and wrapped in a satin sheet. She has an arm around Rowdy, who looks to be equally comatose, his tongue falling limply from the side of his open mouth.

I have every intention of leaving Rowdy right where he is to avoid waking up either of them, but for a moment I admire Paige as she sleeps. Even with her mouth agape and the little spot of drool on her pillow, she's still the most beautiful thing I've ever seen. This girl could climb right out of bed and put every other woman to shame, no problem.

Rowdy must get a whiff of me because he pops his head up, spots me, and jumps off the bed with a purpose.

Time for food.

Paige sits up from the mattress, her eyes wide in momentary panic. She spots me and calms, stretching both arms high in the air with a noisy yawn. The sheet falls to her waist, and the way the t-shirt hugs her body allows me to see her nipples under the cotton. A throb jolts from the pit of my stomach down through my cock. Then she opens her eyes, and I quickly avert my gaze, first to the ceiling and then to the wall.

Smooth, man.

"Get a good look?" she asks with a playful smile. She brings both her feet to the floor. Her long, perfect legs are bare besides the thong peeking out from below her hiked up tee. She grabs a pair of shorts from the floor and pulls them on slowly, flashing me a coy smile. "Why are you watching me sleep anyways, creeper?"

She stands and scoots right past me to the kitchen. Rowdy prances right alongside her.

"Hey now, I just came in," I say as I follow the two of them.

"Uh huh, that's what they all say." She pours two cups of coffee and sets them on the table, then takes a seat, patting Rowdy on the head. Knowing her well enough by now, I grab the Bailey's from the fridge and add some to both of our coffees. Her eyes light up and she nods in appreciation.

"I wasn't watching you sleep, ya know. I was just looking for Rowdy."

"Defensive, much? You're sounding pretty guilty to me," she says as I return the Bailey's to the fridge and take a seat across from her.

"I guess you left him outside last night. He was scratching at the back door and woke me up."

"Okay, one… I watched you sleep for *maybe* a second. Creeper regulations require at least a minute of sleep-watching to count. And two, yeah, I have a tendency to do that."

"When you're drunk, you mean?"

I look down, feeling a bit guilty, but she just laughs. "You had quite a bit last night. I've yet to see you that drunk. I told you to slow it down."

"It was just too much all at once. I guess you were right."

"God, that'll never get old. Can you say it just one more time for me?" She smirks, taking a sip of her coffee.

"That's the only one you're getting out of me! Was I an ass, by the way? If so, I'm sorry."

"You don't remember our conversation"

"Honestly, I remember parts of it, but it all kind of snuck up on me at the end there. Everything's a bit hazy. Was I an ass?" I repeat my question, hoping I wasn't as douchey as my clouded memories suggest.

"Not an ass, per se, but you definitely weren't a happy drunk like I usually see you. You seemed…" Her words trail off, and she glances to the ceiling in thought. "I don't know."

"No, what? I wanna know. Did I do something stupid?"

"No, nothing like that. It just seems like when you drink—I mean, *really* drink—some deeper shit comes out."

"Yeah, that's not the first time I've heard that. Trouble usually starts when I'm drinking with a purpose. I don't know why I get like that." My mind goes to every drunken fight I've ever been in, to my DUI in Florida—and the crying fit that happened in the cell afterward—to the kid I almost killed.

"Well, I think it's because you're holding on to a lot. I think there's maybe stuff you've got bottled up."

And I think you have no clue about the things I've seen and done.

"Well, thanks for the morning session, Dr. Phil."

She rolls her eyes. "Hey, I'm just telling you what happened. Take it however you want to," she says, sounding annoyed.

"I know, I know. I'm just giving you shit. I'm sure you're right."

"I know I'm right." She smiles, a haughty, proud smile. "What's on your agenda today?"

"I didn't tell you?"

She cocks her head and looks at me with confusion. "Not that I know of."

"Well shit…I mentioned it to Jack. I thought I told you as well. One of my Army buddies just transferred to Fort Leonard Wood from Georgia. I'm going out to see him today. Probably leave here in an hour or two."

I want to invite her. I would love for her to meet someone reasonably close to me—somebody I've truly bonded with—but I'm leaving soon, and that's just not something I can change. I'll move on from here, and after a few texts and maybe a phone call here or there, we will forget all about each other. She'll have met the man of her dreams, and I'll be back trying to piece together my broken, fucked-up life, a neverending job she doesn't deserve being subjected to. There's no reason she needs to get more involved in my life than she already is.

"Cool. Have fun," she says, in a manner that makes it seem as if she just read my mind. She gets up and puts her cup in the sink. "You might want to feed your pup. He doesn't look like he's willing to wait much longer." She laughs and points at Rowdy seated at the back door, his tail relentlessly wagging and warm eyes glued to us. Every few moments, he looks out the door and then back at us.

I hear Paige trying to make a quick exit and I turn to catch her. "Hey."

Ask her to go with you. Ask her to go with you.

She stops and turns her head to look at me.

"Hey, what?"

Ask her. Ask her. Ask her.

"I hope you have a good day."

"You too."

The trip to Fort Leonard Wood is the exact reason I love driving so much. The spring air is crisp and floral. It floods the open windows and the sun shines brightly through the windshield. It's the perfect time to think… to go over all the things that have been nagging at me. The more I think, the more I realize I have been letting Paige get too close. I have yet to let a woman do that to me. Until now.

But why her?

I've told her things I haven't shared with even my closest friends—not that I've had many to begin with. This whole situation has gotten the better of me. I shouldn't even be here. I shouldn't have let myself get close, because as much as I need the money and would love to delay seeing my sister longer, the fact of the matter is Paige does do something to me.

She makes me feel again. She makes me feel safe. She makes me feel… normal. But how normal would she see me if she knew it all—if she knew the worst of it? She'd never be able to look at me the same way again. It's selfish for me to continue on with this…with her.

The sight of my buddy sitting outside the restaurant interrupts my thoughts. The last time I saw Chase 'Irish' McGregor's big burly ass he was deploying to Afghanistan. Three months later, I got word from some of our buddies he was shot. He's a sight for sore eyes to say the least.

"Motherfucker!" I shout to him as I hop out of the truck. He stands, reminding me how much bigger he is. I'm no shrimp, but this dude is *big*. Like NFL defensive lineman big, which makes sense considering he started four years at defensive tackle for West Point. Besides a new gut starting to show, he's still a guy you don't want to fuck with. His cabbie hat sits atop his head as usual.

"You look pretty good for a man who got shot." I say. He laughs, pulling me in for a bro hug and letting me go. I feel like a little kid in his embrace.

"Shit, man, call me Forrest Gump, I guess. I got shot in the ass by a sniper. Came out my right thigh without hitting any bone." He sits, lifting his empty beer to the passing waitress he motions for another one.

"Well, it's great to see you, dude." I take a seat, backing the chair up just a bit to retreat from the cigar smoke billowing from the ashtray. Chase is rarely seen without a cigar stoking nearby.

"Great to see you too, man. Didn't think it would happen so soon. Shit, we deployed what… six months ago?"

The waitress returns with two Bud Lights and sets them before us. Chase's eyes follow the waitress's ass as she makes her way back inside.

"Yeah, six months," I say, though his attention is anything but mine. "How the fuck you still drinking that beer piss, Irish? You need to get on the craft beer train."

He reluctantly returns his eyes to me and shakes his head. "Shit, no way I'm paying seven bucks a beer like you do!" He lifts his beer with a smirk.

"It's been too long, man," he adds.

"It has been! How is everything? How's the wife?"

He takes a long pull of his beer and averts his eyes. "Yeah, that shit's over. Divorce is almost finalized." He takes another chug and shakes his head. "Fuck her."

"Shit, I'm sorry to hear that. What happened?"

"Minus all the bullshit you already know about, my dad caught her fucking my brother. Nobody was able to reach her when I got shot. They got ahold of my dad instead and passed on word I'd be heading stateside. He called and called and called… nothing. So he's got an extra key for the house—for emergencies, ya know?—and he goes over there. Finds them both strung out on meth. Dog shit everywhere. Fucking ball gags and anal beads… the works, man. Pops said it looked like some bizarre fucking porno shoot."

I'm speechless. I knew the chick was a piece of shit from the day I met her. Some people just stink of worthlessness. She's one of those people. But this? This is just fucked.

"I'm sorry, dude." It's all I can manage.

"Shit, better to find out now, without any kids or anything. My dad was smart enough to take video of the house and both of them passed the fuck out. She has nothing on me which means a clean break. That's all I want at this point."

"Fucking crazy."

"Anyways, enough with my sob story. What the fuck are you doing in Missouri?"

"Shit, I could ask you the same, man. Fort Leonard Wood?? What the hell is an infantryman doing at a MP base."

"I'm processing out, man. Can't keep doing this infantry shit anymore. I'm tired of it and I just don't know how much more I can take." He looks a little ashamed of his words. Being friends with a big group of infantry fucks for as long as I have, you come to learn quickly the sanctity of the title and what it means to be in that brotherhood. They don't often extend a positive greeting toward a civilian like me, but as is the case with most of my life, my fists earned the necessary respect.

I can see in his face it wasn't a decision he came to lightly.

"Fort Leonard Wood is closest to my family in Iowa, so I asked to do all the exit paperwork down here," he adds.

As he speaks, I can't help but think about our years spent together in Georgia. He was the first real friend I ever made and it's not something I take lightly.

"Fuck, man, you know what just popped into my head?" I blurt out, the rush of nostalgia running through me. "The first time we met."

Chase laughs loudly, holding two hands to his gut.

"Do I ever, man. I thought for a second that one of us wasn't gonna make it out of that bar alive."

"You started that shit, acting like you owned the place."

"What kind of cocky fucking civilian walks his happy ass into a military bar and starts mouthing off?" Irish says, taking a swig of his beer and then shaking his head. "Compared to you, I did own the bar!"

"Shit, you bumped into me, fucker. Funny how quickly shit turned though, huh?"

"Leave it up to some queer-ass sailors to make me forget about you spilling your drink on me."

"I think my favorite part was running away from the cops after beating the living shit out of those Navy fucks. Seven grown-ass motherfuckers jumping fences and slinking through alleys and shit. We used to be so fucked up."

"What's with this 'used to be' stuff?" Irish jokes. "That was only like three years ago. I think I may have gotten worse."

Though I know he's kidding, a part of me thinks there may be some truth to that.

"I'm right there with ya. Hey, at least we're in bed at an earlier time these days."

"You got that right! Cheers to being old, drunk and stupid." He lifts his beer and I do too, though I don't cheers him right away.

"I'm with you on the drunk and stupid part, but remember you've got about seven years on me, you old fuck."

He laughs, his broad shoulders shaking as he does. He orders two more beers and two burgers he claims are the best he's ever had. It's not even close to the first time I've heard him say that. Food is his best friend… and his worst enemy.

"Back to my question you so quickly bypassed," Irish interjects. "What the hell are you doing here?"

"Well, after you guys deployed, I didn't really feel like hanging in Columbus anymore. I was making my way west and stopped in this little town called Truman Valley for the night.

Ended up meeting a family that owns a winery. They needed a hand for a few months, and I needed the money. So here I am."

"Which town? Worth checking out?" he asks.

"It's this tiny-ass town about an hour west of here. Not much going on there, but it'd be good to have you visit either way." My thoughts stray to Paige and the potential of her meeting Irish. As much as I would love him to meet her, and vice versa, I just don't know if it's good for me. Our lives have already become entangled enough.

"Any hot tail? I've been having a hard fucking time getting back into the game after everything, and my dick is *not* happy about it."

"There's a few sexy girls." Brandi momentarily crosses my mind. "One that you'd definitely be down with, and I get the feeling she may be open to the idea."

"Sign me the fuck up! Weekdays I'm pretty much stuck here, but one of these weekends coming up you're showing my ass a good time.

"Just say the word, man. We'll work something out."

"How about next weekend?" Irish is definitely hard-up. He takes a large bite of his burger, eyes still on me.

"Fuck it, sounds good to me," I finally say.

"Alright, that's what I like to hear. I can't stand these MP fucks here, and I need to get my party on. Somewhere I don't have to worry about who will run into my drunk ass. Sometimes I really hate being an officer." He stops for a moment, as if in thought, before continuing. "I should've been in the NFL, man."

"Yeah, or fucking prison." We both laugh, his teenage run-ins with the law are common knowledge among friends.

"Like you weren't a little fuck back then too. Let's not forget the flashlight incident, man." He notices my immediate discomfort and rolls his eyes. "Don't get all chickish on me. It was a long time ago. Nothing to still be bothered by."

"No, I know. It's not like that. I just don't like thinking about it. That was a different me."

"Not a different you, just an immature you. If I remember it correctly, the guy deserved a good beating. Hitting a girl and shit. Fuck that."

"I honestly don't even remember if he hit her on purpose. It all happened so fast. I definitely don't think he deserved the beating he got."

A half dozen or so people from a town over are gathered around the bonfire. Only one of them—Jared—knows me, though still only on a first-name basis. We go to the same weed dealer and have partied a few times together. The guy knows how to get down, and at this point in my life, I like hanging with people who know where the party's at. As it turns out, he's an acquaintance of the only two girls here. The men, all four of them, are complete strangers to both of us. Almost as soon as we pulled up and got out of Jared's van, the dirty looks started.

The fact that we don't know most of the people here is something he failed to inform me. And though this dumbass is too ate up to recognize the problem with a scenario like this, I'm not. I have an analytical personality—overanalytical, to be perfectly honest. I may be eighteen, but they've been a hard eighteen years and I've become pretty adept at smelling out shitty situations. This situation right here is nothing but bad.

As Jared approaches the two girls, I quickly realize the looks have intensified and whispers are being passed between the oth-

ers. I pull Jared back by his sleeve while the girls continue their conversation as if he had never even been there. One whispers to the other, and they both look at me and giggle. I smile and nod, then lean into Jared.

"Dude, what the fuck were you thinking?"

"What?" he asks, entirely too loud. A few of the guys are cracking open new beers, while others engage in obnoxious conversations.

"You don't know any of these guys. Do you not see the problem with that?" Jared's eyes are bloodshot, and he looks at me through squinted eyelids. His breath reeks of whiskey, his motor skills wrangled by THC.

"No, I don't know them. The girls invited me. They're high schoolers, bro. Hot as fuck!"

"Okay dude, that's really great news, but do you not get that we are kind of encroaching on their territory here?" I pass a nod toward the group of guys, who are now working their best game on the two girls.

"What do you mean?" he stammers, his eyes wandering to the girls. "The girls invited me."

I can just shake my head. I don't know which of us is dumber, him for being so fucking blind or me for letting him drive me here. It's not like I have a car anyway, but it sure would be nice to have the option of leaving.

Jared staggers back to the bonfire. He pulls a flask from his back pocket and takes a big gulp, drunkenly stumbling over his feet a bit. He introduces himself to the guys who take his hand without much enthusiasm. Some fail to shake his hand at all, leaving it floating awkwardly in the air.

I turn back to fetch the Jack Daniels I left on the floorboard *of Jared's van. After downing about a third of the bottle, I stow it in my back pocket. If shit's going down tonight, I'm going to be in an 'I don't give a fuck' mental state.*

I can fight with the best of them sober. I'll take someone's ass out with a quickness, but being sober comes with limitations. It comes with a moral code. When I'm drunk, that code vanishes. Limitations cease to exist. I become ruthless and I give zero fucks. If I'm gonna get my ass beat, I'm at least taking a few of these cocksuckers with me.

I grab a lighter from my front pocket, and as I tread slowly back to the bonfire, I pull a Marlboro Light from behind my ear. I slip it between my lips and light it, taking a long drag. It's when the smoke dances back out my lungs in waves that I see Jared thrown to the ground by the biggest guy of the lot.

A flurry of fists rain down on Jared from the guy who pushed him down as two others kick him. The last one watches me. One of the girls bends down to try and pull the big man off Jared, and as he pulls back to throw another punch, his elbow connects with her face. She stumbles back, her hands holding her nose. He doesn't seem to notice as he continues pummeling Jared.

I see red. Before I know it, I've grabbed a Maglite from the van, and within seconds, I've whacked three of them hard in succession. They back off, hands guarding their faces. The big guy sees me with the Maglite and then looks at his buddies bleeding from fresh cuts on their heads. He lets go of Jared, whose face is swelling already and bleeding badly, and he jumps to his feet. He takes off toward his car, but I'm right behind him. The others are in shock, not moving a muscle. The big guy doesn't make it far before he trips and stumbles to the ground.

He turns onto his back but doesn't have time to get up. The

Maglite comes down on his face in quick succession—one, two, three, four. I can't stop. I lose count. I'm blind with rage, and the only thing running through my head is just how much I like watching him bleed. He begins yelping like a dog on the other end of a rolled up newspaper, sad little cries that make this big man now look utterly pathetic. Flesh splits wide open and pours blood. His nose now juts sharply to the left.

I keep hitting him. I can hear the two girls screaming. One of them is crying. I don't care, nor do I pay it any mind. I bring the Maglite down a few more times before I hear his friends' footsteps growing closer.

Jared pulls the van next to me. The door's open and he's yelling at me to get in. I don't want to stop. I bring it down on the dude's face two more times. He no longer cries, but struggles to breathe through the blood collecting in his mouth. I stand, admiring my handiwork for a few moments before I rear back and throw the Maglite full speed at his face. It connects with a loud thump and then falls to the ground. He lets out a sickening gurgle and groan. I hop into the van and we take off, leaving him bleeding in the rearview.

"Jesus fucker, say something. I know you're eating, but shit. Talk between bites or something. You're making shit awkward now." Irish's voice pulls me from my haze as I pop the last of the burger into my mouth and wash it down with a swig of beer. I hadn't realized it, but I finished my entire burger without a word between us. My mind was too busy lost in the collection of memories. That was a different place in my life—a different me.

"Something on your mind?" he asks.

"Nah, man. More or less just trying to figure out where I

go from here."

"Fort Lewis, no?" He knows just enough about my past to understand I would make it up there someday.

"Eventually… or maybe not. I don't know, man. I think I've just gotta figure some shit out before I take all that on. I'm twenty-seven. I've never had a job for longer than six months. I don't like putting roots down anywhere. Three years in Columbus with you guys—actually settling and getting close to people—that's rare, man. I'm learning that the hard way in Truman Valley."

"How do you mean?"

"Just not making too many friends over there."

"No?"

"Not even close."

"You fuck the wrong woman?" he asks, knowing my history full well. Women are trouble for me. I spend just enough time with them to get what I need, and when it comes time to get real—to open myself up to another person fully, to give them all of me—I run. And I run fast. Women are my Kryptonite and love is foreign to me.

"Not quite. There is a girl, and the bullshit involves her, but we haven't fucked or anything like that. I work for her dad. We've made out a few times, but that's it. Nothing serious. This is just a pit stop for me."

There's doubt in his eyes. "You sure about that, man?"

"Positive. She's just got this crazy ex who's been a fucking pain. Him and two of his bitches."

"Anything we need to tend to while I'm in town?"

"No, not at all. Best to try and not let it get to me. I'm too old for all this shit. In the old days, we'd handle this how we've handled any other situation. But now, I'm just over it. He's just trying to get under my skin."

"Is it working?"

"Is it hard to get under my skin?" I ask with an eyebrow raised.

"Well, we did start as enemies."

"Because you're a shit-talking Mick."

"And you're a sensitive prick," he says, laughing as he stands. "There's a real nice strip joint out off Highway Z. A *real* classy place." He takes a quick glance at his wristwatch. "And with it being one in the afternoon, they're really going to have their prime ladies up dancing."

"You mean their fuckin' D squad." I laugh, but his face is nothing but serious. "You're not fucking around, are you?"

He just shakes his head and walks toward his car, a souped-up Camaro that is comically small for a dude pushing 6'4.

Irish motions to the passenger side. "Get the fuck in, you cock." He lumbers into the driver's seat and I reluctantly climb in the car after him, noticing for the first time the Purple Heart license plate. It reads one word… IRISH.

CHAPTER FIFTEEN

Paige

"Lover Come Back"—City & Colour

BRANDI AND I SIT CROSS-LEGGED ON MY BED, THE SUN LONG since set. With a half finished bottle of wine, we're getting our Netflix and chill on hard. It's a nice little reminder that the last time I actually "Netflix and chilled" was more than six months ago.

Rowdy's big head lies on my lap, pulling my thoughts to his daddy and the fact that maybe I've been pushing for too much. It's only been a few short weeks and I know he'll be leaving one day soon, but I can't get him out of my head. I just can't.

I wish he were here. He left nearly twelve hours ago, and I haven't heard a thing since earlier in the day. The thought of something bad happening to him is unsettling.

"So what the fuck do you think Cody's gonna do?" Brandi asks. "That shit last night… Xander calling them out in front of everyone. That's not gonna go over well." Brandi drunkenly twirls her hair as she reminds me of what I already know.

Cody won't let this go. And I'm scared shitless what he may do. I've seen him hurt a lot of people.

"I don't know. You've known him as long as I have." I pause, contemplating what could come. "He's going to get him back. He wanted to last night."

"I saw him follow you guys out! What stopped him?"

"Deputy Johnson drove by. You know he's not an idiot when it comes to Cody. I just worry about Xander."

"How are things with you and hot stuff by the way? I guess we're kissing in public now, huh?" She laughs, but it's the nervous kind. She knows as well as I do that no one keeps secrets in small towns.

"Yeah, that was unexpected. Right in the middle of the place too." I grimace, thinking of all the people I knew in there. At the time I couldn't care less, but now that I've had time to process it, I realize things may get weird around here pretty fast.

"Do you think your parents know already?" she asks, finishing off her glass of wine and refilling both of ours with the rest of the bottle.

"I think it's entirely possible in this damn town."

"Fuck."

"Yeah. Fuck." I take a swig of my wine and glance at the clock... 11:00 p.m.

Without warning, the sound of wood violently splintering comes from outside.

Both of us jump at the noise, spilling wine on my bed and ourselves. I put the wine glass down and make my way quickly to the back door. Rowdy and Brandi follow close behind.

When I open the door, I can't believe my eyes. Xander's truck is positioned a foot into the guesthouse porch, a few of the two-by-fours splitting around the truck frame.

His truck lights are still on and the door is open wide, but he remains seated. He bobs his head slowly to the music on the radio and he's completely unaware we're watching him.

Instantly, my mind goes to my parents. They're both heavy sleepers and are usually dead asleep by ten—at the latest—but the noise was loud enough that it could have woken them. I'm in a near panic as I think of the implications of this. Xander would certainly be thrown out. There's not a doubt in my mind. My dad lost a close cousin of his to a drunk driver, and he'll never forget it.

I creep through the house, listening for any movement. *Nothing.* I peek around the corner and down the hall. No lights are on. I hear Caleb's television, blaring as usual, but there doesn't seem to be any other commotion.

I go back to the kitchen just as Brandi comes through the backdoor with her hands to her mouth.

"Yuck, yuck, yuck. He just threw up. Like bad." She goes straight to my room without bothering to turn back around. I return to the back door and see Xander in the same position, but completely passed out now. Rowdy is up on his hind legs and licking his face.

My mind rapidly sifts through possible excuses as I try to figure out what the hell to tell my parents. I come up empty. Real fucking empty. Each lie seems more ridiculous than the last.

After shutting Rowdy inside the guesthouse, I cut the truck's lights and turn the engine off, sneering at Xander's passed-out ass as I do. I wake him up just enough to support some of his weight and walk him to his door.

"Hey, I'm okay," he mumbles, pushing me away a bit. His eyes are just slits and looking at nothing in particular.

"Okay, my fucking ass. You're far from okay. And I swear to God"—I push him to the bed and he sits hard, looking up at me spitefully when he lands—"tomorrow I'm putting a fucking boot in your ass. I cannot *believe* you'd do something like this. I feel fucking sick."

He still looks at me, but with little understanding. He lies down and closes his eyes, legs still hanging off the bed.

"I'm tired," he murmurs, his face planted in the mattress.

"Tomorrow morning your ass is mine." I turn his lights off, leaving him just as he is and hoping his back and neck pain tomorrow is just as bad as his hangover will be. I leave the guesthouse, anger stirring as I see the mess of vomit I'll have the pleasure of cleaning up.

It's five something in the damn morning. Mom will be up around seven and Dad even earlier than that, so now is the time to wake up Xander. There's a lot to go over. I've got a bullshit story even the dumbest person on Earth wouldn't believe, but I'm rolling with it. I'm praying Dad takes into account that I have never lied to him. Not ever. There has to be some stock in that.

Checking out the damage in daylight relieves me just a little. It isn't as bad as it appeared around midnight, and with the truck already towed, I see only a few of the two-by-fours are split. Regardless, I'm livid.

I find Xander in just about the same position I left him. He snores and twitches violently in his sleep. I storm up to him, and without regard, I shake him. After a few stiff shakes, his eyes go so wide it seems they may pop out at any moment. He bolts upright, his hands blocking his face.

He drops them slowly and scans the room. His sunken, bloodshot eyes finally meet mine.

"What happened last night?" he asks, almost in a whisper. "I think I know, but can you tell me?"

I stand with both hands on my hips, my foot tapping the floor as if I'm a parent disciplining a child. I don't care.

"Well, what's the last fucking thing you remember?" My crassness takes him by surprise. I haven't cursed around him much, but when I'm angry, all bets are off.

"We went out after lunch. Stayed out awhile. And, uh, I…" He rubs his temples firmly, his eyes closed and head shaking. "I remember heading back here. And…and I guess it's spotty after that."

All I can do is shake my head. His carelessness is appalling.

"Can I let you in on something, Xander?"

He nods.

"My dad's cousin was killed by a drunk driver a few years back. He had a wife and two daughters. She lost her husband. They lost their dad. Are you understanding what the fuck I'm trying to say?"

He nods again, his eyes as far away from mine as they'll go.

"I'm so disappointed in you, Xander. And I don't mean that in a demeaning, act-like-your-parent kind of way. I mean, you're someone I truly respect and admire, and I was hoping you were better than this."

He doesn't say a word, so I continue.

"Do you remember anything else from last night?" I ask, wondering if he even recalls running his damn truck into the porch. With the way I found him, I highly doubt it.

"Sort of. I know I hit something. I'm afraid of what that could have been." He finally looks at me, pure shame in his eyes.

"Well, thank God it wasn't a person. Thank God you didn't take somebody's father away. Somebody's son. Somebody's brother. You only wrecked the guesthouse porch… this time."

He puts his face in his hands and groans. Then he stands, staggering a bit before collecting himself and walking past me to the window. He looks out and sighs.

"So, yeah, there's that fun little problem we now get to deal with. I already cleaned up your puke and Ethan's on his way to tow your truck." He looks back at me sharply. "How were the burger and fries, by the way?"

He looks back out the window, cursing under his breath again.

"How the fuck am I supposed to explain this, Xander? My dad doesn't look past stuff like this, no matter how much he likes you."

"I'll just tell him the truth. And then I'll move on."

"I don't want that."

He glances back at me. The shame in his eyes makes my heart ache for him, but I won't let up. Not for something like this.

"I don't want that either, Paige. But you're right. We have no options. This is my fault. I'm a fucking moron, and I need to deal with the repercussions."

"No, I won't let that happen. I don't want you to go. I just don't want you to be a fucking idiot. I mean, seriously, is that like a regular thing for you?"

"No. Not at all."

I'm not sure whether to believe him or not.

"Well, I've got your back this time. This time, and only this time… because I care about you. And I believe people are allowed to make a few mistakes… if you learn from them."

"Paige, how exactly do we explain this?"

"Your truck is old. Brake lines go bad. That's all we've got, and we're going to roll with it. You need to get your ass in the shower, wash some of the hangover off your face and get that damn whiskey off your breath." I pull my phone out and check the time.

"It's 5:32 right now. Dad will be up in a few. We'll meet him in the kitchen for coffee as usual. You tell the story and I'll back you up."

"This will never work, Paige."

"Well, it has to work. Unless you have any better ideas."

He shakes his head.

"Well, alright then. I share everything with my Dad. I always have. I'm his only daughter. He trusts me. And if I back your story up… he'll trust us."

I hope.

"Are you sure about this, Paige?"

"Just get in the shower, Xander."

I leave the guesthouse without another word.

CHAPTER SIXTEEN

Paige

"Just A Kiss"—Lady Antebellum

"So wait, what happened?" Mom looks up from her workstation and eyes me curiously.

"It's an old truck. I guess it had been a while since he changed out the brake lines. Luckily, he wasn't going fast. I'm surprised you guys didn't wake up. It was loud!" I say, as convincingly as I can. I'm naturally a terrible liar, but to my parents? That's a whole other story.

She seems to accept my explanation though and shifts her attention back to her pencil and paper, drawing up plans for her next project.

"Well, you know how heavy we sleep. It's your father's snoring. I've had to train myself," she says with a smirk.

"Oh, trust me, Mom, you aren't the only one who suffers. I can hear it from all the way downstairs. I'm still shocked you didn't hear the wreck. It was pretty bad."

"Is Xander okay?" she asks.

"Yeah, Brandi and I went out there right away and checked on him. He was a little shaken up, but otherwise alright. The guesthouse porch, not so much." I laugh, scanning my mother's face for any sign of doubt.

Her head pops up, her eyes gazing out the front windows in thought. She looks over to me slowly, a wrinkle of concern in her forehead.

"Do you think Cody did something to the brake lines?"

"I thought about that at first, but Xander was at Fort Leonard Wood all day hanging out with his friend. He wasn't even around here. Ethan's got the truck in his shop now though, so he'll probably be able to tell us soon."

She's believing it now. I can tell by the way she looks at me. And I feel terrible for it.

"I bet that's what it was," she says, shaking her head. "Pardon my language, but I'd like to kick that boy's ass. And that's just what he is... a boy."

"I know, Mom."

"What he did to you..." Her voice trails off, and I know without even looking at her that tears are welling in her eyes. They always do when she brings up my past with Cody. "I'll never forget it."

I leave my desk and meet her at her workstation. I take her in my arms and squeeze her, holding her for a few extra seconds for good measure. She leans her head on my shoulder, sniffling.

"It's alright, Mama. That's over now. Never again." I pause a moment. "Mama?"

"Yes, dear?" I release her and sit on a stool beside hers.

"I think I'm falling for him." I haven't mentioned anything to my mother about Xander and I at this point, but she nods as if she's known all along.

"I feel so stupid because it's been such a short time, but—"

"Do you know how long I knew your dad before I was convinced I was in love?"

I shake my head.

"Two days. And I hated him after our first date. The man forgot his wallet, for Pete's sake!"

I laugh, remembering the story she so often tells… my father running terribly late, picking her up in a beater of a truck, getting all the way to the restaurant and forgetting his wallet, my mother having to pay.

"After the next date, I knew he'd be the man I would marry." She smiles

"He was so charming, and dorky, and perfect. He was everything. Don't put a time constraint on your feelings. Trust them. And trust your gut, of course. I like Xander, dear. I really do. I'd like to learn more about him, but I like what I do know. Your father likes him too. I'm not so sure he'll like you all together though."

I know full well if my father doesn't already know, he will not be happy when he finds out.

"A lot of people at Whittaker's last night," she says, catching me off guard.

"Oh god. Does he know?"

Mom nods her head and my heart sinks.

"When?"

"Bryson Whittaker called your dad earlier today. Wants Xander to start playing one night a week up there or something.

Talked about him being your 'boyfriend,' and obviously your father had all sorts of questions."

I drop my head in my hands. *This is not good.*

"So how did Dad react?"

"Well, you know your father. Keeps to himself mostly. Didn't talk to me much about it after Bryson called."

"And Xander?"

"I assume they will talk. But honey, if these feelings are real and this is something you want to pursue, your father will understand. He's got a bigger heart than anyone I know. He'll get it." She rests a hand on my knee.

"It'll never go anywhere though."

"Why's that?"

"Xander's leaving in like a month. He'll never come back down here again. It'll die off eventually."

"Well, why does he have to leave?" Mom asks.

"It's a long story… and not really mine to tell, I guess. He's just had a really rough life and has some unfinished business he needs to take care of. He could stay longer, if he wanted to, but it would be selfish of me to try and keep him here."

"I don't see how it would be. Does he not feel the same?" She looks at me inquisitively.

"Yeah, I think he does." I hesitate, knowing full well that he does feel the same, but still battling some self-doubt.

Could this all be a game?

"He says he does anyway, but there's just a whole lot to it."

"I don't think anything should get in the way of love," she says.

My thoughts stray to Xander and his sister. The longer he stays here, the longer he puts off reconnecting with her. And that… that is what's most important. I just can't get in the way.

"It's complicated," I say, exhaling with a long, drawn out sigh. I think about what it must be like between Xander and Daddy right now as they work, and I almost feel bad for Xander.

Almost.

"By the way… we've gotta talk about Caleb."

CHAPTER
SEVENTEEN

Xander

"I Don't Wanna Die"—Hollywood Undead

I GOT OFF EASY THIS MORNING. BESIDES THE BLINDINGLY painful headache and an unquenchable thirst, Jack seemed to buy the whole brake line story. Hell, he even suggested that Cody could have been involved. I went with it. When I need to act, I can *fucking act*.

We fixed the deck ourselves, putting down new 2x4s and applying finish. Conversation was as frequent and vulgar as usual. It was around noon when things changed. He came back from taking a call in the house and hasn't spoken a word since.

Three hours now.

Nothing.

I've tried engaging in conversation while we work, but all his answers are short and to the point. *He knows.*

I wish he would just say something already. I wish he'd just spit it out.

"Xander." *Ah, fuck.*

"Yeah, Jack?" Here it goes. My time here has come to an abrupt end.

"It's a small town…" He pauses and I brace for it. "Shit gets around." He stops again, scratching his graying five o'clock shadow. "This Cody character. He's a dumb, worthless little prick… but he's dangerous. He's got a lot of dangerous friends. And some of my friends were out at Whittaker's the other night."

He scans my face, perhaps trying to gauge my reaction.

"You just gotta watch your back. Unfortunately, he's just one of many that are taking over this town. It's the kids these days. They're bored after school, so they start smoking. Then they start snorting and shooting up. Just watch yourself, okay?"

"Yeah, Jack, of course. I appreciate that. I've been trying to avoid the guy, but I need to do a better job of not letting him get under my skin."

"It's a hard thing to do. But you also can't go around kissing his ex right in front of him…in front of people he knows." I freeze, hoping if I stand perfectly still, maybe—just maybe—I'll disappear.

"Relax. I'm not going to hit you." He laughs, and shakes the shovel he's holding.

"Fuck. I'm sorry, Jack."

"Listen, I'm gonna let you explain yourself first. I think you should at least get that. Then we'll figure out what's next."

"It was never my intent to disrespect you, Jack. Never. I just… I don't know. I have genuine feelings for Paige. I fought any attraction I had early on because I *didn't* want to disrespect you. Because I didn't want to disrespect your home. But… I don't know... it just happened." *Dear Lord, man, shut the fuck up.*

"I can stomach real feelings and all that. What I can't stomach is the thought of you with *my* daughter, in *my* house."

"Jack, I have never. I would *never*. Nothing like that has even happened. We've kissed, yes. That's it. And that just happened like a week ago. I truly mean no disrespect. I'll stop everything with her completely. I promise, though, we haven't done anything else."

He settles a bit. The creases in his forehead fade. "Okay, but if you could just stop talking to my daughter like that, I'm not so sure how real those feelings truly are."

"I never said it would be easy, but I've felt bad enough as it is. I know in a way I've disrespected you by not telling you myself—by letting you find out from someone else. And I'm truly sorry for that." I gauge his face for a reaction, but it's blank.

"Well, I love my daughter. And all I've ever want is for her to be happy. I want what's best for her—"

"I do, too," I say.

"If that's the case, then we shouldn't have any problems. But just know, if I *ever* find out you have or do sleep with my daughter under my roof, a shovel will be the least of your concerns. Capiche?"

"I would never."

"Anybody else working for me pulls something like this and their ass is fired without question. I want you to know that," Jack says in a matter of fact tone as he starts to dig again. "You're still here because I like you, and though I know the actions of young men all too well, I trust what you're telling me. And I trust my daughter wouldn't do something like that. Just be smart and don't make me regret keeping you here." He stops and looks up, waiting for my respons.

"I won't, Jack. I won't."

"Well, then that's all I got for that part of the conversation."

"That part?" I ask.

"Yeah, that was Whittaker on the phone. He's the one who let me in on your little kiss from the other night, but he was calling for a different purpose entirely."

"What purpose would that be?"

"He wants you to sing there for a few hours on Friday night. His other performer came down with something. Said it could become a regular thing. I told him 'I didn't even know that motherfucker played music.'" He laughs, which is quite the sound after the conversation we just had.

"Surprise," I say timidly.

"You been holding out on us, boy? You some kind of pop star and I didn't know it?"

"Definitely not pop and far from being a star. I'm more at the alternative rock end of the spectrum. My music is too dark to be pop."

"Oh, you're into that type of shit Caleb blares in his room. That emo nonsense?"

"I actually do like that emo nonsense, I hate to admit it. I guess mine could fall into that category."

"Well, if you're interested in taking him up on his offer, Bryce Whittaker's number is on the kitchen counter. I'd be checking this shit out if Teresa and I weren't going out of town this weekend. Next time though."

"Where are you off to?" I take my opportunity to change subjects without hesitation.

"Wine contest down in Kentucky we do every year. 'Best of the Midwest.'"

"Coming home a winner?"

"I always do." He smirks, heaving a dying plant into the wheelbarrow. A still silence sits between us as we continue to work and after the words we just exchanged, I couldn't be more thankful for it.

CHAPTER EIGHTEEN

Paige

"Fast Cars and Freedom"—Rascal Flatts

As far as I can tell, Xander hasn't had a drink all week… and he has the shakes to prove it. I hadn't realized how much he actually drank before he cut it out completely. I guess I haven't been much of a good influence in that department. We're a drinking family, after all.

He's also been very quiet lately—especially at dinner. As Dad pounds back beers, I've noticed Xander makes excuses as to why he can't. That, and he's been faking illness all week… or maybe not faking at all. He doesn't look good, but he's hanging strong.

Now he's waiting backstage while they set up the equipment. Whittaker's is pretty full already. Luckily, Brandi and I got here early and claimed a table in the middle, right where Xander asked me to be.

I'm so glad Brandi's off tonight, since Ethan's sitting across from us in a pissy mood—as usual. If I had to be here alone with him and force conversation, I don't know what I'd do. He's just not the same anymore. He's always been weird, but it was a different kind of weird. It was weird in an endearing kind of way. Now it's just taxidermy, German shit porn weird. It looks like he hasn't showered in a week. He wasn't even invited here in the first place. He just showed up and sat down, handling his Smirnoff Ices like he can't get enough of them.

"You think Xander's nervous? He hasn't had a drink all night." Brandi leans in and whispers, which makes Ethan huff up a storm.

"He's gotta be. He looked sick as all hell earlier." I take a swig of my Coors. "I think that's why he went backstage already. He seemed crazy nervous with all these people here."

"You think he'll shit the bed?"

I give Brandi a dirty look.

"What?" she asks.

"I hope he doesn't. You better knock on some wood." She taps two knuckles on the table and smiles. Just then, a tall, burly man approaches us from my left.

"You Paige?" he asks, a confident twinkle in his eye. He's looking past me though, right at Brandi. I turn and see she's staring right back at him.

"Yeah, hey. Irish, I presume?" He shakes my hand and then leans in toward Brandi.

"And you must be Brandi…" She puts her hand in his, smiling wide, her eyelashes batting just the right way.

"That I am." Her hand lingers there for a moment before he finally lets it go. Then he walks over to Ethan, who doesn't so much as look at him but still shakes his hand. Irish shrugs and walks back around, taking the empty seat to my left.

"So, Irish, you live at Fort Leonard Wood, and you're originally from… Iowa, right?" I ask. Brandi leans in for his response.

"First off, call me Chase. Only my boys call me Irish."

"Well, how long they been doing that for, Irish?" Brandi asks from over my shoulder.

"It's Chase to you, young lady. And for as long as I can remember." He winks before ordering a beer from the waitress. I grab another Coors… and a shot. Anything to quell my own nervousness.

Chase leans back in. "Anyways, yeah, Iowa… Des Moines, to be more specific. My dad lives up there. My grandma too… and my ex."

"Ex, huh?" Brandi asks, and I shoot her a disapproving look.

"Yeah, long, dirty story. One not worth telling. Just know she is an ex." He smiles at Brandi before his attention is drawn by a commotion on the stage. I look, hoping to see Xander, but it's just Bryson Whittaker messing with the mic.

"When's my boy go on by the way?" He scans the stage.

"He should be going on any minute. He's backstage right now" The moment I say it my thoughts go to Xander, who's probably downing shots before he goes on. I wouldn't blame him if he did. I don't know how he could go on stage without some.

"I'm shocked he let you come watch," I add.

"I was one of the very few people who ever heard that dude play. He used to have this habit of getting shit-faced drunk and playing for some of us in the unit. He never remembered it the next day, and we never reminded him. When he tried to pull some shit, saying this weekend wasn't good for me to come over, I got him to talk."

He accepts a beer from the waitress, slipping her a ten and telling her to keep it. The waitress thanks him and sets the other drinks on the table. I quickly down the shot of Fireball and Brandi hurries to play catch-up.

"Well, I'll be damned. I see I'm not the only one that's Irish here," he says with a smile.

"Damn straight," Brandi says through a grimace.

"Ain't nothing wrong with that," Chase says, raising his beer to her.

"So, Irish, what do you do?" Brandi asks. He smirks and takes a long drink.

"Well, Brandi, I'm working on getting out of the Army now. I'm a captain, and I was shot in Afghanistan. Long story short, I'm ready for some freedom." He smiles at her. "What about you, young lady? What do you do?"

"I bartend at this fabulous establishment." Brandi raises her hands and gestures at the bar with a used car salesman's smile. She then puts two thumbs down and blows a raspberry. Chase laughs, and it's one of those deep belly laughs only big guys can produce.

"What are you going to do when you get out?" Brandi asks, twirling her hair between two fingers. Chase is on his second beer and drinking them as fast as I imagine any Army guy would.

"Well, I race cars." Brandi nods her head approvingly. "And I'm a carpenter. Learned from my dad. I do some stuff with that on the side."

"So, you race cars?" Brandi asks, ignoring the last of what he said.

"Yeah, have been for a very long time. Nothing serious. Street stuff. Two things I learned from my dad: one, how to build anything with wood, and two, how to race a fucking car." He finishes the last of his beer and raises it to the passing waitress. Brandi leans in now, her chin in her hands and her elbow on her knees.

"What kind of car do you race, Ricky Bobby?" she asks, just as Xander plugs his cord into an amp, pulls a stool to the middle of the stage, and takes a seat. His acoustic guitar sits in his lap and it shakes in his hands. Though obviously nervous, he looks to be composed at least. If he was drinking, he didn't drink much.

"I have eight different vehicles. I race a lot of them."

"Well, okay! You'll have to take me for a ride sometime." Brandi's flirting is about as subtle as a face tattoo. Chase is eating it right up though.

"Tomorrow, right?" He smiles, the kind of smile that makes sitting between them seriously awkward. "I can drive to the lake house."

"I thought Xander said you were bringing your Harley?" I ask.

"I did, but I heard somebody here happens to have a '69 Chevelle." He smiles mischievously and rubs his hands together.

"Oh you must be crazy. First you make impromptu reservations for my lake house and now you think you're gonna drive my baby? You must be nuts."

"Hey, the lake house was Xander's idea. I just told him I was coming up and he needed to make some plans." He pauses for a moment before continuing. "And I was promised I'd be able to drive a '69 Chevelle so…" He lifts both hands and shrugs.

"Okay, you *and* Xander must both be nuts. Nobody drives her but me."

"Well, that's unfortunate, because there's no way a woman is driving that car properly." He laughs and curls up, waiting to block me from hitting him.

"I see you and Xander are just two peas in a pod, huh?"

I playfully raise my fist and he flinches just as Xander starts to speak into the mic, introducing himself. We clap loudly as he begins his first song. Bryson Whittaker wanted all covers and Xander starts with one of my favorites—*Counting Blue Cars* by Dishwalla. My appreciation of obscure 90's alternative acts is a well-known fact in this town.

Beyond a few hiccups at the beginning of his set, Xander nailed it. He seemed nervous and his eyes didn't often leave the ground—most of the time they weren't even open—but he played. And he played well.

I've also learned I can't drink with Chase. I get competitive when someone questions my drinking abilities. With each shot Chase ordered, he warned me against trying to match him. So, of course, then I'd order a shot of my own… Every. Single. Time.

Lucky for us, Xander still hasn't had anything to drink. Not tonight, not earlier today… not since running into the guesthouse porch. At least not that I know of.

Since the rest of us are good and liquored up, Xander

drives all of us back to the house.

Xander isn't even smiling. He's not angry, but he's not happy either. His hand is on my lap, but it's limp... lifeless. He doesn't say a word. I hope the trip to Twain Lake tomorrow will cheer him up.

The drive to Twain Lake is a riot. I end up letting Chase drive, after a great deal of begging, and I actually don't regret doing so. The guy wasn't lying when he said he could race the hell out of a car.

Xander just smiles, soaking up the sun from the passenger seat, his aviators perched on his face. It takes me a few minutes to realize I'm staring. I'm just happy to see him in a better mood.

We make it to the lake house around noon... perfect time to catch the best of the sun's rays, to ride the jet skis way too fast, and to appreciate the beauty this place has to offer—a place that has given me so much joy over the years. This lake house is as much my home as Truman Valley, and I'm so thankful to be spending the weekend here with these people.

Chase pulls in, parks and is out of the car with his shirt off before any of us can even open our doors. He runs to the water, high-kneeing it through the shallow part and diving in when it's up to his hips. Xander laughs and shakes his head, then he gets out himself.

Brandi hauls her bags inside and proceeds to change into the skimpiest bikini in existence. I'm used to it by now, but it seems Chase is *not*. His eyes are glued to her. Xander averts his eyes as soon as he possibly can. He seems to have only eyes for me and it couldn't make me happier. As Brandi dives into the water, he takes me into his arms and kisses me.

***

Xander still hasn't had a drop of alcohol. The rest of us... well, I can't say the same. I love that Xander is trying so hard.

Chase is a beast. He's been slamming drinks like he's been lost in the Sahara for days—only they're not water. Beer... after beer... after beer. And somehow he still dances like a pro, music playing from the lake house guiding him along. Brandi dances close by. She's wasted but coherent, and moving closer to Chase by the minute. Xander and I sit in beach chairs near the bonfire, both of us watching them dance through the flames.

"Xander... how are you? I know things haven't been easy for you since everything, but just know I do see you trying."

"Thanks." He smiles and then stares off toward the lake. "That night... driving like that. That was an eye-opener." He pauses and looks as if he's trying to think of the right words to say...or whether to say them at all. "That wasn't even close to the first time something like that's happened. I got a DUI in Miami. It was my first day there. You'd think I would've learned from that, but I didn't. I've done it more times than I could ever comfortably admit since then."

I can only shake my head. My thoughts stray to my cousin Katie and the heartbreaking phone conversations we've had since her dad died. Sometimes she cries, other times she curses the drunk driver. What she didn't do for a long time was cope. I don't think Dad ever truly has.

"Honestly, Xander, that's shocking to hear." It's the only thing I can say. I know he's been through some shit, but it doesn't excuse him putting people's lives at risk. Nothing excuses that.

He's healed a lot from his past. I can see that in just the short time I've known him. He's kind. He has manners and he's polite. He's intelligent and self-educated… but this man is still dealing with a lot. It makes me ache for him, but I could never be okay with something like that. Ever.

"Xander." His shoulders drop as if he knows what's to come. "I see you trying. And I love that you're trying. But for someone to drive like you did that night…" My voice trails off. I don't want to be too harsh, because I can only imagine how he's feeling right now.

"You don't think I know?" His eyes are fixed sharply on mine; his tone rising just a bit. "You don't think I've woken up time and time again trying desperately to piece together spotty memories from the night before? That I don't worry about what I may have done? I'm trying here."

"I know you are." I take his hand in mine and brush my thumb softly against his skin. Laughter from Chase and Brandi carries from the shore through the darkness.

"I don't want to be that person," he says, his eyes not meeting mine. I desperately wish they would. "But it's like…" His voice breaks. "When I'm not fucked up… feeling…. It's just too real. It's too much."

"What do you mean?"

He rubs his temples, sighing in obvious frustration. "I can't even explain it."

I grab both his hands in mine now as he tries not to look at me.

"Try."

"When I'm sober, shit runs through my mind... my parents, the Boy's Home, my sister, shit I've done in my life since then... it all sits right there at the center of my brain, fucking with me. When I drink...when I smoke...those thoughts go away. I feel good. I feel free. Like I don't have a care in the world."

He pulls a joint from his ear and lights it, taking a long, slow drag.

"But you can't live like that, Xander. That's not how it's done. You gotta face that shit."

"And what shit do you face, Paige?" He immediately looks regretful as I give him a glance reserved only for the most fucked-up occasions.

"You know that Cody guy, Xander? The one who's about three inches taller and twenty pounds heavier than you? You think he just slapped me around here and there?" He doesn't respond and won't even look at me now.

"Cody fucking beat me until I didn't recognize myself in the mirror afterward. He beat me so bad I wouldn't leave our apartment for weeks until I recovered. My family was so concerned, but I didn't care. I didn't have time to care. I was so fucking scared of him, and yet I was so in love. Do you understand that, Xander? Can you?"

He still doesn't look at me. His fingers intertwined, he rubs his thumbs together feverishly.

"I thought he would kill me, Xander." He finally does look up and right into my eyes. Then he wraps his hands around mine once again.

"I'd kill him for you, Paige."

"I don't want that. I don't want you going to prison and I

don't want him dead. I just want all this to stop." I take a deep breath, fighting back the tears that want to come. "And I want him out of my life."

"Is that even possible?" Xander asks.

"I have no clue." I think about leaving Truman Valley, joining Xander on his journey to Washington. It doesn't sound so bad to me. We sit in silence awhile and I can feel the tension in him. I want to take it away, but I don't know how.

"Paige, do you know what you mean to me?" he asks, catching me off guard.

"Well, I like to think I have an idea. But tell me... tell me what I mean to you."

"So. Fucking. Much. More than I'm comfortable even admitting. I've never gotten close to a woman before. I've dated, yes, but it's never meant anything. Not a single fucking thing. I just never let them get close. But this..." He points to me and then at himself. "This is real. This is different. From the moment I saw you, Paige..."

My thoughts bring me back to that day we met at Whittaker's, the way this complete stranger came to my rescue. It could be the plot of a damn romance novel, for Christ's sake.

"From the moment I saw you, too. But where the hell do we go from here?" I ask. "What happens when you have to leave? I understand you have to, but what happens to us?"

He shakes his head. "God, Paige, I don't know."

I smile, pulling his palm to my mouth, I kiss it softly. This isn't what tonight was supposed to be about. I don't want to think about tomorrow anymore...only today...only right this moment. "Will you come to the house with me?" He hesitates as I stand, still holding one of his hands. I pull it lightly. "Come with me."

When he doesn't move I let go of his hand and start walking toward the house.

"Paige," he calls from behind me.

"Just come." I walk inside, leaving the door open, and head straight for my room.

I don't turn the lights on; I don't need to. I've been coming to the lake house for as long as I can remember. I stand next to the bed, waiting for Xander to find his way through the dark stillness of the house.

"Xander?" I ask.

"Yes." His voice comes from just outside the door.

"What are you doing?" I ask as I strip everything off but a tank and panties.

"I don't know. But we shouldn't do this here. This is still your father's house, Paige."

"Who said I wanted to do anything with you in the first place?" I scoff. "I just want to cuddle. Now, get your ass in bed."

He walks into the room and stands on the opposite side of the bed. He pulls off his boots and jeans and then takes his shirt off, exposing his broad, muscular chest and rippled abs in the dim moon light. He slides under the covers and I join him there. I scoot myself back until my body meets his warm, solid chest. Before I completely settle in, he throws an arm over me and pulls me into him. I can feel his dick throbbing against my ass. He runs his fingertips up and down my arm in soft, delicate patterns.

I'm powerless against how wet my panties have become. I grind my ass into his stiffening dick again. He groans, and taking my earlobe into his mouth, he lightly nibbles it. He trails kisses down my neck and that sensitive spot behind my ear that sends tingles throughout my entire body.

My panties are almost completely soaked through now, but at this point, I don't care because two of his fingers have pulled them to the side. One of them dives recklessly into my entrance, and my body is owned by a pleasure and anticipation I've never felt before.

CHAPTER NINETEEN

Xander

"Smoke"—A Thousand Horses

I DIDN'T WANT TO BE HERE. I MEAN, I WANTED TO BE IN THIS situation with her, but not *here*. Not anywhere Jack Watson owns. But holy fuck, what the hell am I to do? She's insatiable. And though I know how wrong this is, my cock doesn't seem to care.

My roaming hands unintentionally rub up against her panties. Shit, she's completely wet. Now I'm aching at the idea of being inside her.

My mind fights to rationalize the situation, but my dick is like a laid-back pool shark who already knows what's coming.

I pull her drenched panties to the side and thrust two fingers in. She squeals first, and then it turns into a moan as my fingers meet her G-spot. I just want to fucking taste her.

I *need* to taste her.

I trail kisses down the side of her neck, along the curve of her waist. Her body tenses as I kiss over her stomach. II pull my fingers out and grab her thighs, spreading them apart gently before diving my fingers back deep inside of her. My lips hover over her pussy and I blow a long breath across her delicate skin before I run my tongue against her clit. She lets out a breathy, fervent moan.

Her moans make my cock twitch.

I feel her body shudder and then stiffen. Her hands grab desperately at my hair. I know she's about to come and I want to feel its warmth against my tongue. Her body arches off the bed wildly as she screams and moans my name. Her legs shake against the sides of my head as she watches me clean her up… every last drop.

I work my lips up to her stomach—to her neck, and then I kiss her. She's in a lustful haze coming out from the fog of her orgasm. She looks at me hungrily and grabs a handful of my hair. I can't fight the urge to taste her again. I want to savor every bit of it. I push her panties to the side and slowly swipe my tongue over her.

God, she tastes so fucking good.

The second my tongue circles her clit, her heels dig into the mattress, and her back bows away from the bed. "Shit," she breathes, fisting my hair. "You gotta stop."

My tongue reluctantly parts from her insatiable pussy and she pulls me up toward her, and I kiss her. Knowing she can taste herself on me, makes me grow harder by the second. Both her hands grab my triceps and she digs her nails in as I work my mouth over to her neck, sucking and biting.

I rip her panties completely off and throw them to the

floor. She pulls her shirt over her head, nearly tearing it in the process, and her hands meet her hardened nipples. The sight of her playing with them makes my dick beg to be inside her. With the sexiest look in her eyes, she tugs on my briefs now soaked with precum.

I fight the urge to lose myself in her. I know in just a few moments I will be inside her. I'll feel all of her. And once I've had her, I fear I'll never want to leave. The desire to be inside her is running as high as it could ever be.

Paige shouts out, "Fuck me, Xander. Oh god, please just fuck me already!"

Nope. Scratch that. I was wrong.

I pull off my briefs and throw them to the floor. I rest the head of my cock against her clit and then lightly rub, teasing her. She squirms beneath me as she grips my arms tightly.

"Please," she says, breathlessly, her face completely flush. "I need you inside me."

Paige closes her eyes the moment I slip the head of my cock in, and she throws her head back as I go in just a little more. As she settles her legs around my waist, I shift my weight off her just enough that I can watch myself fuck her . I can feel my cock pulsate and swell against her walls; it makes me feel as if I may come any second. But I fight the urge and slide in ever so slowly. Her pussy is warm and inviting. My body is charged with anticipation and pleasure I'm not sure I've ever felt before.

Paige releases a little whimper that makes me want to thrust harder and faster, but I don't. I take my time running my throbbing cock in and out, but it's as if the slower I go, the hotter she gets. Her nipples are stiff and waiting eagerly for my mouth. I take them in, one at a time. I bite them lightly and then circle my tongue around them as I continue to tease her.

In... Out... In... Out... slowly, meticulously. Just enough to get her to squirm. But I'm only getting started. My dick settles into the perfection of her pussy and the building pressure fades just a little, the feeling of complete ecstasy still going strong. I pick up speed. The faster I go, the wetter she gets.

She grabs for handfuls of hair, but I hold each wrist to the mattress. She fights back as I continue fucking her... In. Out. In. Out... Picking up speed, I take both of her wrists into one of my hands and pin them above her head. My other hand grabs a fistful of her curly blonde hair, pulling just a little bit more with each thrust inside her.

"Oh God, Xander, don't stop. Don't fucking stop. I'm so close!"

The throbbing at the base of my dick is not something I can control anymore. Her intensifying moans will me to thrust harder and deeper. Her restrained hands ball up into tight little fists and she drives her hips up into me. The barrage of warm come sets off my own release—a release that makes my entire body shake and floods my brain with so many endorphins it feels as if I may float away at any moment.

I lower myself and pull Paige into my arms, and she rests her head on my chest. The only sounds in the room are our ragged breaths and the pulsing of our heartbeats. No words are spoken between us. None need to be said.

I kiss the top of her head as our breathing evens out. She snuggles deeper into my side, sighing peacefully. I lie awake long after she falls asleep, wondering what I did right in my wretched life to deserve someone like her.

It's dark. Mommy and Daddy are away. Sissy is crying from the crib again, but I can't reach her. I try my hardest. I want to try harder, but my tummy won't stop growling. I want to eat, but there's nothing in the kitchen.

Mommy comes home first and she's crying. She's always crying.

I don't think she sees me. She walks right past me. I hope she hears Sissy at least. Sissy is so sad.

Daddy comes home and he's angry. He's always angry. He's throwing things and they're breaking. Mommy is screaming and she's holding Sissy. Daddy breaks more things and it's loud. I cover my ears and close my eyes, just like in hide and seek, but they're still there when I open them.

Daddy has Mommy by the hair. He's shaking her and she's scared. Sissy is about to fall, but Mommy catches her and puts her on the table. Daddy is yelling so loud. I hate when he yells this loud.

Daddy hits Mommy over and over again. I don't think he'll ever stop. I grab my wiffle ball bat—the one Grandma gave me before she went to live with the angels—and I hit Daddy on the leg as hard as I can with it.

He turns around and I cry at the sight of him. I can't help it. He looks like a monster. I back away from him, but he comes closer. I'm against the wall and there's nowhere to go. Mommy's crying, but she isn't moving.

Daddy grabs my arm, and it hurts so bad I drop the bat. He pulls a knife off his belt. It's the one I play with when he leaves it out.

I shut my eyes and squeeze them tight. I want it all to be a dream.

But it isn't.

It feels like my arm is burning, like the whole thing is on fire. I scream until my voice goes away. There's blood everywhere.

I can't feel my fingers.

I wake up in a cold sweat, my heart pounding in my chest. Paige lifts her head from the pillow with a look of concern on her face.

"Are you okay, baby?" The way the light shines through the window and hits her face settles me. The glow is almost angelic. The way she looks in my white button-up, and *only* my white button-up… that's a whole other story.

"Good morning, gorgeous. Yeah, I'm okay." I smile and rub a hand against her cheek. "I'm not complaining about waking up to this face *one bit.*"

She leans over and kisses my chest, my neck, and finally my lips.

"I could say the same about you. Were you having a nightmare, hun?" She sits up and pulls my hand into her lap.

"I don't know. I never really remember my dreams or nightmares. Why, was I tossing and turning?"

"You were doing a little more than that."

"Yeah, I've heard I'm a pretty violent sleeper."

"You kept grabbing for your arm…" She sets her hand gently against it. "Where your scar is."

"Really?" I know, I dream it damn near every night, though I won't tell her that. She's better off not knowing.

"Yeah, really. Do you want to talk about it?"

"One day, baby, I swear. Okay?"

"Okay."

"Did my crazy sleep wake you?" I ask, looking over at the alarm clock.

"It did, but it's completely okay. I didn't mind watching you sleep."

I sit up, taking her face with my hand, and I give her a long, deep, passionate kiss. Then I pull away, flashing a coy smile.

"What?" she asks.

"Who's the creeper now?"

"Oh, shut up. I was well within the creeper parameters," she says, pushing me away.

"I don't know. Seems like you crossed a line. And for that, you should probably be punished."

"Oh, you think so, Mr. Evans? I'm thinking you're the one with the punishment in store. Don't make me get my horse whip and ball gag. Mistress Paige will be all over that shit." She snaps her fingers back and forth.

"That just sounds wrong. You know I like a submissive chick."

She puts up two fingers. "One, I'm not a chick. I'm a woman. Two, submissive in the bedroom, boss bitch everywhere else. Just don't get shit confused."

She dramatically brushes her shoulders off and cocks her head, and I can't help laughing. She is so adorably *not* gangsta.

"As long as the whole submissive in the bedroom thing sticks, baby, you can be whatever the hell you want out there." I point to the bedroom door.

She looks at me, still obviously in dominatrix mode, and then pushes me back down. I try and lift myself up, but she does it again.

"You stay." She points to the bed as she uses the other hand to rip the covers away. She motions to my briefs.

"Those. Off. Now."

"What are you doing?" I ask, not sure if she's just kidding around or if shit's really about to go down.

She lightly slaps my face.

"No talking. Just get naked," she demands, and I comply, tossing my briefs at her. She slaps my thigh, harder than she did my face.

"Don't move." She holds each arm down to my side.

"Yes, ma'am."

"That's better."

She brings her mouth down to my thigh and bites gently and then she works her way up, sliding her tongue against my constricting abs. Her hands continue to hold my wrists to the bed and I fight against them, but each time she pins me right back down. She looks up at me, a sultry look in her eyes. "*Don't. Move*," she repeats.

She teases me for what seems like a century, my muscles flexing and releasing with each pleasing touch. She runs her tongue from my chest down slowly to where I yearn for it to go, which has me begging and writhing beneath her. I want her mouth around my cock more than anything at this point and she's doing her best to use it against me…to toy with me. I need to be in her, a part of her, one with her.

She does finally take me into her mouth, gliding it in and out, her hot tongue sending jolts of pleasure throughout my body. My body is buzzing as she takes me closer and closer to complete satisfaction. A rush of adrenaline strikes. Blood surges to my head.

It's not even the pleasure of it all that gets me off. It's the look in her eyes. It's how much getting lost in those eyes captures me. It's a feeling my ice cold heart has never felt before.

It's a new beat.

New life.

It's the realest thing I've known in my twenty-seven years, and as I throw my head back in undeniable ecstasy, I can't help but know—right in this moment—that I love this girl.

CHAPTER
TWENTY

Paige

"Mayday"—Cam

THE NIGHT WAS PERFECT. I'M NOT JUST SAYING THAT.

I'm not just some middle school girl with a crush. The things he makes me feel and think, the way he touches me at just the right time and in just the right way.

It's everything.

Going back to normal work life is going to be tough. The monotonous morning routine has me in a zombie-like state as I dress with the usual early Monday morning sluggishness. Rowdy's barking outside lets me know Xander is up now, and I can't help but wonder if he had as hard of a time as I did sleeping alone.

He comes through the back door, Rowdy at his feet, as I enter the kitchen. He smiles and then glances in the direction of the stairs. I turn and look too, listening closely. My parents are up and moving, but not yet heading for the stairs.

When I turn back around, I feel his lips meet mine. He swoops me into his arms and holds me chest to chest. Heart to heart. He puts the other hand against the small of my back, and he kisses me passionately. Then he let's go. Another gorgeous smile and he's on his way to pouring both our morning coffees.

"Good morning, gorgeous," he says from over his shoulder.

"Good morning, handsome." I smile, taking him in as he pours coffee and then my usual Baileys.

He hands me the mug and then pours a cup of his own—without Bailey's of course. "Plans tonight?" he asks, smiling like he knows something I don't.

"No, sir."

"So you're mine then? Date night?"

"You better believe it." He embraces me once more and then takes a seat at the table. Just as he does, my brother's yelling comes tearing down the stairs. I can hear my mother attempting to calm him.

"Jesus, I can't be a part of this right now. I'm gonna head into work early." I lean down to him and kiss him on his cheek. "See you tonight, babe?"

He kisses me once more. "See you tonight."

———

Flustered, and cursing my own stupidity under my breath, I walk down the small dirt road that leads to my driveway. My car is a mile back with a flat and no spare. My phone is dead in my pocket, just as it has been since I got off work at seven.

Mom's staying late and I had no desire to do the same—not any later than I already had, at least. I didn't want to miss my date with Xander. As I walk the long stretch of road to my driveway, I'm hoping like hell Mom doesn't stay as late as she planned.

I haven't been walking *that* long, though the sun has begun its descent into the horizon, but it sure feels like I have. I had to ditch the heels about a mile back, but the gravel against my bare feet isn't much better.

Just as twilight hits, and with home just a few hundred yards away, headlights shine from behind me. At first, I think it must be Mom. This road is often empty unless it's someone going to and from our house. I stop and turn, waiting to see what kind of vehicle it is, peering into the headlights and fighting its harsh glare. I can't make anything out and I'm eventually forced to cover my face to rest my eyes.

I hear the vehicle slow and then stop just in front of me. I drop my arm but still can't make it out. Though, I can see it enough to know it *isn't* Mom.

The door swings open.

Maybe it's Xander.

But it's not.

I see his face just before he snatches me into his arms. I fight, but Cody is too strong for me to get away. I try to bite him, and he punches me twice in the face—hard. I lose awareness. Just darkness and the blood red glow of the brake lights.

My body feels like it's floating, and my limbs are hanging weightlessly, outside of my control. My back meets hard metal with a thud. I feel a jolt of pain race up my spine, but I can't move. I can't respond. My head spins. I fight for my eyes to open, but they don't.

I try again with everything I have, and I see Cody on top of me, an angry, drunken look in his eyes. I suddenly realize my pants are around my ankles. He tears at my panties just as he realizes I'm looking straight at him.

He hits me two more times.

My eyes close. Stars circle the darkness. His angry grunts just distant and muffled.

I feel a surge of energy, a powerful burst of adrenaline that takes over my body. I force my eyes open. His head is buried in my stomach, his tongue looping in circles around my belly button as he makes his way to where he shouldn't go.

The feeling returns to my arms. They feel extremely heavy, but I'm at least able grab each of his ears and I pull as hard as I fucking can. I pull them so hard I feel they may tear from his head at any moment. Cody rears back with a desperate scream, holding his hands to his head. He stands, wobbling as he tries to gain balance. I pull a naked leg back and I thrust my right heel into his groin as hard as I can.

His eyes roll as he immediately clutches his balls. He drops to both knees and howls in pain. I don't waste another second watching. I leap off the truck, disregarding my pants and flats, and I take off running for home as fast as I can.

Dad and Xander are in the family room when I rush through the door. Xander is dressed in a button-down and jeans, presumably ready for our date, while Dad is still in his work clothes, dirty as hell.

They scan me from head to toe, and I see the moment they realize I'm without pants and my face is beaten to shit because their looks of concern transform to ones of horror. Dad immediately runs over, cradling me in his arms, and it's right at the moment he touches me that I completely break down. All of the strength I mustered to escape Cody is gone. I am a child again weeping in my father's arms.

He grabs a blanket from the couch and wraps it around me, kissing the top of my head. "Baby, what happened?" Dad asks, setting a hand on my shoulder. Through tear-clouded vision, I see Xander starting to put two and two together. His face is a combination of anger and confusion.

"Paige, please, what happened?" Dad repeats.

"Cody…" It's all I can muster. A thick lump sits at the base of my throat. The tears stream.

"What did he do to you? … Goddamn it, what did he do?" Dad's voice shakes. His jaw is trembling.

Dad helps me to the couch before going to my room for pants. Xander sits next to me and pulls me in close. I rest my head on his shoulder and his lips meet my forehead. I want to stay right here in his safe arms forever.

"I'm so fucking sorry, Paige," Xander whispers.

"It's not your fault. There's nothing you could've done."

"I should have gone looking for you. I should've known." He shakes his head.

Dad comes back with the pants, hands them over and then sits on the other side of me. Xander removes his arm.

"Paige, I need to call the sheriff. You have to tell me what happened." Just as he says this, the front door opens and Mom walks in. She catches sight of me and puts both hands to her mouth, slowly shaking her head from side to side.

"I got a flat and my damn phone was dead. It was just down the road…" My voice trails off as I replay what just happened in my head. Mom still stands by the front door in shock, the door wide open.

"I walked for a little bit and then a vehicle came up behind me. I thought it might be Mom… but it wasn't."

"What did he do?" Mom asks, finally sitting on the love-seat beside us. She's crying, but I can tell she's doing her best not to break down completely.

"He didn't rape me. But he tried. He hit me in the face… so hard. So many times. My head hurts so bad." The act of talking even makes my head pound.

"Honey, call the sheriff." Dad hands his phone to my mother and she dials quickly.

"I'm going to kill him," Xander announces, standing to his feet. "I'm going to fucking kill him."

"Xander, we have to let the sheriff handle this. This is serious," Dad says calmly.

"Damn it, Jack, what's he going to get? A few years in some white collar prison. And that's if some shady-ass lawyer doesn't get him off. Fuck that. That's not enough."

"Xander, that's not how this is gonna go down." Dad stands and takes a few steps toward Xander. "You think I don't want to kill him too? I'd like to rip the motherfucker's head off, but we can't. We have to get him locked up. That's the priority here."

Xander looks at him, disappointment in his eyes, and says, "I'm so sorry, Jack. I really am." He bends down and kisses me on the forehead. "I'm sorry, Paige."

With that, he heads for the door.

"Xander! Xander, damn it, come back here!" Dad yells, but it's too late. Xander's already out the door and in his truck. We're left with the sound of his spinning tires against the gravel drive.

Xander's been gone for at least two hours now. The sheriff's deputy came and took my statement, and he's already on his way over to Cody's. The deputy was not told anything about Xander, and I worry about what he's doing—or what he's already done. I just hope he doesn't get in trouble.

Mom, Dad and I sit at the dining room table waiting for Xander when Caleb comes in. He nearly bypasses us to go upstairs, but instead turns and comes back.

"What happened to your face?" he asks with a look of disgust.

"Excuse me?" I say, barely able to contain my annoyance.

"Caleb, just go to your room. This doesn't involve you," Mom says, rubbing my shoulder in an effort to calm me.

"Well, it wasn't her business to tell you about my PlayStation, and she did that. So fuck her."

Dad immediately stands. I've never seen him so angry. "Caleb, tonight is *not* the night to start with your shit," he barks.

"*My* shit? My shit?! You all don't give two shits about me. Poor little Miss Paige has a run-in with a fist, and you're all over her like she's fucking dying. I've been getting beat up my whole fucking life. Where the hell have you been?" With each word spoken, Caleb's anger intensifies. "You're not even my real fucking family. I don't have any family."

"Honey, you never told us about anything like that. We care just as much about what happens to you as we do Paige. We just have to know," Mom says, trying to remain calm.

"You never care to listen. None of you do. None of you fucking care about me. About what I've been through."

"Of course we do," Mom responds.

"Fuck all of you. When I'm eighteen, I'm fucking gone. I'm done with this place!" Caleb tries to turn and leave, but my dad rocketing out of his seat draws his attention.

"Then leave! If you think you've got it so fucking bad here, fucking leave. We've given you everything, son. And if you think somehow we aren't giving you enough, by all means, just go. But I refuse to let you treat your sister or anyone else in this family like that. I refuse to let you talk to us like that. You have so much more than many others do. You need to grow the fuck up, Caleb."

Caleb is in complete shock. He doesn't say a word, but just stands in shocked silence. I'm left speechless as well. As much as I had to say to Caleb before Dad spoke, it's all evaporated now. I'm thankful for my father defending me, but I'm also sad. As much as I hate Caleb right now, I just wish we could connect sometimes like normal siblings do. I wish I understood what he's been through.

He turns and heads for the stairs, and I want to cry at the look of regret on Dad's face.

———

Xander returns some time later without a word. Though I pester him for information, he tells me nothing. I don't push it. I'll get it out of him eventually, though his swollen knuckles tell me enough. He came back right about the time Caleb packed a few bags and took off. Mom raced out after him, but he was in his friend's car and gone before she could try to make him stay.

CHAPTER
TWENTY-ONE

Xander

"Wolves"—Phosphorescent

IT'S BEEN ONLY A DAY SINCE PAIGE AND JACK HEADED UP TO Truman Lake. And God, I miss her already.

It's not the same around here without her. After her run-in with that piece of shit Cody and hearing what good ol' Caleb had to say to her that night, it's not surprising Jack thought it best to take her away for a bit. She fought against it, but Jack insisted. I selfishly wish she had stayed, as a week away from her is not my idea of a good time.

Late-night thinking has me wide awake and dying for some alcohol. Anything to give my restless mind a break. The weed is doing the job at the moment, but I still toss and turn relentlessly. Not that that's anything new these days. I could be dead tired after a long day's work, eyelids fighting to close, and I'll still lay my head on the pillow only to have sleep evade me.

I think too much. That's the problem.

The bright red numbers reading 12:01 on the alarm clock mock me from the nightstand. I think about Paige and the feelings that have undeniably taken up residence in my heart, forcing me to reevaluate everything I thought I knew.

My life, with all its confusion and uncertainty, has suddenly become a bit clearer. I've always wanted love, but there has never been a woman before who has made me feel it—who has made me question my wandering ways. No woman has ever made me want to settle… until her. It makes restless nights like these that much more unbearable.

Letting people in is not my thing. It took a lot to become close to my military buddies, to allow them into my headspace, to accept that I could actually get close to another person. This is different, though. This involves matters of the heart. Am I truly even able to love? Had you asked me that question a month ago, I would have firmly told you no. But now… now everything is a mess. So much about love makes no sense to me, and tonight, I guess, is my night to try and figure it all out.

God, I wish I could just sleep.

The muffled sound of glass shattering rings from the main house. A scream follows—a horrible, ugly scream that tears from the house in waves and sends shivers down my spine.

Teresa.

I jolt from my bed, waiting a moment to make sure I wasn't just hearing things. I'm high, so it's possible my brain was playing tricks on me. I hear nothing else.

I slip on my house shoes anyway, grab a bat from beneath my bed and head out into the still night air, cautiously making my way to the back door. I try to convince myself it couldn't have been a scream; it must have been my imagination. But I know what I heard…as much as I wish I didn't.

I open the door as quietly as I can. My entire body tingles just below the surface. I fight to control my breathing, creeping ever so slowly through the laundry room and into the kitchen. That's when I feel the crunch of broken glass beneath my shoes. That's when I spot something in the middle of the kitchen floor.

It's Teresa. I can tell by the nightgown.

I feel for the light switch and flip it on. What I see nearly knocks me off my feet. Teresa is facedown in a pool of blood that's quickly spreading out around her. The room is filled with the faint smell of copper. A butcher's knife stained crimson lies just beside her body and puncture holes dot her nightgown.

I drop to my knees, immediately pressing two fingers to her throat. The feel of the blood against my skin turns my stomach upside down. There's a pulse, but it's faint and fleeting. I panic, fighting a mess of emotions that make it hard to process a single thought. I search the house, the bat in one hand and my phone in the other, and I dial 911.

CHAPTER
TWENTY-TWO

Xander

Present

"If You Only Knew"—Shinedown

"**X**ANDER, YOU STILL WITH ME?" WARDEN NARANJO ASKS, though his words seem distant.

"Yeah, yeah, sorry."

"Did you hear what I said?"

"No, sorry," I repeat, slouched in the chair across from him in his office. I can't help my thoughts continuously returning to that night.

It haunts me—it *consumes* me.

"I said, we really need your assistance with this."

"With what?"

"Xander, have you even heard a word I said? The guy's throat was slit from ear to ear. That was after he had been fucked to the point of his colon rupturing. Child molester or not, we can't let this kind of shit go down in here. And I think you know more than what you're telling." He folds his arms and leans back in his chair.

"Warden, I told you, I'm just trying to fucking survive. I'm trying to make it through this shit the only way I know how. That means keeping my head down and not getting involved. I don't know any more than you all do." I'm not completely lying. I really do try my best to keep what goes on in this place out of my headspace, but I'm not blind. The guy had it coming for a long time, and there's one group of individuals who paid him extra special attention when he arrived.

He was a shitty cellmate anyway.

"We know who it was, Xander. You know who it was, too. All we need is a statement. We know you saw something."

"I wasn't in the cell, Warden. I saw nothing." I cross my arms now.

He drops his head, shaking it slowly back and forth. "That's some bullshit if I ever heard it."

I say nothing, and a look of acceptance settles on his face.

"Fine, Xander. If that's how you're gonna play it, that's how we'll play it. I've been easy on you. I've looked past a lot not-so-kosher things because I know you're one of the few good ones in here. One of the ones not stirring up shit. But you think that dip you're using is within regs? You think if I flipped your bunk I wouldn't find contraband? Drugs? We can make it quite a bit harder on you from now on if that's how you want it."

"Is that a threat, Warden?" I try my best to keep a look of disdain off my face, but with no luck.

"I don't make threats. But if you aren't gonna work with

me, I'm not gonna work with you."

"We done here then?"

He says nothing for a few moments, observing me for any sign that I'm going to give in. Whatever he thinks he's going to get out of me… he's wrong. No matter how much I like the guy, I'm no snitch.

He sighs, interlocking his fingers atop his desk.

"Just about. But don't for a second think this is over. We'll be coming back to this."

"Okay, so what else?" He's not very happy with my tone, but at this point, I couldn't care less.

He pulls an envelope from his top desk drawer. "There's a program, in this prison and most others, where family members of the victims have an opportunity to communicate with the perpetrator."

My mind races with his last words. *Did he just say what I think he did?*

"Now, we need your approval before any communication happens, and we will be analyzing everything that comes in and goes out. It's for the protection of the victim's family. Do you understand?"

I can only nod my head. I'm speechless.

"And do you approve?" Another nod.

He hands me the letter, but before I can snatch it away, he pulls it back from me.

"Xander, you need to think about what I've said here today. This kind of shit will not go down in my prison. And people who can help but won't are only going to get away with it for so long."

"I've got nothing to say, Warden." I eyeball the letter turned upside down, and anxiously wonder who it could be from. Jack, Caleb... *Paige*?

"For now, you don't. I have a feeling that'll all change real quick." He hands me the letter, and I take it from him without hesitation.

I hold it in my hands for a moment, scared to see who it's from—and even more scared about what it might say. I turn it over and read the words, but can't for the life of me believe what I'm seeing.

Paige Watson

PO Box 10461

Truman Valley, MO 36833

The walk back to my cell couldn't possibly feel longer. I hold the letter tightly in my hands as if it could be stripped away at any moment. It feels like I'll wake up in a cold sweat to find that none of this is real. But it is. And the exhilaration I feel runs like electricity throughout my body.

I get back to my cell to see who I presume is my new cellmate lying on the bottom bunk. I give him a nod and climb to the top, hoping desperately that he'll leave me to my letter. But he doesn't.

His head pops around the side of my bunk. He has disheveled copper hair and a thick, matching beard.

"Not much of a talker, eh?" He's got a slight country twang, one like I used to hear in Georgia. Not enough to make one truly southern, but enough to let you know they come from below the Mason-Dixon.

"Nah."

"Shit, they put you with the wrong guy, I guess. I don't fucking stop." He flashes a toothy grin, and that's when I notice finely etched scars on his face. There's some on either side of his nose, others creeping out from the top of his beard.

"Brighton Young's the name. But most call me Twitch."

"Why Twitch?" *Why do I care?*

"On account of my ADHD, I guess. I'm always moving. Always fidgeting." I don't say anything. I could tell him to fuck off, but that might make for shittier time served if I'm stuck with this guy for awhile.

He rests both hands on my bunk and I see tattoos line his right arm—an American flag, a UT Longhorn, a Mizzou Tiger and a can of Copenhagen.

"So, you got a name?" he asks.

"Xander."

"Well, Xander, what's a guy gotta do to get a pinch of dip around here?" His eyes wander over to my tin of chewing tobacco on the window sill. "But don't get me twisted, I ain't sucking no dick." He laughs loudly.

"You can grab one. If a man is dip crazy enough to get a tin tattooed on his arm, I guess I can help out." He takes no offense, though it was definitely a jab. After he grabs a pinch and puts it in his bottom lip, he then returns both arms to my bunk.

"I love me some fucking dip, but not enough to have it inked on my body, friend. This sleeve is for my guys."

"Your guys?"

He points to the tin. "Corporal Ryan Jackson, KIA January 14th, 2007." Then to the Longhorn. "Specialist Chad McGinnis, KIA March 18th, 2007." And finally to the Mizzou Tiger. "Staff

Sergeant Jimmy Reardon, KIA June 1st, 2007."

"Fuck, I'm sorry, man. What branch?" I reluctantly slip the envelope into my pocket and sit up, leaning back against the wall.

"Army. Special Forces. Nine years of service, three deployments. And don't worry about it. Ain't the first time people have questioned my tats. Sure as fuck ain't gonna be the last."

"What the hell is a guy like you doing in a place like this?"

"Well, that's quite the story." He removes his arms from my bunk and takes a seat on top of the stainless steel desk bolted to the floor. He puts his feet up on the matching stool. Though I'd give anything to read the letter right now, I'd be lying if I said I wasn't intrigued.

"Well, I've got a life sentence, so start talking" I say, smiling.

"I've only got ten years, but I don't think it'll take quite that long." He laughs. "I was wounded in my last deployment. Medically separated from the Army and moved back home to Arkansas. Fucking hated it. Hated all the millennial pieces of shit making fucking excuses for everything. Hated the mundane nine-to-five life I found myself living. Hated the fucking boredom of being normal." As I watch his hands go from clasped together to crossed to his knees and back, I can't help but think 'Twitch' is a fitting name for him.

"Found myself enjoying a life outside the law. Started simple… forging checks, making counterfeits, that kind of thing. Not outta greed or anything like that, just for the thrill of it all. Though the thrill died off quickly. There ain't no adrenaline rush that comes with forging fucking checks."

"Nothing like serving in combat, I'm guessing."

"Precisely. So what's an old Army vet to do? Next best thing… I start robbing armored carriers. A few banks here and there. I fucking got off on that shit. I used all the shit the Army taught me to fuck the system. And I got pretty damn good at it."

"So how did you find yourself in here?"

"I wasn't as good as I thought I was, I guess." He smirks, his hands finally settling behind his head.

"Picked the wrong accomplice, and the fucker turned me in to save his own ass. That was a couple years ago though. I've escaped from two other prisons since then."

"Damn, dude, that's impressive."

He shrugs. "It's what I do."

"So you said you were wounded. What happened? If you don't mind me asking…"

"Nah, you're good, man. One thing you learn as a wounded veteran… you better get used to telling your story." With one quick motion, he pops a row of dentures from his mouth and a prosthetic eye from his right socket. He smiles, showing the empty space in his mouth nearly three inches wide. I try my best to keep the look of shock from my face, though my efforts are futile.

"Crazy, right?"

"Dude, I had no idea. I mean, I saw the scars, but I didn't expect *that*."

"No one usually does, though a lot of the time I do have some Forest Whitaker eye going on."

He laughs and I can't help but laugh too, though I feel like shit for it.

"I got hit by an IED in Baghdad. I was the gunner in my Humvee. Shrapnel came up through the roof of my mouth, shattered my jaw, blew out my teeth and lodged in my eye."

"Holy shit. You lucky fuck!"

"Yeah, it was fucking crazy. I was in a coma for a month. Didn't even know what happened until I woke up with a big-ass metal contraption holding my jaw in place and bandages covering my right eye."

My mouth is gaping. I'm blown away at how nonchalant he is about this. Though the letter is about the only thing I can think about, I'm both impressed and saddened by this guy's situation. He seems to not have a care in the world as he slips his dentures and prosthetic back in.

"Anyways, I noticed you had a letter with ya when you came in. I know what that means in a place like this. Sorry about keeping you. I'll leave you to it."

"No issues at all. I'm honored to be sharing a cell with you. I've made quite a few military friends over the years and respect the hell out of what you all do."

"Appreciate it, my man." He grabs an extremely thick book from the desk and holds it up. *11/22/63* by Stephen King. "Now I've gotta get back to this girthy bitch."

He climbs back on his bunk, and for a moment, I almost forget about the letter entirely. I'm still awestruck by this man's story. It takes a few moments to regain composure, but when I do, I pull the envelope from my pocket and tear it open. For the first time in a long time, I have a feeling of hope and optimism. She reached out, and no matter what this letter says, it means she hasn't forgotten me. It means that maybe—just maybe—I have the chance of convincing her of the truth.

Xander

It's taken me a year to write this. Three years to build up the courage. As I sit here and write, my hands are shaking. I'm filled with so much anger. So much hatred toward you. Do you realize what you've done to my family? How the fuck could you do this to me? I thought I knew you. I thought you cared about me. I thought you cared about my family. You surely pulled the wool over all of our eyes. I'm just so confused and so incredibly heartbroken. I miss my mother every single day. I ache to talk to her again. To hug her again. But you stole that from me. And why? Why my family? Why my mother?

You are a fucking monster. I will never forgive you for what you've done, but I at least deserve a reason why. You owe me that much. My mother cared for you... she really did. We talked often about the things you've been through in your life. She wished so much that she could've taken your pain away. Little did she know. Little did any of us know.

How could you take the life of someone else? How could you rip my family apart like this? Our winery is gone. Watson Metalworks is gone. The land and home we had for two generations... gone. Seized by the bank after repeated non-payments. My dad has completely given up on life.

So what, your life was shit so you decided

to make someone else's life shit too? How could you? God, I just want to fucking kill you. I think about it sometimes. You deserve to rot in that place. And I hope you do. I hope you spend every single day remembering what you did.

Just tell me why. Please, just tell me why.

Paige

The letter falls to my mattress and I feel the tears roll down my cheeks. If I could only make her see the truth.

I pull a notepad and pencil out and do my very best.

CHAPTER
TWENTY-THREE

Paige

"Future Starts Slow"—The Kills

IT'S BEEN TWO WEEKS SINCE I SENT THE LETTER, AND I'VE regretted it since day one. How can I expect to get anything out of a cold-blooded killer? For all I know, everything this man ever told me has been a lie. He's a monster, and that's all there is to it.

I'm just finishing my eight-hour shift at Whittaker's. After what happened, I can't run numbers anymore. I can't sit in front of a computer and do accounting bullshit when all I ever think about is her. With the phone call from the sheriff playing over and over in my head, how would I concentrate?

I pull up to our apartment complex, one that nearly every dollar of my paycheck goes to. Dad hasn't worked since the loss of my mother. If it weren't for him—and Brandi—I would've offed myself a long time ago. I'd be lying if I said I don't think about it often. I just don't think my father could stand losing anyone else. My death would almost certainly result in his own. As it is, he's drinking himself to death anyway. He sleeps in until late in the day and wakes up just to get drunk and pass out again. Every single fucking day.

I don't blame him. The only way I can go in to work and put on my fake smile is because of all the shots I take while I'm there. I've become an alcoholic myself, but at least I'm a functioning one. When I'm sober, all I feel is pain. The liquor quells my ability to feel—at least for a little bit—though most nights I cry myself to sleep anyway. I just don't want to exist anymore.

I don't want to think about that day. I don't want to think about being at her funeral, breaking down in front of her closed coffin, having to be dragged out of that place. This pain is deep and visceral. It's everlasting.

I walk into the apartment to find my dad passed out on the couch as usual. An empty fifth of Jack and a plethora of empty beer cans litter the coffee table. Dirty dishes are stacked two feet high in the sink. The apartment has a filthy musk that hangs in the air from lack of cleaning. I can't bring myself to do much when I'm home. As for my dad, he rarely leaves the couch for anything other than pissing and grabbing more beer. He rarely eats.

Caleb moved back soon after Mom's death, but he's never home other than to sleep and eat. He doesn't work and he dropped out of school a year ago without much resistance from Dad, so I'm not sure what the hell he does. I've seen him deteriorate quickly, with constant bags under his eyes and a sadness he carries with him always. He has a thousand-yard stare that most often is attributed to drug addiction. I've had a sneaky suspicion that he's gotten into the harder stuff, but I haven't even spoken to him much in long time.

As I grab a beer from the fridge, I remember the letter and wonder if perhaps the fucker has decided to write back. I haven't really checked the mail in quite some time, and now seems as good a time as any.

I check the mail slot beside our front door and find a mess of envelopes and coupons. I pull them all out, set them on the counter and rifle through them. Most are overdue bills, which I toss into a pile of mail I'll never open. It's far easier to ignore them than to face the facts. We're sinking, and we're sinking fast.

I've gone through most of the envelopes, and there's no sign of anything from Xander. Would I even want to ingest his bullshit? I'm about to toss the remaining envelopes to the side and head to my room when I see it. Written in pencil, scribbled on the front of a plain white envelope is Xander's name.

For a moment, I think about crumpling it up and throwing it away. But I can't. I grab a bottle of vodka from the freezer and carry it, along with the letter, to my room.

After a few nerve-settling shots, I open the envelope and pull the letter out. I take a deep breath, another shot, and I unfold it. *Here goes nothing.*

> *Dear Paige,*
>
> *What can I say that would convince you of anything other than what you already believe? I'm no killer, Paige. And I loved your family. You have to know that. I would never want to hurt any of you. You don't know how difficult this all*

has been on me too; how difficult it still is. They found shit in the guesthouse—shit I didn't put there. They found weed in my system. They told me I had no chance of convincing a jury I was innocent. I had no idea what to do. They were going to send me to my death, and right about now, I'm wishing they would have. I thought I was sparing you the pain of going through a trial—of seeing what I saw that night.

Paige, I can't erase my memories of finding your mother that way. I couldn't put you through that. I couldn't put your family through that. I thought accepting the plea deal was my only option. It's the only thing that made sense at the time. The sheriff, the DA… they had it out for me. They were out for blood. What was I supposed to do?

I understand this probably sounds like a load of shit to you, but it's the truth. I've spent the past three years running thinking about it constantly, and I still can't make sense of it. I thought I did what I had to do. I thought I was doing what was right. I knew what the loss of your mother would do to you, and I didn't want to put you through even more. I'd give anything to bring Teresa back. I'd give my life for hers in a heartbeat.

You don't have to believe me, Paige. I probably wouldn't believe me either. But just know that I truly loved you, I loved your family, and I would've never done anything to hurt any of you. I was set up, plain and simple. I don't know who and I don't know how, but I was. I'm a slave to these thoughts, and they own every second of my life. Believe me.

Everything I ever told you was the truth. Everything I ever felt for you was real. I don't ask you to take my word, I just ask you to truly think about it. I hope you can at least open yourself up to the possibility of someone setting me up. I had a lot of enemies, Paige. You know that.

I feel I've said too much already. I don't want to cause you any more pain than you've already experienced. I just need you to know, on God, on my life, on my undying love for you, I DID NOT kill your mother. I pray one day you can see that. I pray one day you're able to heal from your wounds, though I know these are wounds that will never truly heal. I pray I'll hear from you again, even if it is just to wish more hell upon me. I'll take it. I'll take it all, because hearing from you, no matter the context, is the best thing I've felt in years.

If you could see my eyes and hear me out, I know things could be different. But since I can't, I wish you the best, Paige. And if I never hear from you again, I'll understand. This is my life now, and though I am here for a crime I didn't commit, it somehow feels like I'm right where

I belong. It's where I've always belonged. I'm a nobody, and I deserve to rot as nobodies do.

Xander

Teardrops coat the letter as memories of my mother flood my brain. I ball the paper up and toss it to the floor, then tip the bottle of vodka back and drink as much as my taste buds will allow. The drunker I get, the more I sob. I look to the drawer where my 9 mil is stowed away, and I contemplate pulling it out and shoving the barrel into my mouth. I think of pulling the trigger gently, letting the memories disappear into a splatter of brain matter on the back wall.

I don't though. I just drink until I can't feel a thing. And then I fall fast asleep.

I wake up with a skull-splitting headache. It takes a moment for me to gather my thoughts… to remember the events from last night. When I do, I quickly snatch up the crumpled ball of paper and unfold it, doing my best to flatten out the wrinkles. I read the letter over and over again.

Then I cry harder than I have in a long time, so unsure of what to think. The truth is, beyond the loss of my mother and the complete collapse of my family, one of the hardest parts to swallow about this whole ordeal has been believing Xander could kill my mother. What I felt for him was one of the realest things I've ever known. Everything about him seemed genuine. Every word seemed so honest. He opened himself up to me,

and I could feel his love for me. People that kill aren't like him—
at least I never thought they could be.

But why give up his life to spare me the pain? Why not
at least try and convince a jury of his innocence? My head is
filled with so many questions—questions I feel may never be
answered. But what if I were to go see him? What if I gave him
a chance to explain himself… to get it straight from the horse's
mouth? Would it even do any good? If he were lying to me before, cloaking his evil with sweet words and actions, why could
he not do the same now? I would've never even thought about
it before, but having read his letter, a small part of me wants to
see him. Maybe even *needs* to.

I ready my computer to respond, though it seems about
the hardest thing I can imagine right now. I sit and stare at the
flashing cursor, the words stuck somewhere deep in my gut.
Uncertain what to say and how to say it, I close the laptop and
make my way to the fridge for my first beer of the day.

I pop the top and take a long swig while opening the door
and grabbing the *Truman Valley Times* from my doorstep. The
headline catches my attention right away.

Another murder rocks Truman Valley.

Immediately, I recall Xander's words. *I would've never done
anything to hurt any of you. I was set up, plain and simple.*

I flip the paper open and scan it and see a picture, all too
familiar, on the front page: a body wrapped in a body bag being
removed from a trailer. I begin reading, the paper shaking in
my hands.

*At 9:08 p.m. on Tuesday night, the body of Mandy Little
was found by a relative. She'd been stabbed twenty-one times and
decapitated. Her head was missing from the crime scene. This*

makes the third murder in Truman Valley over the last three years. Investigators are puzzled as the crime scene was free of any fingerprints, and there was no noticeable evidence.

"We are doing everything in our power to catch this killer. I've seen nothing like this in my eighteen years as Sheriff of this town, and I ache for the victims' families. We will catch this madman as swiftly as possible. Our investigation is ongoing, and at this time, we have no leads," the Sheriff stated at a press conference last night.

We've heard similar responses from the Sheriff's department over the last couple of years, and the citizens of Truman Valley are becoming understandably restless. Many local businesses are reporting a sharp decline in revenue as citizens spend more and more time in their houses.

The sheriff stated they are looking into possible connections between the three murders. All victims were stabbed and their bodies mutilated.

The last line makes my stomach turn in tight circles. I've been following these latest murders, and each one reminds of what my mother must have gone through that night. The possibility of a connection between these murders and hers sends a chill down my spine. Then the tears start again. Crying is all I seem to do these days. Then, once again, Xander's words replay in my head…. *I was set up, plain and simple.*

I toss the paper aside and head back to my desk, disregarding the computer this time and pulling out a pad of paper and pen instead.

CHAPTER
TWENTY-FOUR

Xander

"Fire Away"—Chris Stapleton

"WAIT A SECOND. YOU'RE TELLING ME THE DUDE drained from his asshole… continuously?"

Twitch looks up from his steaming bowl of ramen and shakes his head.

"Not all the time. But on foot patrol, in one hundred and twenty-degree heat, yeah, he did it continuously."

For two weeks now, Twitch has been my cellmate, and I'm still surprised by the shit that comes out of his mouth. Most of it is both disgusting and surreal. He served in Afghanistan and Iraq. He's seen best friends take their last breaths beside him.

"So what the fuck did he do? Just let it run in his pants?"

"No, man…" He laughs. "Who the fuck is just gonna let shit drain in their pants on a combat patrol?"

"Well, fuck if I know! I've never heard of rectal discharge

before. So what the fuck did he do?"

"He stuffed paper towels in his ass crack. Kept a roll in his pack, and every half mile or so, he'd have to pull the shitty paper towels from his ass, throw them to the ground, and stuff more in. All while he's still walking."

My uncontrollable laughter, the kind that knots the stomach and makes it hard to breathe, is broken up only by CO Hansen arriving at our door. He holds up a letter and immediately my mind is taken away from Twitch's story and to the possibility of the letter being from Paige. The only other person who has ever written me is Irish, and I take so long to respond and I'm so short with him, I think he's finally given up. I haven't heard from him in quite some time.

It has to be Paige.

"Xander, ya got mail." He tosses it to me and I catch it mid-air.

"Thanks."

I flip it around, read her name, and my heart lodges in my throat.

"Something good?" Twitch asks, still chewing the last of his Ramen.

"Something great," I say, tearing the envelope open and unfolding the letter.

> *Xander,*
>
> *I've thought a lot about this. I've written and rewritten this letter many times. I still don't fully understand why you would just confess. I would never confess to a murder I didn't commit. But then again, I think of the alternative—the*

possibility of getting the death penalty—and it confuses me all over again. I get why you would confess, but then I don't. It's hard for me to fathom.

I balled your letter up and threw it away when I first read it. I want to hate you. It feels good to hate you. It keeps me focused. I've thought of you dying many times. And I've thought about doing it myself. But this morning I put two and two together.

There have been three more murders here. All three deaths are very similar. And while I want to continue hating you, and I don't understand clearly why you confessed... I think there's reasonable doubt. And as much as I want to feed this hate, the possibility that it could be someone else who killed her completely overwhelms me. I couldn't live without knowing. I need to know.

What if I were to meet with you? I want to talk to you about all of this and see your face when you tell me. I want to read your body language. That's where I'll start. Just let me know.

Paige

For the first time in three years, I feel some semblance of hope. Three miserable years here, and for the first time I'm feeling something other than pain. If I could talk to Paige, she'd hear the honesty in my words. She'd understand.

"Twitch, throw me that pad and pencil, will ya?"

He tosses them and I write just about as fast as I ever have.

CHAPTER
TWENTY-FIVE

Paige

"Call To War"—The Lone Bellow

PULLING INTO THE PRISON PARKING LOT, MY HEART POUNDS in my chest. I've never been so nervous in my life. I downed two shots before I got here, and I throw back one more for good measure before exiting the vehicle.

The process of getting inside is unlike anything I ever expected. I've seen it on TV shows, but they never show all the necessary procedures. It really is a pain in the ass.

I take a seat in the little nook, one of two dozen on either end of the room. The thick plastic barriers separating old-style telephones is dirty and opaque. I tap my fingers feverishly against the weathered metal booth. My mouth is dry, my tongue is numb, and there's a lump in my throat that feels almost suffocating. I don't know if I'll even be able to get a word out.

When Xander rounds the corner, I gasp softly at the sight

of him. Not because of how he looks—he still looks damn good… and he's bigger—but because it feels familiar yet incredibly foreign to lay eyes on him again after so long.

The moment the officer ushers him to a seat and heads back toward the door, a few tears roll down his cheeks. He looks quickly at the metal dividers to his left and right as he wipes the tears away. Then he lifts the phone and pulls it to his ear. I do the same. Neither of us says a word. Another single tear rolls down his cheek and he leaves this one be.

"Hi," he says weakly.

"Hi."

"Did you have a hard time getting in?"

"It was okay," I lie.

"Thanks for coming to see me."

"It was hard." My eyes have yet to meet his directly.

"I can only imagine."

"I want to know what happened that night," I blurt out.

His mouth gapes for a moment before he collects himself. He clears his throat.

"I heard her scream." He pauses and waits for my eyes to meet his. I nod for him to continue and then look away.

"A loud crash and a scream. I went in the back door, and I… I saw her." He stops again and puts his head in his hands.

I fight back the tears. "I read all the police reports. Read the whole damn thing. I already know the details. I already lived that nightmare. I still do. I want to hear it from you."

He lifts his head and looks at me again. His face is etched with terrible sorrow. "She was on the floor. She wasn't moving."

"What did she look like?" I can barely breathe. My throat constricts and tears well in my eyes. And through the tears, I see he has a few more of his own. He puts his head back in his hands and wipes his eyes. He's leaned in against the metal counter as far as he can go.

"She looked really fucking bad. I checked her pulse and… and it was really slow. I moved the knife. I don't know why I did. It didn't even feel like I was there. It felt like a dream… or a nightmare. Like an out-of-body experience. I threw it in the sink, grabbed the phone and dialed the cops. Then I searched the house. There was nothing. Shit was fucked up in the house. Drawers everywhere. Clothes everywhere. But nobody was there."

All my tears have dried. I'm here for a reason. I compose myself the best I can.

"How did my parents' shit get in the guesthouse, Xander?"

"Paige, I don't know! I hadn't touched my luggage since I moved in." He shakes his head. "I have no clue."

"And why would you confess?"

"I told you, they wanted to throw me to the fucking wolves. They promised me—my own fucking attorney promised me—the death penalty would be a guarantee. The evidence was stacked against me. I was high that night when it happened. Really fucking high. I… I don't know. They had the case locked down, and I had a shit lawyer. They all had it out for me."

The officer returns and nudges Xander. "Time's up, Evans."

"Paige," Xander says, rising to his feet. "Just do me a favor. Check Cody's friends. Just check them out for me. I have no one else, Paige. *Please.*" He stands but keeps the phone to his ear. "I swear to you. I'm innocent…"

"Let's go, Evans," the officer interrupts sternly.

"I didn't do it. I would never want to hurt you. I would

never hurt your family. Just please, Paige."

His eyes are desperate as he hangs up the phone and backs away. Then he's gone.

CHAPTER
TWENTY-SIX

Xander

"The Funeral"—Band of Horses

"ALRIGHT MAN, WHAT THE HELL'S UP?" TWITCH CALLS from the bottom bunk. "You've been depressed since you got back."

I'm stretched out and facing the wall, trying my best to fight the anxiety that's taken over. Seeing her again was both the best *and* worst thing I've ever felt.

"I know you ain't sleeping. Spit it out. You know I can't stand the quiet."

"C'mon, man." I say, hoping he'll just leave me alone.

"C'mon, man, what? Spill it."

"It's a long story."

"And I've never shared some long-ass stories with you?" He asks with a sarcastic tone.

He's got me there.

"The girl that visited… that wrote me those letters. I'm in here for her mother's murder."

"Holy fuck." He comes off of his bunk and leans in on mine, his eyes wide.

"Yeah, but I didn't do it. I was set up."

He scoffs and rolls his eyes. "Okay, so were you really set up, or were you set up like everyone else in here was?"

"I didn't do it," I say, annoyed and giving him the look that says "don't fucking go there".

He puts a hand up. "Okay, okay, so what did she have to say?"

"Just wanted to talk about that night. She didn't believe me… probably still doesn't. I tried my best though."

I sit up from the bed and lean my back against the wall. I look at him curiously as he's got a mischievous smile on his face.

"Wanna break out with me?"

I try to read his face, but can't tell if he's serious or not. "You kidding me, man?"

"I think you know me better than that," he says. "I ain't serving ten years, friend. I'm out of here as soon as I find the opportunity. And this time, I'm not getting scooped back up."

For a moment, I actually consider it. I have a life sentence. What the fuck do I have to lose? But what if Paige could help? What if she could clear my name?

"Nah, man. I can't risk it."

"You got life in prison. What do you mean you can't risk it? What are you risking?"

"The hole, man. I don't do so well in the hole. And then, what the fuck am I going to do on the outside? I'll be a fugitive.

Always having to watch my back. Fuck that."

His smile is beaming now, almost giddy, and he rubs his hand together as if formulating a devious plan. "There's ways around that, my man. Many ways around it."

"I'm not trying to talk about fantasy worlds, Twitch. That's not my shit. I can't live like that." I scratch the scruff on my chin, my mind only really on Paige and I ask the only thing I can think of that'll change the subject. "Hey Twitch, you ever been in love, man?"

He scoffs as he sits down on the stool and scans the musty yellow walls. "You're talking about fantasy worlds. Love is a fucking fantasy, my friend. It's God's never ending practical joke." He chuckles, a miserable little chuckle as he looks longingly out the barred up windows. "I was in love once. She's the mother of my kids."

"Shit man, how did I not know you have kids? How many?"

"You never asked, fucker." He puts three fingers up. "I have three boys—Able, Cayden, and Jude."

"Three fucking kids, man? Three boys at that? *Damn* your swimmers must be strong."

He laughs and leans forward, elbows to his knees.

"Their mom's a cheating, lying bitch who hasn't let me see my kids in years. And now that I'm a felon, I've put the final nail in the coffin my own damn self. Love is a façade, Xander. We love who we can't have, and when we do find love, we don't want it anymore. It's the twisted life we live."

"Fuck, man. I'm sorry."

"Don't be sorry for me. I did this to myself. I got fucked up and cheated on her. I caused her to lose it. She was never the same after. Love? Don't ask me about love." He laughs, but there's a lot of pain behind it.

Out of nowhere, Twitch perks up and nonchalantly nods toward the door. Three lifers—we call this particular trio the beast queens, or BQs, on account of their bodybuilder stature and penchant for rape—are standing outside our door. The leader—Joker, I think they call him—takes two steps in and crosses his arms. He's covered in prison ink, as bald as Mr. Clean, and he's got meth mouth like a motherfucker. He ignores Twitch, who looks like he's about ready to pounce, and he focuses solely on me, jabbing a finger in my direction.

"You the little prick talking to the warden about me?"

"I haven't said shit. Nor will I. The guy got what was coming to him."

"That's not what I've been hearing."

"I'm sorry, then you've been hearing wrong." He tenses up, but I remain calm. He wants a reaction—that's why he's here. But I'm not going to give him one.

"Oh, you think so?" He turns back to one of the guys standing behind him. "Hey Chester, this guy right here's calling you a liar. How does that make you feel?"

The equally large and slightly ginger Chester steps forward, shaking his head. With his long hair and gym teacher goatee, he looks like he belongs in the WWE… or on *To Catch a Predator*.

"Nah, I don't like that one bit, Joker."

"And look at you." Joker says, grabbing a handful of crotch and licking his lips. "Such a sweet little bitch you'd make. That pretty head of hair you got, it'd be good for holding onto while I'm fucking your face."

"I can promise you"—I look him dead in the eye—"none of that is going down. Not in this lifetime. And not in the next."

"Oh, we can arrange that. We can take care of you just like we did your last fat fuck cellmate. We made that boy squeal for us, didn't we, Chester?" He laughs, slapping the back of his hand against Chester's chest, who grunts in response.

"Listen, I haven't said shit and I'm not going to say shit. You've been misinformed. That's all I'm saying."

"We'll see now, won't we?" He pretends to suck a dick, stroking a hand toward his mouth before departing. Chester follows close behind after blowing a kiss my way.

"Well, that was fucking interesting." Twitch says with a smile. "Friends of yours?"

"I guess we are now. Before today, they didn't know who the fuck I was. Look's like it's my lucky day."

It's been three weeks since I last saw Paige, and a week since we spoke on the phone and she told me she'd come. I've tried not letting it get to me, but the wait has been excruciating. A day in here is like ten on the outside. I can't imagine how those like Twitch with kids back home deal, though I don't think he even knows where home is anymore.

As I approach the booth, I spot Paige's curly hair, which is pulled up into a ponytail. It's by far my favorite look on her. She smiles when I approach, and although it's a weak smile, it's still a nice change from the last time I saw her.

"Hi, Xander," she says as I lift the receiver to my ear.

"Hi, Paige. It's so good to see you again."

"You too. How have you been?" She looks at me with apologetic eyes. "I mean…"

"No, you're okay. I haven't been bad, all things considered. Life just is what it is in here. You learn to appreciate the small things. I've got a good cellmate finally. Army Special Forces, wounded, all that… you know how well I mesh with that type."

"Speaking of which, have you spoken to Chase recently?"

Even though I haven't thought about him in months, memories of our times together bring a smile to my face. It's my fault it's been so long.

"It's been at least a year and a half."

"Damn. Really?" She asks.

"Yeah. I wasn't too keen on talking to people on the outside for a long time. Envy, I guess. Or maybe I just didn't want him to see me like this. Maybe a little of both."

"Well, do you know he proposed to Brandi?"

"What?! I didn't even know they were seeing each other!"

"Yeah, pretty much since they met. They live in Truman Valley. You should really reach out."

"I know." I shake my head, as I'm well aware I haven't kept up my end of the bargain in that friendship.

"I hope they're well."

"They are. Brandi works with me at Whittaker's still…and yes, I'm working at Whittaker's now. I don't want to hear it." A smile tugs at the corner of her mouth and it excites me as it's the first time she's joked around with me. I miss that so much.

"Chase started an online carpentry business which is doing well and he's still racing regularly. He's a little upset that he has to go all the way to St Louis to do it though. I don't think the country living is quite for him." She lets out the lightest laugh, but it's enough to make me forget all about this place.

I want to continue the small talk, it's what makes me feel normal again in a place like this, but the dwindling time is ever present in the back of my mind. I need to know if she found out anything. She is the only chance I have.

"Paige, sorry, I hate to change subjects, but we don't have much time." I immediately regret my words. I want to relish our chance at a normal conversation. But I just have to know. "Did you look into Cody's people for me? Rusty and Benji?"

"Yeah, I asked around a little. They moved a town over… to Wainwright. Word is that they're controlling pretty much everything drug related in the county. Pushing stuff out of St. Louis. Producing some too. And Xander…"

"Yeah?"

"I looked into Cody, too." She lets her words linger and I fight to keep my face expressionless. I know what's coming next, and I hope to God she's mindful of what she says in here.

"Thinking he'd obviously have more motive than anyone… you know, with all that had happened around the same time. After everything with my mom, we never pressed charges against Cody. We just didn't have it in us. But it turns out, they could never locate him anyways. They still haven't. His truck was still there. Everything was still in his trailer. He just vanished."

"He could've easily went into hiding after the attack. Maybe Russ and Benji are hiding him. I think we gotta focus on his friends."

Paige looks inquisitively at me. "Is there something I should know?"

She tries to read my face and it feels like she sees right through me. I can't tell if she knows or if she doesn't, but this is not the time or place for it anyhow.

"Not at all. With everything that's happened with you and Cody, with what he's capable of, I don't want you anywhere near him. And Paige…"

"Yeah?" she asks.

"Please be careful. You have no idea what your help means to me, but I would never forgive myself if something happened to you."

"I honestly don't know why I am helping. I still can't wrap my brain around that." She shakes her head.

"Do you still think I did it?" I'm afraid of what her answer will be, though I wouldn't blame her if she did. How could I?

"I don't know, Xander. This hate for you has been in my heart for a long time. It's not something that can just go away. But the possibility of your innocence is there. And if there's one thing that's remained consistent, it's that I've had a terrible time seeing you as a killer. I knew you. It was a short time, but what I felt for you…" Tears build in her eyes. "What I felt for you was real. I didn't want to believe it was you for a long time. I fought it. My family is falling apart piece by piece, Xander. Don't ask me what I think. I don't know what I think. I don't know anything anymore."

I stand and put my hand to the glass as the CO calls that our time is up. I look at Paige and see the tears swallow up her beautiful doe eyes and it breaks my heart completely. In this moment, I want to pound this plastic until it breaks and take her into my arms. I'd never fucking let her go.

With every ounce of sincerity in me, I say, "Paige… I *didn't* do it."

I set the phone back on its cradle and walk the path back

to my own personal hell on earth.

The days have been unbearably long—four of them since I last saw her.

If I didn't have Twitch, I'd be a fucking mess.

Paige is all I can think about. The feeling of seeing her again only to be ripped away in ten minutes is so very bittersweet. It's something though, and on sleepless nights, thoughts of seeing her again are what get me through.

The book in my hands does nothing to take my thoughts away from her. The hustle and bustle of normal midday prison activity doesn't help much either. Without Twitch here to bullshit with, I find my mind running away from me. It makes it even worse that he got to go outside the gate for some denture work this morning. He still isn't back yet. Chained and handcuffed or not, seeing something other than barbed wire and concrete would be incredible. I'd almost be willing to give an eye and some teeth for it. *Almost.*

I'm right at the part in *Shutter Island* where US Marshall Teddy Daniels discovers that his wife drowned all four of their kids in a lake and it guts me in the way I love how books do. I set it on my lap, absorbing what I just read when I notice Joker and his crew lingering near my door, not looking in but back over their shoulders. My stomach squeezes into a tight ball. An icy chill travels throughout my veins. I know what's coming, and it's not going to be pretty.

Just past the BQs, four others in their posse start attacking each other, throwing wild, arching punches. COs swarm them in seconds, and that's when Joker's crew makes their move. I'm off the bed with a shank held tightly in my hand when Chester and Sanchez enter, hungry looks on their faces. Two more follow behind them and come immediately for me. I slash them across the face and arms, which moves them back, but the other two come at me immediately, grabbing at my arms. Sanchez buries a shank into my stomach, just above my hip. The pain is almost unbearable. It's as if hot coals have been burrowed under my flesh. Blood pours from the wound and puddles on the floor. Chester then grabs my wrist, hard enough to make me drop my shank, and in one quick motion, throws me down onto the concrete floor, face first.

They kneel on either arm, and it feels as if my arms may snap like twigs at any moment. The concrete floor pushes the shank in deeper, taking the breath from my lungs completely. I start to fade in and out of consciousness.

I feel two more sets of hands cinch each leg. Chester grabs a fistful of my hair and slams my head into the concrete with full force. My ears start to ring.

Darkness.

I fight my eyes back open. A deep, mind-numbing throb ravages my entire head. My vision is blurry, and my taste buds detect only blood.

I feel Chester's hand clutch my hair again. In my head, I beg him to stop, but words can't be formed. Thoughts barely process. My head hurts so badly.

As he holds my head up, I see Joker through clouded vision laughing maniacally as he walks toward me, his hand pulling his dick out of his pants.

I feel my own pants being pulled down. I try to kick, but I

can't even tell if I've moved.

The darkness comes again as my face meets the concrete one final time.

CHAPTER
TWENTY-SEVEN

Paige

"Lost"—Liza Anne

FOR THREE WEEKS, I DIDN'T HEAR BACK FROM XANDER. I sent him letters and even went as far as including my number in one of them, which I said I would never do. Still nothing.

But today I finally received a phone call from him and found out what happened. His voice, gravelly and weak, absolutely killed me. For the first time, I wish I could just get him out of there. For the first time, and for reasons I can't comprehend, I believe he's telling the truth.

This evening, I'll have the chance to finally see him, but first, I have business to carry out. I've been tracking Benji and Russ for a few days now. I know where they live, and I've seen a few of the people they've done business with, but no sign of Cody. I don't imagine he'd stay anywhere around here, but if there's a chance…

This neighborhood is not one you want to be hanging out in after dark. I stay parked far enough down the street to not be made out. I give one last good scan before I head over to the prison, hoping I can get any sort of information for Xander. Anything that could clear his name.

There's been a lot of activity around this house, but Benji and Russ rarely leave it.

I don't want to believe my eyes when a distinct '96 red Civic pulls up to their house. My heart clenches in my chest when my biggest fear becomes reality.

Caleb exits his Civic and approaches the house. Benji takes a step out, greeting him at the door. Caleb shakes his hand then pulls the backpack from his shoulders as he enters.

A slow-moving F-150 and suspicious eyes scare me from my spot. I've seen enough for now, anyway. I can't stomach anything else today. I pull out and make my way back home to get ready to see Xander.

At least that was my intention. I can't help but roll my eyes when I see Ethan sitting on our stoop, smiling with that odd little smile of his. He's still wearing his Whittaker's uniform, which is a nice little reminder that he quit his job at the garage so he could work with Brandi and me. Never mind that it was very much unwelcomed.

Here we fucking go.

"What's going on, Ethan?" I ask, hearing the attitude in my voice though I tried to stifle it.

"I just got off work. Hadn't seen you in a while and thought I'd drop by and say 'hi'. It's weird, but we haven't really been scheduled together lately."

"Yeah, sorry, man. I don't make the schedule." But Brandi does. Of course I'm not going to tell him I asked her to not give us shifts together. "And unfortunately, I'm just a little bit busy. Would you mind if I hit you up later?"

He motions for the door. "Just for a second? I wanted to talk to you about something really quick."

Here it comes...

"Okay, Ethan, but only for a second. I really gotta hop in the shower."

"What, you got a hot date?" he asks defensively as I unlock and open the door.

"Dude, Ethan, it's three in the afternoon. Who the hell goes on a date at three in the afternoon? Is that what you came here to ask me?" I walk in and throw my keys onto the kitchen table, waking my dad up in the adjoining living room—but only for a moment. He'll have to sleep through our conversation because Ethan *is not* going anywhere near my room.

"Do you want to sit?" He looks over his shoulder at my dad. "Or go in your room?"

"I'm fine here, Ethan. What's up?"

He leans back awkwardly against the kitchen counter.

"You know, I've just thought a lot about you and I, and with what you've been through, and..." He still hasn't looked me in the eye. Taking a big gulp, he digs his hands into his pockets.

"I just think... we make sense. I think it's something we both have been fighting for way too long."

Dear Lord, are you kidding me right now? It takes everything in me not to cringe.

"Ethan, you're a really great guy and I really appreciate you as a friend, but I think you've got this situation all wrong. I don't look at you like that."

"Paige, c'mon. We both know there's something here. I want to protect you and take care of you. I want to be the best husband for you."

I'm completely taken back. I knew it would be something along those lines, but I wasn't quite expecting this.

"Listen, I'm not trying to be a bitch in any way, shape or form, but I'm not into you like that, Ethan. You have to stop talking like this."

He pushes off from the counter, and his sudden movement startles me. A tingle trails up my neck.

"*Why* are you denying us, Paige?" His brows furrow and there's a look of pure disdain on his face.

"I'm just telling you the truth. That's it. Now, I think you need to leave." I look at my dad. He's still passed out and snoring. Ethan takes a step forward and puts a hand on my hip. I pull away.

"Ethan! I don't like you like that. Please, now I have to get ready."

"Going to see him again, huh?" he mumbles under his breath.

"*What* did you just say?"

"Nothing. I said nothing. I'll leave you be. Just think about what I said."

"Nothing, my ass. You just asked if I'm going to see *him* again. Who the fuck did you mean by *him*?"

He nervously picks at his arm, his eyes on the floor. "Xander, the fucking murderer," he blurts out. "What in the world are you doing seeing him anyways?"

"How do you know about that? I've told *no one*. Not even

Brandi. How do you know?"

"I'll leave you alone. I just misspoke." He tries to walk out, but I stand in front of the door.

"None of this 'misspoke' bullshit. Tell me now, Ethan, or I'll never talk to you again. I swear to God."

"Listen, I just don't want anything to happen to you, Paige."

"So what, then, you watch me?" I can't hide my revulsion. I can feel my lips curl back in disgust.

"Not all the time. Only when I'm concerned for your safety. I'm protecting you, Paige." He takes my hand and tries to pull me toward him. "I've always protected you," he says in an almost whisper.

I push him off and his back slams into the counter.

"Get the fuck out, Ethan!" I point my finger to the door, noticing my father still hasn't moved a muscle. At first, neither does Ethan. He just looks at me wide-eyed as if he's a little kid being scolded by his mother.

"Paige, I just want what's best for you."

"Get. Out," I say once more, opening the door for him this time.

"Paige…"

"Now!"

Dad stirs in his sleep, which scares Ethan enough to leave. I shut the door quickly and lock it.

I spent about an hour in the shower cleansing myself of that wretched conversation. I've always known Ethan was into me, but nothing like that has ever happened between us. He tried to kiss me once long ago, and I hit the brakes on that real fast. It's hard to believe with everything I have going on in my life, he would choose now to pull this shit. I can't let it bother me though. I'm going to see Xander in just a few minutes, and I'd be lying if I said I wasn't a little excited. Even if he will be in a hospital bed.

Xander looks bad, though not as bad as I thought he would after talking to him on the phone. But still pretty fucking bad. Both arms are in casts and his sunken eyes are black and blue. Gauze is wrapped around his forehead. He smiles weakly as I approach. I start to cry and he shakes his head just barely, but it still causes him noticeable pain. It makes me want to cry that much more.

"No crying, lady. I'm good." A guard stands close by, and it makes me uncomfortable and a little embarrassed for shedding tears. I try my best to fight the feeling.

"You don't look too good."

He laughs and then grimaces in obvious pain. He takes my hand into his the best he can, pulling me closer.

"I don't feel too good," he says with another feeble smile. I can't help but feel awful for him. The look in his eyes—it's the same sweet look I remember. Genuine. Kind. Honorable. He's no killer. He can't be. My mother's words come immediately into focus.

The eyes tell the truth.

"How did you get me in here? Is this even allowed?" I scan the hospital ward. Hospital beds line either side of the room, and only a few of them are occupied. Handcuffs prevent the patients from leaving their beds. My eyes land on Xander, who only has his feet cuffed to the bed frame.

I'm overcome with sadness. To see him here and to feel like he doesn't belong… it's heartbreaking.

"No, not usually. But I gave the warden what he's been trying to get for awhile. Got to see Twitch, too."

"He's your cellmate, right?"

"Yeah. He saved my fucking life." Tears begin to well in his eyes. "Saved me from a lot."

"Are you okay?"

"Yeah, I'm good. I haven't felt good in a while. But I'm starting to." He lifts both casts in the air. "Two fractured arms." He motions to his head. "Concussion, fractured orbital. That one was the worst." He shakes his head, but he's got a half smile on his face. "They missed all my vital organs with the shank by three fucking millimeters."

"Damn." It's all I can muster.

"Yeah, but it could have been a lot worse. And being in here"—he scans the room—"isn't so bad."

"Well, I'm just so happy you're alive. And that Twitch was there to help."

"Yeah, me too. I don't remember much of it. But he and the Warden filled me in." Xander pauses and takes a deep breath. "Motherfucker tried to rape me. And he fucking could have. I had four guys holding me down. I couldn't process a lot of what happened after they slammed my head into the concrete." He looks to the walls in thought, as if fighting to find the words. "But I guess Twitch intervened before anything could happen. Beat the ever-lovin' shit out of all fucking five of them. And the guy that tried"—he swallows hard, unable to look me in my eyes—"to do that shit, Twitch nearly fucking ended his life."

There is a quiet stillness between us for a moment before he continues. "Have you found out anything else, Paige? Please tell me you have."

I look back over at the guard, who has his back against the wall and head down. I don't know why talking about it makes me nervous. Shit, this entire place makes me nervous. The prison hospital isn't as bad as the prison itself, but it's not far off either.

"No … not yet. But I'll keep looking. I did find out that Caleb's mixed in with Benji and Russ. I thought maybe he was on drugs for a long time now, but I never expected this. I think he's dealing. I have no doubt he's using too." I shake my head, unsettled by the whole situation. "I didn't find out much else because I got scared and left."

"I'm sorry, Paige. I should've never had you out there. This is my battle to face. You don't deserve to be caught up in it." He stretches as far as he can, and taking my hand, he brings it to his lips and kisses my palm, just like we used to do with each other so long ago. I don't want to like it, because there's still so much I don't know and still so many questions left unanswered. But the thing is I do like it. I like it a lot. And the moment his lips touch my palm, so many familiar feelings completely overwhelm me.

He looks at me inquisitively, perhaps taking in the complete and utter uncertainty I'm projecting or the fresh dose of tears that run freely down my cheeks.

"Paige." He swallows hard, looking me dead in my eyes. "Do you still think I did it? In your heart, do you?" His eyes are pleading with me. I don't want to cause him pain, but the truth is, I don't know what to think…or what to believe. I want to trust what he says, and every day I've seen him since we re-connected I've noticed more and more of the old Xander show through, but a few weeks of reconnection can't erase three plus years of pain. Sorry Xander, I don't know a goddamn thing in this life anymore.

"No, Xander. I don't think you did it. I really don't." Tears begin to roll down my cheek, and he tries to gently wipe them with his casts. It makes me cry even harder.

"Xander…" The corrections officer approaches, pointing to his wristwatch.

"Alright, boss. Thanks." He looks to me and grabs my hand again. He gives it a light squeeze.

"Will you come see me again?" he asks, his eyes desperate and pleading.

"Of course."

"Promise?" Another kiss to the palm.

"Promise."

He brings my hand to his lips and kisses my palm once more. As I walk away from him, the tears streaming harder than ever, I'm hit with a powerful and undeniable feeling that there's no way this man is a murderer.

There's just no way.

CHAPTER
TWENTY-EIGHT

Paige

"Save You"—Turin Brakes

IT's BEEN TWENTY MINUTES SINCE MY BROTHER LEFT THE apartment. It's the first time in two weeks he hasn't brought his backpack with him. He's hard enough to track as it is, spending most of his time sleeping, or out doing whatever it is he does in the middle of the night.

It takes a few shoulder heaves to bust his bedroom door from its lock, but lucky for me, we live in a dirt cheap apartment complex. The doors are paper thin. It's also a good thing my dad's a heavy sleeper.

If Caleb has nothing in his room, I'll apologize, but I have a feeling I'll find something. He's showing all the signs.

I look around the room first, but I don't see his backpack. I look under his bed…still nothing. I slide open the closet doors, and though I still don't see it, I do notice a large, beat-up chest, secured with a padlock.

After grabbing some bolt cutters from the utility closet, I pull the chest out and then cut the lock, tossing it to the side. I flip each metal clasp up and the chest lid creaks open slowly. My hands tremble. My pulse races.

The very first thing I see is the backpack. I pull it out and open it carefully. I find exactly what I expected. Inside are hundreds of tiny little bags with white powder in them, along with a wad of filthy cash. There's also a needle, spoon and a lighter.

I can't tell if I'm sad or angry, but I'm shaking all over. I take a moment to collect my thoughts, so impossibly worried for my brother and scared he may be too far gone. And I'm so very angry at his complete disregard.

I put the backpack to the side and reach into the chest to pull out a large duffle bag. When I open it up, I see a half dozen or so notebooks. I pick them up and set them down next to the backpack, then take the first one off the top. Flipping it open to a random entry, I begin to read.

March 15th

I bought formaldehyde today. I may have even gotten high off some lol! The previous tokens just aren't doing it. To say I'm excited would be the understatement of the century. Now the search begins. The best part by far, if I do say so myself. Soon... very, very soon.

In the meantime, I have Benji and Russ right where I want them. They're like my best friends. I steal to pay for the drugs myself, give them the money and keep the drugs, and they think I'm the world's best fucking dealer. I'm something alright! So much more than the shit in this town. So much more than the bullshit the people in this town spew. Fuck them all.

I flip a few pages and begin to read again.

March 27ʰ

I found her today. She's perfect. Looks just like Mom. Every-thing is ready. I just need to find the right time. There's nothing anyone can do. This is my destiny. This is what every second of this horrible life has been for. My undeniable vengeance.

I flip the page.

March 30ʰ

I took her today. I kept her in an abandoned cabin in the Twain Lake woods. She struggled more than the last ones, but I stabilized her eventually. She was so damn sexy. It was hard for me to keep my hands off of her... even after death. I see her head in the jar now, and I get an erection all over again... Is that messed up journal? lol

I drop the notebook to the ground, putting both hands to my mouth in disgust. I can't even believe what I'm reading. I don't know how, because my stomach is turning over on itself, but I pick the notebook back up and flip a few more pages.

April 3ʳᵈ

I feel so compelled to cause mayhem. To make people fear me, to fear my every movement. I don't know how I got here or why, but this is my destiny. I am here to turn this fucking world upside down.

I hope beyond hope that this is just some sick form of fiction, but the memory of the newspaper article about Mandy Little and her missing head is gnawing at the back of my mind.

I reach back inside the duffel bag and grab the first thing my fingers touch. It's a manila envelope. I open it and pour out its contents. I'm horrified as I shuffle through driver's licens-es of people I know—people I grew up with—with names I've read about in the paper.

My shaking hands reach back into the duffel bag once more and pull out a small cardboard box. Fearful at this point of what exactly I might find, I open it cautiously.

The cardboard box falls and I'm left with only a jar in my trembling hands. The air is ripped out of me. I want to run, but my feet are planted firmly to the ground. My muscles won't respond to my brain's commands. I'm forced to look at it…to come to terms with exactly what I'm looking at.

There's a human head in the jar, ghastly and bloated. Filmy eyes protrude from it. If I hadn't known Mandy Little my whole life, I may not be able to recognize that it's *her* lifeless eyes staring back at me.

I lose all feeling in my hands, dropping the jar to the floor with a loud crash. Glass shoots in every direction, as does the liquid the jar contained. Mandy's head rolls across the floor and settles with her eyes back on mine. At once, I'm petrified and revolted. It's hard to even process a thought, let alone figure out what to do next. A stench has taken up the room that makes me nauseous. I stumble a little, my vision beginning to blur. My face is flush and tingling. I fight the urge to pass out, but it's overwhelming.

I close my eyes and take deep breaths, willing myself to get it together. Some feeling returns to my legs and the icy chill has left my face. I open my eyes, keeping them on the wall and nowhere else, and I'm relieved to find that my vision is clear.

It's the creak of the floor behind me that draws my attention. As soon as I turn around, a baseball bat comes barreling into my face. I can hear the bones crunch and feel the teeth loosen as it connects. Then I fall for what seems like forever before landing on the duffel bag… and on the rotting head. I can feel it squish beneath me.

I don't black out immediately. My eyes are open, but it feels as if they're spinning in circles—as if I'm outside of body, clinging to the ceiling and watching all of this play out. It can't be real. This cannot be my life.

I can see just enough to identify my brother standing over me, getting ready to swing again. I can see the hunger, the pleasure and the sickness in his eyes. I can feel just what my mother felt before her life was ripped from her.

With everything in me, I scream. And I scream louder than I ever have in my entire life.

Wrongly convicted man released
St Louis Post Dispatch

Three years ago, the small town of Truman Valley in southeastern Missouri was rocked by the fatal stabbing of Teresa Watson, a wife, mother and beloved member of the community. A twenty-seven-year-old man went to prison for her murder. He signed his own confession. However, at 10:56 a.m. this morning, Xander Evans walked out of Missouri Correctional Facility a free man, his innocence found through a family torn apart.

Two months ago, Paige Watson lay bleeding on her brother's bedroom floor, her skull fractured and three teeth knocked out. As Paige's adopted brother, nineteen-year-old Caleb Watson, stood over her with a baseball bat to strike her once more, their father shot him twice in the back, piercing his heart and killing him instantly. Paige was taken to the hospital in serious condition while investigators tried to make sense of it all. Paige is out of the hospital now, but could not be reached for questioning.

What investigators found in the teenage killer's closet at 413 Wipperwill Way rocked the town of Truman Valley to its core. They discovered an arm bone, an ear, and the head of Mandy Little, who was killed in late March. Three "tokens" from victims he had taken over his three-year reign. DNA evidence has confirmed the ear belongs to 36-year-old Danica Andrews from Truman Valley, whose mutilated body was discovered last July in an abandoned trailer. The arm bone was taken from victim Rachel Simmons, 48, from Wainwright. The rest of her remains have yet to be found.

As if that wasn't enough, the young Watson documented all of his heinous actions in seven different journals. The journals depicted animal abuse at a young age, kill lists from high school, and a deteriorating mental condition. They also told, in detail, the murders he committed, including the one that Xander Evans was sent to prison for back in 2013.

The one unanswered question in the Xander Evans-Teresa Watson case was the victim's ring finger. It had been removed from the victim but was never discovered. Today, investigators know why. Mrs. Watson's finger bones weren't found with the others. They were recovered from Caleb Watson's pocket in a pouch along with his mother's wedding ring. People that knew him say he never went anywhere without the pouch. They claim he never talked to them about it and that they never asked. DNA analysis positively confirmed that the bones belong to Teresa Watson.

EPILOGUE ONE

Xander

"I Won't Lie"—Go Radio

HOW THE FUCK AM I SUPPOSED TO FEEL?

Of course I'm happy. I'm *fucking* ecstatic. But for two months now I've waited on the judicial system to get their shit together and I've worried about Paige constantly. All the while I've been rehabilitating from my injuries. I'm better now and two seconds from walking out of this prison a free man, but there's still an emptiness inside. I feel selfish when I get down about what's transpired over the past three plus years. I know I shouldn't take this second chance for granted, but it's just so hard sometimes. I didn't kill Teresa, but maybe if I hadn't ever stopped in Truman Valley she'd still be alive. Maybe Paige would still have her family. It serves no purpose to think like that. But I still do.

I can't presume to know what it'll be like out there. This place changes you. It breaks you down and hardens your heart. I love Paige. I know without a doubt in my mind. But who's to say I can even make love work out there? Shit, can she even? The things she has been through go beyond even my tortured past. Time will tell.

The burst of sun from the opening door forces me to shield my face. I've been out in the sun for rec time, but it never felt like this. Not even close. The feeling of warmth charges my body with excitement. For the time being at least, all the questions and doubt fades. The concrete walkway between barbed wire fences is the longest, most anticipated walk of my entire life. The chill spring air whips against my arms and I lean my head back, soaking it all up.

"Why you walking so slow, man? I'd be running the fuck out of here," I hear a familiar voice call out. I turn and see Twitch in one of a dozen or so cages, each one with a small basketball court and an inmate. He lets the basketball bounce away and approaches the side of the cage, his hands gripping the fence. I slow my pace and smile at him. I haven't seen Twitch in a couple months as I've been in rehabilitation. They keep us broken fucks in a different cell block. The goofy-ass smile he flashes is a welcome sight.

"Hey, Twitch. Good to see you, fucker!"

"Good to see you too, man." He looks around as if about ready to tell a secret and then leans in closer to the chain link. "I'll be seeing you again *real* soon."

"Alright man, I'll keep an eye out for you."

"Damn, why do you gotta make it about eyes? You trying to say something?" He pretends to be offended, but then cracks up laughing, sticking two middle fingers in the air.

"That's fucked up, man. You can't keep using that. It's not fair to the rest of us." Twitch shakes his head from side to side.

"No way. As long as I got it, I'm using it." He picks the basketball back up and starts to dribble. Turning to me one last time he calls out, "Now, fuck off, you free bastard!"

"Hey, keep your head down in there, but don't go sucking any dick."

"But what if I want to?" He yells, loud enough for the whole damn prison to hear.

"I'll see you on the other side, Twitch," I say before starting to walk again. There's no doubt in my mind I'll be seeing that crafty bastard sooner rather than later. He hollers out some more nonsense as I head down the remainder of the walkway, but I just ignore him. I have an appointment in the parking lot with a beautiful woman that I just can't miss.

I almost can't believe it when I see her. Paige is leaning against the hood of her Chevelle, and her smile, big, authentic and beautiful, takes my breath away. There's pain in her eyes though. So much pain.

Here she is, this girl who not two months ago was in a hospital with a severe injury, and now she's picking my lousy ass up from prison. I'm so incredibly lucky. If three years of my life had to be served to finally have this woman in my arms again, so be it.

She doesn't just hug me, she hops up and wraps both legs around my waist. I instinctively grab them, getting turned on by just the feel of her toned legs against my fingertips. She kisses me, a deep, everlasting kiss that makes my lips tingle. She takes my bottom lip between her teeth and pulls back. I fight for our lips to meet again, but she stubbornly continues to pull back until finally giving in.

It's a kiss I never want to end. It's the perfect combination of passion and freedom. This is what I spent sleepless nights thinking about. This is what got me through the longest days of my life. These lips were worth waiting for. These lips were worth fighting for.

I finally do pull away from her, and her eyes look at me with so much innocence. She's the most beautiful thing I've ever seen.

"How are you doing, gorgeous?"

"I'm okay." Her eyes almost instantly dart to the ground. They well with tears. "It's just a lot. Nothing you haven't been through, though."

I wipe the single tear from her face and then kiss her once more. "It's so good to see you." I let her go and open her door for her, stepping aside so she can get in.

"It's so good to see you," she says without moving. "Hey, Xander?"

"Yes, Paige?"

"I'm sorry... for everything."

"Hey, Paige?"

"Yes, Xander?"

"Get in the damn car."

I smirk at her, then make my way around to the passenger side and climb in. She follows soon after.

"Let's get the fuck out of here." I say, so ridiculously ready to rid my life of this place.

The disappearing barbed wire and chain link in the rear-view fills me with so much exhilaration I feel I just might burst.

We're an hour from Truman Valley, on our way to meet up with Brandi and Irish. I haven't seen him in so long it's going to be unreal. I was hoping to see Jack too, but I guess he's just not the same anymore. Paige thinks it's best I don't, that he may still see me as associated with his wife's murder somehow. I don't blame him. With the tragedy this family has seen, I don't know how any of them are getting by. I really admire Paige for her resilience. She's still the same Paige. Her soul's a little weathered, but it's still her.

We pass a sign for Twain Lake, and I can see the tears rolling down her cheek from the reflection in the window. I don't know why I decide to tell her. Maybe to take her mind away from the pain of all the memories she's made here, and all the ones she'll never make. Maybe to get it off my chest. I don't know, but it feels right.

Honesty feels right.

"Hey, Paige?" She wipes her eyes and looks over at me, sniffling.

"I believe in honesty. With friends, in relationships, whatever."

"Okay?"

"When you visited me in prison…I think it was maybe the second time. You asked about Cody, right? About him disappearing?"

"Yeah."

I nod my head in the direction of the lake. She looks out, scans, and then looks back, her forehead crinkled in confusion.

"What?"

"You were wondering where Cody was."

"So where is he? At Twain Lake?"

"No…" I don't want to say it—I really don't—but I have to. "He's *in* Twain Lake."

The car swerves and she looks at me with her mouth wide open. I turn away. I just can't look at her right now. The silence is unbearable.

"Xander, are you shitting me right now?"

I clear my throat. "Unfortunately, no. And I didn't want to tell you because I was too chicken shit. I got the feeling you already knew, though, and that the questions would come."

"A part of me did know." Her hands tremble against the steering wheel. "But I didn't want to believe you could do something like that. *Why* would you do something like that?"

"It was an accident." I stop and take a deep breath. "I didn't mind killing him. I really didn't. He deserved it. But I didn't mean for it to happen."

"So, what did happen?"

I race to his trailer, my hands white-knuckled on the steering wheel. I only have a little bit of time before the sheriff and his deputies make their way there as well. Then again, with the rage I'm feeling right now, I'd likely beat the ever-loving shit out of him right in front of them.

Thankfully, he lives only a few miles away and the trailer park is quiet and still. I creep to his trailer, hoping to God none of these people spot my truck. It's not hard to identify this old thing in such a small town, but I know full well how trailer parks work. They keep quiet about things. They mind their business.

As I pull up to his trailer, I can't believe my eyes… and my luck. His truck door is wide open, dome light on, and he's passed out drunk in the driver's seat. Country music still plays low on his radio.

I cut my lights and pull up alongside him. I slink from the truck with a stun gun, a roll of duct tape and some rope from my glove compartment. As I approach him, he still doesn't move a muscle. An empty fifth is by his side, and the rank smell of piss fills the cab.

In one quick motion, I pull him out and throw him to the ground, face first, between our trucks. He grunts and mumbles something unintelligible.

Before he can say anything else, I duct tape his mouth shut, going around his head with the roll a few times for good measure. He starts to wake so I hit him with the stun gun. His body goes rigid and then limp. I take his arms and legs and hog-tie them together.

As quickly and quietly as I can, I lift him and throw him on the bench seat. I turn his truck off and close the keys inside and then drive slowly back out of the trailer park—to where, I have no clue.

Only a few miles down the freeway, I find the perfect exit. There's nothing here. Not a soul to be found. There are endless miles of thick, thriving woods. The only sounds are the echo of crickets and the occasional croaking of a frog.

My high beams pour light on his hog-tied body. I can see him, but he can't see me. He's crying and struggling to see through the light. I grab him by his hair and pull his head up. He cringes with every movement I make.

I don't know how many times I hit him, I just know each one feels better than the last. His face is humorously contorted with welts and gashes, and his nose points sharply to the left. I keep going. I think about Paige, half naked, beaten and dirty as she ran through the front door. I think about him trying to rape the woman I love. It fuels me.

I am a man on fire.

I don't know when he stopped breathing...but he did. The duct tape and mess of crushed bone and cartilage blocked both of his airways. It's not hard to see how it happened after the fact, but at the time I didn't fucking care. I wanted to teach him a lesson.

Then again, maybe a small part of me wanted him dead all along.

I don't panic. I can't panic. I can only act. And that's what I do.

I make him disappear.

She still hasn't said much since I told her. With the uncomfortable silence fucking with my head, I'm thankful to see her pull into a long drive leading to a beautiful house on a plot of land just outside of Truman Valley.

"Damn, is this the place?" I ask.

"Yeah."

As the Chevelle comes to a stop, Irish's big teddy bear ass comes out of the house. He's holding hands with Brandi, who looks as if she hasn't aged a day, and the sight of him nearly brings tears to my eyes. The feeling of being free is still so incredibly surreal. It's not like anything I've ever felt before.

Rowdy comes sprinting out after them, his tongue flopping freely from his mouth and his eyes bugging with excitement. I get out of the car and he jumps up on me, his paws meeting my chest and I hold him there. He slathers my face with dog kisses and the tears really do start to fall.

I let Rowdy down when Irish approaches, a broad smile on his face. As Rowdy makes his way to Paige, sniffing up a storm, Irish grabs me up in a big hug. He holds the hug for a moment and I feel like a little kid in his bear-like arms. In most circumstances I'm not about any male-to-male contact, but this right here…this is the real thing.

"Dude, so fucking good to see you." Irish says as he finally lets me go.

"Good to see you too, my man." I hug Brandi as well and squeeze her just a little tighter than I ever would have before.

"How's it feel to be free?" she asks.

"Like a fucking dream." I laugh, taking it all in for a moment. "What do I gotta do to get a beer around here?"

Irish laughs, throwing an arm around me.

"We're gonna get you good and fucked up tonight, my friend."

"I like the sound of that."

———————

It was one of the best nights of my life. I kept it pretty chill on the alcohol, keeping a good buzz going most of the night, but after a blunt or two of Cali's finest, I was flying. Freedom tasted really fucking good.

This feeling right here though, waking up next to the love of my life, being able to cradle her in my arms until she wakes… it's everything. It's still going to take some getting used to being out of that place, but it helps having her next to me.

Paige is still passed out cold on my chest, but I don't mind at all. She did her own bit of partying last night, and it was a nice reminder of just how fun this woman can be. I pull her in tighter. Her beautiful amber curls splay out in every direction, and even though some of her hair is in my face, it doesn't bother me one bit. The smell of it is distinctly her, and breathing it in is instantly comforting.

She wakes up and smiles as her sleepy eyes adjust to the light. When they finally do she takes me in and then kisses my chest. I love the feeling of her lips against my skin.

"Good morning, baby." One of her eyes remains closed as she says it.

I could really get used to waking up like this.

"Good morning, gorgeous." I kiss her forehead and then pull back. I try and read her face, wondering if I should say what's been on my mind all night or not.

"Paige?"

"Yeah?" She leans up on an elbow and traces my arm with her fingertips. "What's up, babe?"

"Whatever happened, whatever needed to be done, just know it was for you. It was all for you. I couldn't let him get away with it."

She smiles, placing her hand against my cheek and rubbing softly.

"I know, baby. I know."

Irish has done well for himself. Retired from the Army and racing full time, he's made a shit-ton of money while I've been away. As I scan the massive kitchen, I can't help but shake my head. Three years I ate breakfast chow in my cell. Now this.

"Not too bad, huh?" Irish asks, shoving a piece of toast in his mouth.

"This place is amazing, man." Rowdy's head is lying on my

lap, and though he's no doubt waiting for me to drop a piece of bacon, he also hasn't left my side since I've been back.

Irish shoots a glance at Paige, who's picking at her own breakfast right next to me. I get the feeling there's something they have to say to me. Brandi is still comatose in the bedroom upstairs.

He takes a swig of his coffee and clears his throat. "So, you know you need to go see your sister, right, bro?"

"Yeah, I will, man. I figure I'm gonna stay here with Paige awhile and get used to being out." I pull her in close, but I notice she won't look at me. "Is everything cool here?"

"Of course, babe," she mumbles.

"Yeah, here's the thing, man. We only ever scratched the surface with your sister. I didn't realize how much you've been hurting over that situation. Since you've been away, and since Brandi and I started seeing each other, Paige and I have gotten really close. She's like a little sister to me now. So we've talked a lot about you… a *whole* lot. Both before and after, you know, we knew everything."

He takes another long swig of his coffee.

"I've been keeping tabs on your sister. She's out of the military now. Back home in Wyoming…" He looks at Paige and then at me. He hesitates and then says, "your sister's in some trouble, bro."

"How so?"

"Well, as massive as the military community is in numbers, it's actually pretty tight. I've got some buddies that served with her. A few buddies that still talk to her. I knew you didn't fucking murder anyone. I knew you didn't do that shit, bro. So I wanted to keep an eye on her for you. For when the system got their shit together."

"So how is she in trouble?" My concern is growing with each second he puts it off. I may not have seen my sister in twenty something years, but I love her. I love her with all my heart.

"She got out of the military on some sketchy grounds. An MST from a higher-up."

"Huh? That's Chinese to me, man."

"MST means Military Sexual Trauma, and a higher-up means, in this case, an officer and she was enlisted."

"Fuck."

"Yeah, that's not the worst of it, unfortunately. They didn't believe her. Gave her some shit position in the middle of no-where. She got fed up and discharged. She moved back near her hometown in Wyoming. Started running with the wrong crowd, dealing heroin and arms and shit. It's just not looking good, man."

He nods his head to Paige.

"Paige and I have talked a lot about it since we found out you were being released. We think you need to go see her… the sooner, the better. Paige has to stay down here with her Dad and take care of him, but I think you know that. We will all be up to visit soon though, my brother. I promise you that."

I know he's right, but the thought of not being with Paige makes me sick. How can I ever be expected to spend more time away from her than I already have?

"We know it's the last thing you wanna do. We don't want your ass to leave either, but we also know this thing with your sister is really important. And we want you to see her"—he looks to the table and swallows hard—"before it's too late."

"Xander." Paige takes my hand in hers, squeezing it. She's not often soft spoken, but in this moment, it's hard to even hear her.

"I want nothing more than to go with you, and I'd love nothing more than for you to stay. But neither is possible. It's the hardest thing in the world sending you away. But the thing is, you have to go. If—God forbid—something happens, I don't want you to regret not seeing her again"

The reality of it all settles in my gut, making me feel sick.

"How am I supposed to get there? They impounded my truck a long time ago."

"I've got an extra Harley. It's now your Harley," Irish says, rifling in his pocket and pulling out a set of keys. He slides them to me.

"Are you serious?"

"As a heart attack."

"What about Rowdy?" I ask, petting his head as he nuzzles in.

"Brandi and I have really grown to love him over the past few years. We definitely don't mind watching him for you."

I pat Rowdy's head and he nuzzles in close. I don't want to say goodbye, but I know I need to. I will regret it the rest of my life if something happens to her before I can see her again. I'll blame myself. I have no option.

I kiss Paige on her forehead, breathing in her scent before pulling away. I gaze into her beautiful blue eyes and get lost in them. Tears begin to roll down her cheeks.

"I love you, Paige."

"I love you, Xander. So much."

EPILOGUE TWO

Paige

"Burning House"—Cam

TWO MONTHS AGO XANDER LEFT FOR WYOMING TO SEE HIS sister. We've talked every day since then, but god how I need his touch. Especially now as I feel myself slipping further and further into the nothing.

That's why the four of us are hitting the road to Wyoming, me in my Chevelle with Brandi and Rowdy, and Chase on his Harley.

Of course, that's not the only reason we're on the road. My desperate need to see Xander is matched by an equally desperate need to get away from Truman Valley… forever. I have nothing left here. No one. The only thing I have left are these people. Without them, I would crumble.

It's been a month since I read the note. I knew just what it was when I saw it taped to the front door, though I didn't want to believe it at the time… I still don't. It told me not to go inside, but who listens to something like that? Father, mother, sister, brother, it doesn't matter. You read a letter like that from family and you're going inside. No matter what it says.

Sometimes though, I wish I hadn't gone in. Sometimes I wish I'd listened to his words of warning. Then other times I wonder if I would've regretted having not seen him one last time… even with the way he looked.

I don't blame Dad for hanging himself. There are many times I want to do the same thing. He'd been holding onto a lot of guilt, and all he ever did was grieve.

He gave up a long time ago.

I want to give up too… but I don't. I need Xander and he needs me. We're all each other has, two broken souls fused together. He was made for me, and only he can get me through this. It's just so damn hard sometimes. I'm always so sad. Always mourning. I hope beyond hope my love for Xander can change that. I hope his touch brings my heart back to life.

This is my life now. My entire family is gone. Xander is my home.

Xander is my *only* fucking home.

ACKNOWLEDGEMENTS

Thank you, first and foremost, to my readers. Without you, I would never be able to live out these dreams. If you had asked me five years ago—hell, even three years ago—if I thought I'd have people that actually wanted to read my work, I would've probably burst out laughing. To have your support, your appreciation, and your love means the world to me. A thousand thank yous wouldn't be enough.

A big thank you to my BTU Beta Babes: Angela, Nikki, Jenn, Cat, Barbara, Stefanie, Jen, Jennifer, Amy, Amanda, Holly, Cara, Kristen, and Lucy. What can I even say that would do you all justice? People scoffed when I took on foureen betas. They thought it would be too much. I'm happy you all proved them horribly wrong! This book would not be what it is today without your insight, your passion, and your support. You added so many different elements to this book and to the writing process in general. Just know that I am extremely grateful and I look forward to working with you for a long time to come.

Thank you Pops, Britto, and Bradford. Ten long years I've fought this battle and you have always been there. You've never left me to fend for myself. I'm thankful, each and every day, to have you guys in my life. I may not have a lot of family, but I have as much as I'll ever need. I love you!

To my friends who are pretty much family: Krotch, Rob, Josh, Andrew, Johnson, Randy, Belch, Beth, Stevie, Harvey, Jenn, Jennifer, Gideon, Michael, and Wills. You all mean so much to me. The time we spend together is always a riot and incredibly fulfilling. To have friends like you is to truly know what life is all about. You watch my six and I watch yours. When I'm feeling down, I remember you guys and how much our friendship means to me. You are the best friends a guy could ever ask for. Love ya'll.

A special thank you to Chris with CJC Photography, cover model Gideon Connelly, and Marisa with Cover Me Darling for capturing exactly what I was looking for with this cover. Chris, not only is your work incredible, but you have become a fast friend I have truly come to respect, appreciate and admire. Thanks for being so awesome, down to earth, and supportive. Gideon, bro, what can I say? You came in at the absolute last minute and you crushed it. I consider you a true friend and coming through like that really showed me a lot. Not only that, but you took who I thought Xander was going to be and made him a million times better. You, sir, are going far and I'm so excited to watch your ascent. Your dedication is second to none and something I have been inspired by and impressed with since day one. Keep doing you, brother. Sky's the limit. Marisa, you never cease to amaze me. Your talent is undeniable. I have never seen someone create so much raw emotion with covers. I'm happy to have found my designer for life. Well, you and my girl, Cassy, over at Pink Ink Designs. I can't forget her. Thank you both for inspiring all these stories through a simple Facebook group.

Thank you Heidi McLaughlin for being a dear friend, constant inspiration, and a wonderful mentor in this writing business. I cherish the time I get to spend with you and your family and admire what you all have so much. I truly appreciate and respect the road you traveled, and how you never stopped fighting for your family. Much love, always!

Golden, I can't forget about you. We've been on this fun ride together with our separate solo releases and watching your incredible success in the writing realm has been a real pleasure. You've been nothing but supportive since I met you and just know that I appreciate it very much. As for the news today about the Journeyman Series spin-off, I could not be more honored. Thank you for including me in such an amazing project!

Harper, from the get go, I knew two things about you: one, you are the best person in the world to party with, and two, you are loyal to the end for those you care about. I'm so happy that our relationship didn't just end at author and cover model. I genuinely value our friendship, admire your immense success and tireless work ethic, and appreciate the amount of support you give. There is absolutely no one in this world quite like Harper Sloan! I love ya, lady.

Kirby, you're always there when I need you. You always have the right advice and you couldn't be sweeter when having to help my rookie writing ass. I love the stories we create together and can't wait to continue the journey!

A very special thank you to Michelle, Jake, and all the Threshers for opening up your home, your arms, and your hearts to me. I miss David every single day, but to be able to see you guys, to be able to spend time with you and watch little Jake grow up…it's everything. I CANNOT wait to watch Jake play high school ball!

To David, you've been here all along. You guide me when I'm lost, comfort me when I'm down, and empower me when I'm struggling. I've mourned you since you left us, but I'm comforted in knowing you're watching over me, Michelle, and Jake.

I'm so glad we could finally share that beer. It only took ten years! You will never be forgotten for as long as I live. Rest in peace, sir.

Last, but certainly not least, thank you to my Lord, for showing me the way. He never left my side even when I left His. He lifts me when I'm down and humbles me when I get too sure of myself. I'm forever grateful for my second chance at life. I owe everything to Him and I will never forget that.

ABOUT THE AUTHOR

BT Urruela is a former US Army Infantryman originally from St Louis, Missouri. In 2006, while conducting combat operations in Baghdad, he lost his leg to a roadside bomb. Upon retirement, BT co-founded the non-profit organization, VETSports, and became a *USA Today* Bestselling romance novelist.

Made in the USA
Charleston, SC
21 July 2016